MW01491793

"I really nee[d]

Ivy released a h[eavy sigh.] "I understand."

As the sun magnified the color of his eyes, it came to her which paint hue she would need to fully capture them. *Gold.* Just a hint to bring out the true rich color of his eyes. Ivy cataloged his face in her mind. It would stay there, along with the wonderful memory of this afternoon with him, but one thing was missing.

As if he'd read her mind, Jaxon leaned in. His hesitation was a silent question, asking her if she was on board with what he was about to do next.

She was.

He brushed his mouth over hers. The firmness of his lips paired with slow, soft kisses had a drugging effect on Ivy. As she slid her hands up his chest and around his neck, he settled his in the curves of her waist. Jaxon gently sucking her bottom lip prompted her to release a small sigh, allowing him to glide in past her lips. As his tongue caressed hers, she was lost in a rush of delicious heat. She rose on her toes for more as he explored her mouth.

A long moment later, the kiss reluctantly came to an end. Ivy's heart bumped in her chest. He rested his forehead to hers and she closed her eyes, soaking in the wonderful aftereffect as they both breathed unsteadily. Those electric-like sparks of desire she'd wondered if she would ever experience again. Oh, she'd felt them all right, but with someone she wasn't going to see again. The unfairness of it all hit with a bittersweetness that turned into sad disappointment.

"Come to the Wavefront tonight," he said.

Dear Reader,

Welcome back to Bishop Honey Bee Farm, located in Bolan, Maryland. As the sign just outside of town says, Friends and Smiles for Miles Live Here. If you've visited before, it's great to see you again!

Sweet on a Younger Man is the second book in the Bishop Honey Bee Farm series. In this story, you'll find out where Brooke and Harper's aunt, Ivy Daniels, landed after flying off and leaving them in charge of the bee farm. I'll give you a hint. She ran into her former fiancé. The ending of their engagement over a decade ago was amicable. Now they possibly have a second chance, right? Maybe... or maybe not.

While vacationing with a friend in Hilton Head, she meets Jaxon Coffield, bartender and former business entrepreneur. The difference in their ages isn't a problem. She's turning forty in a few weeks, and he's in his late twenties. According to her friend Amelia, he checks all the boxes for the perfect younger guy relationship.

Their night together is supposed to be a onetime thing, but fate leads to a reunion in Maryland. What starts out as a happy coincidence ends up being overshadowed by family, past relationships and expectations. Staying away from each other is impossible. Seeing each other in secret while enjoying a few fun adventures together is the perfect solution. Jaxon is leaving in a few weeks, and no one will be the wiser. But there's a problem. They can't hide what's taking hold of their hearts.

I love hearing from readers. You can reach out to me through the contact page on my website, www.ninacrespo.com. While you're there, sign up for my newsletter and follow me on social media. Instagram and Facebook are two of my favorite places to share about my books and upcoming appearances. I look forward to seeing you there.

Happy reading!

Nina

SWEET ON A YOUNGER MAN

NINA CRESPO

H Harlequin

SPECIAL EDITION

If you purchased this book without a cover you should be aware that this book is stolen property. It was reported as "unsold and destroyed" to the publisher, and neither the author nor the publisher has received any payment for this "stripped book."

Harlequin®
SPECIAL
EDITION™

ISBN-13: 978-1-335-18020-9

Sweet on a Younger Man

Copyright © 2025 by Nina Crespo

Recycling programs for this product may not exist in your area.

All rights reserved. No part of this book may be used or reproduced in any manner whatsoever without written permission.

Without limiting the exclusive rights of any author, contributor or the publisher of this publication, any unauthorized use of this publication to train generative artificial intelligence (AI) technologies is expressly prohibited. Harlequin also exercises their rights under Article 4(3) of the Digital Single Market Directive 2019/790 and expressly reserves this publication from the text and data mining exception.

This is a work of fiction. Names, characters, places and incidents are either the product of the author's imagination or are used fictitiously. Any resemblance to actual persons, living or dead, businesses, companies, events or locales is entirely coincidental.

For questions and comments about the quality of this book, please contact us at CustomerService@Harlequin.com.

TM and ® are trademarks of Harlequin Enterprises ULC.

Harlequin Enterprises ULC
22 Adelaide St. West, 41st Floor
Toronto, Ontario M5H 4E3, Canada
www.Harlequin.com

HarperCollins Publishers
Macken House, 39/40 Mayor Street Upper,
Dublin 1, D01 C9W8, Ireland
www.HarperCollins.com

Printed in Lithuania

Nina Crespo lives in Florida, where she indulges in her favorite passions—the beach, a good glass of wine, date night with her own real-life hero and dancing. Her lifelong addiction to romance began in her teens while on a "borrowing spree" in her older sister's bedroom, where she discovered her first romance novel. Let Nina's sensual contemporary stories feed your own addiction to love, romance and happily-ever-after. Visit her at ninacrespo.com.

For Elizabeth Rose

Chapter One

Having a fabulous time in the Caribbean. Can't wait to hear about everything that's happening as soon as I get back from my cruise!

Ivy Daniels added a kissing emoji to the text. Searching throu
gh the photos on her phone, she chose one of her smiling on the beach. In the picture, she wore a crimson-and-gold bathing suit with a long, matching wrap skirt. The wind swept her dark hair back from her face. Behind her, the expanse of azure-colored ocean looked crystalline, perfect, and refreshing…unlike her conscience at the moment. It was cluttered with guilt because where she sat, alone at a table, the ocean or a ship were nowhere in sight.

A couple of yards away, a group of children happily shrieked as they splashed around in a hotel swimming pool while their parents and other guests relaxed in lounge chairs nearby. Tall palm trees shading the outdoor space at the resort swayed in a light summer breeze, partially obscuring the sun and the other highrise buildings located in downtown Miami.

Ignoring a pang of self-reproach, Ivy included the photo with the text and tapped Send. Her message wasn't a complete lie. She was wearing a similar blue bathing suit and skirt, and she actually *had* been vacationing on that ship.

Since the ending of the cruise eight days ago, she'd been hanging out at the resort. But altering the truth was an extra deterrent, just in case her nieces, Brooke and Harper, were thinking about contacting her. She couldn't mediate a dispute if she was away on a ship. Her absence was the only way to prompt her nieces to work together in running Bishop Honey Bee Farm and encourage them to repair their fractured relationship.

After losing their mom and dad to a tragic car accident years ago when they had just been teenagers, Brooke and Harper had grown apart. As soon as Brooke was old enough, she'd left the family bee farm and distanced herself from everyone. For a few years, she'd traveled from place to place doing temporary work and had only come home once a year to fill in as beekeeper for a few weeks so Ivy could go on vacation.

Meanwhile, Harper had become a workaholic, practically tying herself down with the running of the farm, and she resented Brooke for not being there to help full-time.

When Brooke did return to help out, from her sullen attitude, she seemed to view it as a punishment. And worse, as soon as she walked in the door, the farm transformed into a battleground with she and Harper sniping each other.

By the time Ivy would return from her vacation,

they'd usually reached a chilly détente primarily based in silence. No amount of talking or trying to help them resolve their differences had been able to allow the two sisters to understand each other. Ivy had grown more concerned about it every year until finally, she'd decided to take action.

As Ivy mulled over the worrisome situation, a server from the bar dropped off the drink she'd ordered earlier.

"Thank you," Ivy said.

"My pleasure." The young woman flashed a friendly smile. "Can I bring you anything else?"

"No, this is perfect for now." The lemonade cocktail in a tall frosted glass promised coolness to beat the heat.

"Just let me know when you're ready for another one."

"I will." If only she could order what her nieces needed from a menu just as easily and send it to them. *I'll take a heap of understanding with a few helpings of listening and communication on the side to go, please.* Unfortunately, she couldn't. Abandoning them had been the best way to handle things.

But even as she justified what she'd done, more guilt piled on as Ivy remembered the looks of panic and disbelief on Brooke's and Harper's faces when she'd told them, almost three months ago, that she would no longer help manage the family enterprise in Bolan, Maryland. She'd signed over everything to the two of them, fifty-fifty. Right after delivering the news, she'd promptly rolled her luggage out the door and gone to the airport.

Brooke had just arrived at the house for her usual stay-for-a-few-weeks visit to fill in as beekeeper when she'd found out she would need to stay long-term. Harper had been caught off guard as well at the prospect of her sister as her new partner in handling day-to-day activities at the farm.

Leaving and then practically ignoring them afterward had probably felt unfair, especially to Brooke. She no longer lived in town and had planned on being at the farm for only a few weeks. But Ivy had needed to avoid them talking her out of the decision to leave. It wouldn't have taken a lot to change her mind. Ever since becoming Brooke's and Harper's guardian when their mom and dad died twelve years ago, they'd become like her own children. She loved those girls so much. *No.* They weren't girls anymore. They were women capable of solving their own problems and handling the legacy left to them by their parents. The time had come for them to start communicating with each other instead of letting hard feelings or unresolved grief completely erode their sisterly bond.

Still, it was hard sometimes not to just see them as the young girls they once were.

On her phone, Ivy scrolled through past photos of her nieces from years ago and paused on one of them. When it was taken, Brooke had just turned seventeen years old. Harper had been fifteen. They were standing in the honey extraction room at the farm dressed in white hairnets and blue coveralls. Nowadays, most of the farm's honey processing was done at a cooperative facility in another town, but back then, they'd all had to pitch in at the farm to get it done on site.

In the photo, the sisters' personalities were on full

display. Brooke grinned as she skillfully balanced three full jars of honey in her hands. She was free-spirited and trusted her intuition when it came to making decisions. Harper was more methodical and restrained. She held one jar with both hands wrapped tightly around it. Even today, she was careful and disciplined and relied on facts as her guide.

As teenagers, the two had squabbled over borrowed clothing, which TV shows to watch, or one of them hogging the bathroom. But eventually, they'd always forgiven each other. She'd never envisioned her nieces growing so far apart.

A wistful smile tugged up Ivy's mouth as she scrolled through more photos of Brooke and Harper from past holidays, birthdays, and other occasions. It pained her not to have more recent pictures of her nieces happily posing together, but there was hope. According to a friend in Bolan who was discreetly keeping an eye on them, Brooke and Harper had become a bit closer. And there was a major change in Brooke's life. She had gotten together with their new neighbor next door, Gable Kincaid, and apparently, their relationship was serious.

Ivy toyed with the straw in her glass. She had planned on spending a few days with her friend Amelia and then taking a train tour across the country. After weeks of traveling on cruise ships, she'd wanted to change things up. Maybe, instead of taking the tour, she could pop back in at the bee farm. Even though she hadn't decided where she was going to live yet, she still needed to pack up her things and choose what came next for her.

In addition to wanting to push the girls together,

something else had prompted her to take such a humongous step. Her fortieth birthday was on the horizon. For the past year, she'd felt the need to break from responsibility and find out what she wanted more of in her life.

While she was figuring out what she was going to do next for a career, she could check in on her nieces and make a few friendly suggestions to Brooke and Harper about how they could navigate the changes they were facing. Nothing too heavy-handed, just a nudge in the right direction.

Or you could continue to stay out of it, and trust them to figure things out on their own... As the voice of reason resonated within her, Ivy sat back in the chair and sighed. Her nieces *had* made a lot of progress over the past few months. Pride in their accomplishments, along with sadness at the idea of having to let them go, formed a lump in Ivy's throat. She washed it down with a sip of her cocktail. Tart, sweet, and with just the right amount of alcohol, it tempered some of her concern. *They're okay without me, right?*

As if in answer to her half musing, half prayer, a soothing breeze ruffled her hair over her shoulders. With it, a calming sense of rightness washed over her.

"Ivy...?"

The familiar voice caused her to glance up. "Von! Oh my gosh." Shocked to see her former fiancé, astonishment pushed her up from the chair.

Over a decade had passed since the amicable ending of their engagement. He looked different. He was older, of course, and instead of a full head of black hair, he had a shaved head. It suited him, and so did the neatly trimmed dark beard that brought contrast to his deep-brown face. But his wide smile was the same.

"It's so great to see you," he said as they embraced.

"You, too."

"Are you here on vacation?" They both spoke at the same time then laughed.

"You first." He graciously gestured to her.

"Yes, I'm here on vacation, or at least I was. I'm leaving for South Carolina day after tomorrow."

She and Amelia, who lived in New Jersey, were spending a week at a town house they'd rented in Hilton Head near the ocean. Lounging on the beach, girl chat, sipping cocktails, and shopping were on the agenda.

"What about you?" she asked.

Dressed in a crisp pullover and shorts, he looked as if he was headed to the golf course. "A vacation with business mixed in. Unfortunately it's been heavier on the business side of things than I'd hoped. I haven't gotten much relaxation in." His expression softened. "Enough about me. How have you been?"

The answer to that question spanned so many years, starting from the moment they'd said goodbye to each other after agreeing they should end their engagement twelve years ago. Where did she start? "Well, I'm a retired beekeeper now—"

His phone chimed. Glancing down at it, he sighed. "I'm sorry. I want to hear all about it, but one of my clients is impatient to discuss a business matter. We're meeting for lunch this afternoon, but I'm free later on. Have dinner with me tonight. I'm flying back to New York in the morning."

The genuine interest in his expression prompted her response. "I'd love to."

After exchanging numbers, Von hurried off and Ivy sat back in her chair, caught in the pleasant spin of un-expectedly running into him. She had just been won-dering if Brooke and Harper would be okay without her. Maybe seeing her former fiancé was a sign she could stop worrying about them and focus on her own life.

Chapter Two

Six days later...

Ivy sat with Amelia inside the Wavefront Bistro in Hilton Head. They were enjoying an early Saturday lunch after spending another glorious morning lounging under umbrellas on the beach.

The white, ruffle-strapped cami Amelia had on accented her skin, which was lightly kissed by the sun. Her dark auburn coils not secured by her messy bun or the sunglasses on top of her head brushed her light brown cheeks.

Ivy wore her favorite tangerine sundress. After spending most of her time in practical boots, jeans, and button-down shirts at the farm with no makeup and her hair firmly pulled back out of the way, the chance to wear her hair down and put on a pretty outfit, sandals, and makeup was a refreshing change.

Amelia poured citrus dressing on a grilled salmon salad with arugula and cherry tomatoes that looked almost too perfect to eat. "This restaurant is great. I'm glad we found it."

"I agree. This place was a good pick."

The food was excellent, and the establishment had a relaxed, enjoy-the-moment vibe. A variety of plants thrived in the space with walls and furnishings in soft purple, white, and yellow hues. An outdoor dining area at the back of the restaurant was nestled in the midst of trellises with raised garden beds filled with budding plants.

That part of the restaurant reminded Ivy of the flower field at the farm. At this point in the early summer, forager bees from the apiary would make several visits to the nearby field. They would collect nectar and pollen from the array of blooms to take back to the hives for the worker bees to produce honey.

Despite her many years working as a beekeeper, she never got jaded to watching the beauty of that symbiotic relationship between the bees and the flowers unfold. It always left her in awe. She was hit with a wave of homesickness, missing the farm, but day after tomorrow, she would be a part of it again.

And she knew that she would return to find things even better than when she'd left, because Brooke and Gable were engaged now. This next step in their relationship had happened quickly, but from the way they'd looked at each other during a video call with them, clearly, they were in love.

Gable, an up-and-coming country music singer, was going on the road. Brooke wanted to take a couple of weeks off to join him. She'd asked Ivy if she had time to fill in as head beekeeper while she was gone, and, of course, she'd said yes.

Feeling pleased about how it was all going to work

out for everyone, including her, Ivy smiled in between bites of the best carnitas tacos she'd ever tasted. Brooke and Gable would get some much-needed time together. Harper would still have the help she needed at the farm, and as far as herself, she would get a chance to peek in on things while spending time with the bees. Plus, she wouldn't have to figure out what to do on her fortieth birthday.

After all the traveling she'd done, being in one place and enjoying a simple celebration with Harper would be nice. Yes, turning forty was considered a milestone, but she didn't need a big party to celebrate. A few friends had already sent her virtual gift cards, and Amelia had also given her a present the first day she'd arrived in South Carolina. A beautiful pair of gold heart-shaped earrings.

"This week has flown by," Amelia said. "I'm so glad we got a chance to do this, but I still haven't made up my mind if I'm giving you a pass for taking away a day from our vacation to spend time with Von." Although she was teasing, there was a hint of real annoyance shading her tone.

The decision to spend an extra day touring Miami with Von had been last-minute and had seemed like a great idea, at first.

"It wasn't a full day, just a few hours," Ivy replied. "I got here early Sunday morning instead of late Saturday night."

"That's still not a good excuse. Anyway…" Amelia breathed out the word. "You never said what it was like seeing your ex-fiancé again after all this time."

As Ivy took a sip of zinfandel from her glass, she debated on how to respond. She hadn't brought up the subject because Amelia, who would have been her maid of honor twelve years ago, hadn't been completely in favor of Von back then. Even though she'd had doubts if he'd been a good fit for Ivy, she'd supported her decision—but when the engagement had ended, she hadn't seemed very sorry to see that part of her friend's life come to an end.

And now, Ivy couldn't help thinking that maybe Amelia had been right about it. Seeing him again definitely hadn't been the sign she'd thought it was.

Ivy put down her glass. "He asked me to marry him."

Amelia sat back in the chair. "He did what?"

As her friend stared at her from across the table, Ivy related to the look on her face. Jaw-dropping shock. That was what she'd felt when Von had popped the question. It had come so far out of left field. The first night she'd shared dinner with him at the resort, they'd chatted and laughed like no time had passed, but their interaction had felt strictly platonic. They'd enjoyed themselves so much, he'd delayed going home to New York, and she'd put off her departure to meet Amelia so they could have a little more time to catch up.

The next day, playing tourist around the city had been fun. When he suggested taking a sunset cruise on Biscayne Bay, she'd envisioned them happily parting as friends afterward. It had seemed like the perfect ending to their time together…right up until Von had asked her to marry him.

"So how did he take it when you said no?" Amelia asked.

"He pled his case. He pointed out that he had more than enough money for me to live a life of luxury with him in New York, and that my time would be my own to do with as I please."

"Being all alone in a relationship." Sarcasm flooded Amelia's tone. "Oh wow, isn't that appealing."

Although Ivy understood Amelia's reaction, Von's remembered sincerity prompted her to add, "From his point of view, it made sense. He's the head of his own firm. He has a lot on his plate. Since I know what it takes to be successful, he assumed I would understand his intense work schedule and wouldn't be put off by it. And as a bonus, neither of us would have to face loneliness."

"Bonus?" Amelia huffed a breath. "Married people can still be lonely, especially if their spouse is never around, and it sounds like that would be the case with Von. What did he expect you to do? Just sit around and wait for him?" She shook her head. "It sounds like he was negotiating a business deal, not making a marriage proposal." Her eyes narrowed a bit as she studied Ivy's face. "The life of luxury part, didn't it tempt you just a little? Be honest."

"No, of course not." Amelia's slightly amused, brown-eyed stare was like truth serum. Ivy laughed. "Okay, maybe for a brief second I was tempted, but friendship is the only option for me and Von at this point." A fact that had become evident to her after dinner that first night when what was supposed to be a peck on the cheek had accidently turned into a light kiss on the lips.

Years ago, for her, just being near him had been as heady and explosive as fireworks. But after he kissed her, she'd felt…nothing. The chemistry they'd once shared was gone, and honestly, she hadn't experienced it with anyone since Von. Butterflies of anticipation fluttering in her belly. Electric-like sparks of desire making her heart race. Would she ever feel those things with someone again?

"Friendship, huh?" Amelia jabbed a piece of lettuce with her fork. "Von is lucky you're giving him that option considering how he broke off your engagement. He was all kinds of wrong for leaving you when you needed him the most."

"In all fairness, Von didn't break things off. He and I agreed to end our engagement. Remember? And as far as needing him, I don't know if he could have helped. He wasn't in the headspace to raise two teenagers."

"Neither were you, and you still managed to pull yourself together and step up. Becoming Brooke and Harper's guardian plus running the farm were two of the biggest changes of your life."

"It was, but knowing Dion and Lexy's wishes helped me through it. I knew I had to get over the shock of losing them and keep going."

She'd been twenty-two years old when Dion and Lexy had asked if they could legally designate her as the one who would raise their children should anything happen to them. It had felt like a huge ask at the time, but she'd understood why they'd made it.

Dion's parents had been advanced in age when they adopted him as a baby and were in poor health. As far as her and Lexy's parents, unfortunately, they weren't a good choice.

Their parents managed to stay together fifteen years despite each of them feeling they'd sacrificed more than the other. After the divorce, they'd shared custody of Ivy and her sister. Although they'd cheered their daughters' successes, Ivy and Lexy had sensed their parents wished they'd made different choices, and they'd resented the way marriage and family life had held them back.

If they hadn't been together, they could have pursued whatever dreams they believed they'd lost out on. When Lexy died, even their grief seemed to be more about themselves. They preferred to focus on their personal grievances rather than considering what anyone else was going through. They wouldn't have been able to provide the love and support their granddaughters had needed. Other than sending checks for Brooke and Harper on their birthdays, they'd rarely stayed in touch.

As Ivy mulled over the past, it felt like a strange mix of yesterday and years ago. That sad and chaotic time when she'd followed through on Lexy's and Dion's wishes for her to nurture their children just five short years after she'd made the promise was like a muted echo, remembered but not as painful.

On the other hand, Amelia's loyalty to her was just as fierce as it had been when the tragic accident occurred— and apparently so were her ill feelings toward Von.

"Taking on the responsibility of raising Brooke and Harper was a natural step for me," Ivy reasoned. "I couldn't imagine doing anything else, but Von could. He'd just landed his dream job with a prominent law firm in Manhattan. I couldn't ask him to give that up to run a bee farm."

"He expected you to put your career as an artist on hold once you were married. How is that different?"

"I didn't exactly have a career. I was just a struggling painter with two part-time jobs working in a small art gallery and an art supply store."

"You were a talented artist with dreams of showing your work in art galleries." Amelia shook her head. "How can you still be so generous when it comes to his lack of support or consideration for your situation? I stick by what I said earlier. He was wrong. You were too good for him then, and you're too fabulous for him now. You're radiating best-self energy, and you don't need him ruining it." From the stubborn look in her friend's eyes, she wouldn't be swayed from her opinion.

"Well, I must admit, I do feel fabulous." Ivy wiped her hands on a napkin. "Why dwell on what happened? It's in the past. Von did what he felt he had to do, and I did what I needed to do, and here we are today. Honestly, I feel sorry for him. He's successful. He has money, but he has no one to share it with. I hope he finds someone…"

Amelia's fake snoring cut into the conversation.

Staring at her friend, who had her eyes closed, Ivy nudged Amelia's leg with her foot under the table. "What are you doing?"

"Sorry." Amelia pretended to shake herself awake. "I dozed off somewhere between you making excuses for Von and imagining some poor woman sharing a torturously boring future with him."

A smile slipped past Ivy in spite of herself. "You really need to stop."

"I need to stop? What about him and his insane marriage proposal? Why would he even think loneliness was a factor for you? You're too amazing for that to happen, and on the good karma side of things, I think it's time for you to start exploring your creative dreams again. You should find a really gorgeous man to paint." Amelia nodded and smiled at her own idea. "Girl, bringing someone like that to life on canvas could be more than just inspirational, do you hear me?"

Ivy gave Amelia a friendly, mini dose of side-eye. "Yes, I hear you. And yes, I do feel amazing. But picking up a brush and diving back into where I left off as a painter isn't that easy. And let's be real, eligible guys just don't fall out of thin air or onto a paint canvas."

"Maybe they do. That guy over there has been checking you out since we walked in. If I were an artist and single, I wouldn't mind *painting* him one bit." Amelia's smirk said it all.

"Painting, huh?" Ivy couldn't help but smile as she took a bite of food. She also couldn't resist a glance to where Amelia tipped her head. The only guy in that vicinity was the bartender.

He definitely was worth the pause. A dark T-shirt accented his wide shoulders and solid-looking chest. His movements as he went from one task to the next were effortless. Smooth, confident, no second-guessing. Did those instincts translate into *everything* he did?

Suddenly, a vision of him pressing her against the

wall as they indulged in a fiery kiss set her thoughts aflame.

Whoa! Where did that come from? Ivy gave herself a mental shake. Luckily, no one in the room could read her mind, especially him. But what if he could? Would he be on board with her fantasy? As her mind continued to explore more erotic territory, his stare collided with hers. It felt as if he could see straight into her thoughts—and past her clothing, leaving her bare to his gaze.

A heated jolt laced with a delicious thrill ran through Ivy, and she dropped food in her lap. "Crap…"

"Oh, here." Amelia quickly handed her a napkin.

"Thanks." As Ivy cleaned food from her dress, she couldn't stop herself from glancing over at the bartender. He was still staring.

The color of the sauce stain on her dress reminded her of one of the pigments she used to include on her paint palette. *Venetian red…* That would be the perfect color to pick up the faint amber hue in his light brown skin. But what color would best capture his eyes?

Wait, why was she thinking of capturing anything? In the past decade, the only artistic thing she'd done was doodle on a notepad at her desk during a phone call. Amelia's comments had put silly ideas in her head.

As her attention kept wandering back to the bartender, Ivy's cheeks flushed. Averting her gaze, she dipped the end of the napkin in her water glass and intently focused on dabbing the stain.

Amelia chuckled lightly. "Why are you sighing and

biting your lip? Does the thought of someone checking you out make you that nervous?"

"No, of course not. But even if he was checking me out, I'm sure he's not interested now."

"Why don't you ask him?"

"Oh sure." Ivy set the crinkled napkin on the table. "I'll just go over there and ask him if he's attracted to women who spill food all over themselves."

"You won't have to." Amelia gave her a self-satisfied smirk as she picked up her mojito. "He's on his way over here now."

"He's coming to our table? No, he's not." Too panicked to look for herself, Ivy leaned in and lowered her voice. "You're joking, right? But why is he coming over here?"

Chuckling, Amelia released a weary sigh. "You really have been out of the mating game for too long."

"Says the woman who's been in a committed relationship for the past six years."

"Actually, seven." Amelia shrugged. "But who's counting."

"That's not the poi—"

"Excuse me," the bartender interrupted. "I thought you could use this. Club soda, for your dress." He put a glass with clear fizzing liquid in front of Ivy.

As his deep voice poured over her, her heart did an odd flip-flop in her chest. Needing a moment to collect herself, she dropped her attention to his dark Timberland boots. Curiosity made her gaze travel from his boots up his long, black-jean-clad legs to the shirt that perfectly hugged his torso, and then farther up. The chiseled angles of his clean-shaven face were model-worthy and just as captivating as the rest of him.

Mentally shaking away the vision of capturing him in vivid color on canvas, she found her voice. "Thank you. I appreciate it. How thoughtful. I shouldn't have been so clumsy."

"Accidents happen. Especially with those loaded tacos." As his slow smile emerged, Ivy was the one who was captured.

"Yes, it's great." She felt at a loss for words. "Really great."

"Well, I'll let you get back to your meal." He moved to walk away but turned back around. "You know, if you like tacos, a friend of mine makes some of the best in town. He has a food truck. Actually, he's cooking in a competition later this afternoon near the beach, a couple of blocks from here. I'm helping him out. You should stop by. My name is Jaxon, by the way."

"Hi, I'm Ivy." A smile that felt a little too wide for her face suddenly emerged. She struggled to tame it, sure that she looked ridiculous. Or insanely excited about tacos.

"And I'm Amelia." She smiled and gave him a small wave. "That sounds like fun. So what type of competition is it?"

"It's the Food Truck Versus Restaurant Face-Off," Jaxon replied. "It's happening every other weekend for the next couple months. Local food trucks and restaurants are going head-to-head, showcasing items from their menu, and the crowd gets to vote on who's the best. Part of the proceeds are going to a local food bank."

"Supporting a great cause while enjoying good food is a fantastic idea," Ivy said.

"It is." His hazel-brown-eyed gaze rested solely on her. "Plus it gives people a chance to check out food from local places that maybe they haven't tried before."

"And it's a win for visitors like me who are only in town for a few days." As soon as the words left Ivy's mouth, she mentally kicked herself. *You could have skipped that last part. Like he cares how long you're in town.* But another one of his slow, heart-stopping smiles muted her inner critic.

"It's definitely a win for everyone," he said. "The restaurant my friend is going up against has a spicy chili salmon ramen dish that's addictive."

"That does sound good," she replied. "But wait a minute. Does your friend know you're advertising for the competition?"

Holding his hands up in defense, he laughed. "I'm just sharing a little helpful information."

"So where is this happening?"

He told her, and Ivy recognized the name of the beach and surrounding landmarks that he described. She and Amelia had gone to an art gallery in that area the other day.

Jaxon glanced at the bar where servers waited for him. "I should get back to work. It was nice meeting you."

"It was nice meeting you, too," Ivy and Amelia both said.

His gaze held Ivy's a few seconds longer before he

walked away. The back view of Jaxon was just as appealing as the front of him.

Ivy took a sip of wine, but it failed to cool the growing flush engulfing her inside and out.

Amelia's kick to Ivy's foot was as sharp as her short laugh. "Told you he was interested."

"Say it louder. I don't think he heard you." Amelia opened her mouth as if prepared to tell the entire restaurant, and Ivy pointed at her. "Don't."

"What? I was just going to say he's cute."

"He is cute. And he's probably a minute older than Brooke."

Amelia raised her brow with interest. "You know they say that twenty-seven is considered the magic age for being with a younger guy in a relationship." She counted off the reasons using her fingers. "One, he's old enough to have had some life experiences. Two, he's not afraid to step up and date an older woman, and three, there's a very good chance he knows how to heat things up between the sheets. Now, *that's* a bonus. And I doubt he'll mess up your date by proposing marriage."

There was a magic number? Not that Ivy needed to know any of those details. "Date? What date? He didn't ask me out."

"Uh, yes he pretty much did. 'I'm helping with food prep. You should stop by'—what did you think he meant?"

"He was just inviting us to the event."

"Us? He barely looked at me."

Their blonde server smiled as she dropped a leather

bill holder at their table. "Take your time and enjoy your lunch. There's no rush."

Amelia opened it and chuckled.

"What?"

"Our lunch as well as our drinks have been paid for, and I was right. Again."

Ivy accepted the bill from Amelia. It had a sticky note attached with a handwritten message.

Hope to see you this afternoon. I'll be saving you a plate of tacos.

Jaxon

Chapter Three

Jaxon Coffield looked outside the service window of the Taco Tornado food truck, searching for Ivy. *She's not coming.* He released a heavy sigh of disappointment. He'd really hoped he would see her again.

In front of him, people attending the competition mingled on either side of the long, wide aisle separating booths with various vendors selling arts, crafts, food, and local services. Flavor Fusion, the restaurant his friend was competing against, had a large tent set up on the other end of the aisle.

Since he'd arrived close to three hours ago, he'd been subconsciously counting the minutes as they ticked by, hoping that Ivy might show up.

Milo, his friend who was the chef and owner of the food truck, speared the order slips on a metal spike near Jaxon.

"One chicken, one shrimp, and one chicken, no onion." Milo joined his right hand, Grace, back at the service window.

Milo and the petite redhead, with long braided hair and a series of delicate-looking gold rings in her nose, worked together effortlessly as they took and distributed the orders. She and the dark-haired chef were also alternating shifts cooking on the flat-top grill.

Jaxon was in charge of preparing the orders.

He took the slips off the spike. After memorizing them, he removed soft flour tortillas for the tacos from the warmer and put them in the prepped disposable food boats. As he took a spoonful of chicken from a pan in the warming table, the fragrance of garlic and spicy seasonings rose with the steam. It mingled with the scent of cilantro he'd recently cut for garnish.

Milo and Grace sharing a laugh together drew Jaxon's glance. Both in their midthirties, the two chefs loved creating experiences, not just meals, with food. They claimed they were only friends. But Jaxon had known Milo for close to four years. He looked really happy with Grace. Maybe, he was even in love with her.

Gladness for his friend mingled with a slight stab of envy in Jaxon. Years ago, he thought he'd been content in a relationship until he'd realized the woman he was with valued money over everything else. Since then, he'd dated around, but Ivy was the first person in a while who'd caught his interest after just one glance.

The memory of her walking into the restaurant earlier that day rose in his mind. She'd radiated a sense of confidence, but not in a self-conscious way, and during their brief conversation, she'd been genuine. She hadn't been trying to impress him or play the flirting game.

At first, he worried that maybe he'd embarrassed her by noticing she'd dropped food on her lap. When he'd gone to her table, and she'd looked away from him, all he wanted to do was assure her that it didn't matter.

She could have dropped the whole plate on her lap, and he wouldn't have cared. He'd just noticed her, period.

He'd heard other people describe someone as a breath of fresh air, but he'd never fully understood what it meant until he met her. Happiness, interest, and attraction had risen inside of him every time she laughed. And the hint of sultriness that had entered her tone when she'd teased him about promoting the competition had made him wish he could capture her words in a kiss.

For his own peace of mind, Jaxon slid that last thought aside. He shouldn't have just paid for lunch and sent a note. He should have gone back to the table and asked Ivy out directly. But maybe she wasn't interested in him. That could be the reason why she hadn't shown up that afternoon.

"Whoa, ease up a little with the portions. I have a crowd to feed." Milo thumped him on the arm. "And one of those orders is for shrimp, not chicken."

Jaxon glanced down at the tortillas he'd overloaded with spicy chicken. "Sorry."

Milo's thick brows dropped with a questioning frown as he studied him a few seconds longer. "Are you okay?"

"Yeah, I'm good. I just need to stop rushing and pay more attention." Jaxon fixed the order, then slid the food over to Milo, who was still looking at him with a curious expression.

More customers showed up at the window, but sometime later, the flurry of activity died down to a trickle.

Milo wiped his hands on a white kitchen towel as he stood next to Jaxon. "I finally figured out what's up with you. Who is she?"

Jaxon cleaned food from the prep counter with a cloth. "Who's who?"

"The woman who made you confuse chicken for shrimp all afternoon."

Jaxon couldn't deny the confusion part. He had messed up more than a few times in the past three hours. He debated whether to answer his friend's question, though. It probably wasn't worth mentioning Ivy, considering she was a no-show, but for some reason he felt like telling someone about her. "Her name is Ivy. I met her today at the restaurant and invited her to come by the truck. She hasn't shown up. I guess she wasn't interested."

"There's still time. She might make it."

"I don't think so." *Ivy's not coming.* Jaxon repeated the thought in his mind. He needed to get used to the idea that he wasn't going to see her again.

"Well, this is new." Milo flipped the kitchen towel onto his shoulder.

"What do you mean?"

"You being caught up on someone enough to care if they show up to see you. Usually, you're like a non-stick pan. One woman slides away and you're ready for the next one."

Jaxon laughed. "Nah, that's not true." A face in the crowd caught his eye. *Ivy!*

Milo chuckled. "Let me guess, she's here?"

"Yeah, she is." Jaxon couldn't stop a smile as he took off the apron tied around his waist and laid it off to the side. "Are you good with me taking an extended break?"

"Sure, you might as well take off now instead of

later this afternoon. Grace's friend will be here in a couple of minutes." He waved him off. "Go ahead. We can handle it."

Jaxon grinned. "Thanks." He went out the back and turned toward the side where the service window was located.

Ivy stood a couple of yards away dressed in a loose purple T-shirt and tan shorts.

His gaze automatically traveled down her satiny-smooth-looking legs to her wedge heels, and all the way back up again. He hadn't realized he'd stopped walking until Ivy spotted him and her smile jump-started his steps.

She met him halfway. "Hi."

"You made it."

"I did." She glanced around before looking back to him. "It looks like a good turnout. I hope you still have food left. I would have gotten here earlier, but Amelia and I went shopping, and then we had to lug everything we bought back to the town house." Looking down a moment, she laughed softly and shook her head. "You don't want to hear about all of that."

"Of course I do. But don't worry, there's plenty of food left." He tipped his head toward the truck. "I'll grab some for us, and then you can tell me all about your shopping trip."

"Okay."

He led the way, but as they moved closer to the truck, the crowd began to separate them.

On a reflex, he reached back for her, and a second

later she slipped her hand in his. The soft warmth of her skin made Jaxon's heart kick in a few extra beats.

His physical build created a path for them, but the charm she naturally radiated easily did the same. Ivy wasn't holding onto him because she had to. She wanted to hold his hand. The realization of that made his chest puff out a bit as he guided them to Milo's food truck.

When they reached it, he reluctantly let go of her. "I'll be right back."

She smiled. "I'll be here."

Inside the food truck, Jaxon snagged a couple of larger take-out containers near the prep counter instead of the food boats.

Based on what Ivy had ordered at the restaurant, she wasn't afraid of heat or spiciness. He prepared a container for him and one for her with a little bit of this and a little bit of that, plus small containers with extra condiments.

As he picked up the closed containers, Milo called out to him. "Hey, you can use the VIP pass if you want."

"Thanks." Jaxon snagged the plastic-covered card with VIP written on it and rejoined Ivy outside.

She glanced at the closed take-out containers then looked around. Most people just carried disposable food boats and ate as they walked, but they wouldn't be able to do that comfortably. "Where should we go to eat?"

"The VIP tent. It's to the right behind the booths."

In the tent, after grabbing drinks, plasticware, and napkins, they sat next to each other on a bench at one of the outdoor tables.

Jaxon handed Ivy the food container he prepared for her.

She opened it. "This all looks so good. I'm not sure what to try first. What's in them?"

"The one on the left is a chili spiced chicken taco. The two in the middle are shrimp. I recommend you try those with Milo's signature pineapple and avocado salsa. And as promised, carne asada topped with guacamole, cilantro, and crumbled queso fresco."

"I'm definitely trying the carne asada, but shrimp with pineapple and avocado salsa sounds too good to pass up."

"Go for it."

Ivy put some of the salsa on one of the soft-shell shrimp tacos then took a bite. "Oh my gosh. This is so good." She moaned, and the hint of sultriness humming through the sound raised goose bumps on his arms.

"It is," he agreed. As she loaded on more salsa and took another bite, Jaxon tore his gaze from her mouth and smiled. She wasn't shy about eating in front of him. He liked that. It made it easier for him to dig in, too, knowing she was satisfied.

A few bites into their meal, she said, "Your friend Milo definitely nailed the balance of spices in that salsa. It has just the right amount of heat. I like spicy things, the hotter the better, but it's a waste of everything else if that's all you can taste."

"I feel the same way. So are you a taco connoisseur or do you just like Mexican food in general?"

"Both. But no matter what type of restaurant it is, if they have any kind of tacos on the menu, I usually order them. The other day, Amelia and I went to this Thai Mexican fusion place. The tacos were good but they made the best—"

"Tableside guacamole?" he guessed, finishing her sentence.

"Yes! You know the place?"

"I do. They just opened up. Right now, they're the best-kept secret in town."

"I have a love/hate relationship with best-kept secrets. I'd hate keeping a good thing a secret but at the same time I'd love to just enjoy it for myself." She laughed. "I know, that sounds bad, right?"

"Actually, I get it." Enjoying Ivy all to himself was his new favorite thing. "You said you go for tacos at any kind of restaurant? That's adventurous. What's the most unusual kind you've ever tried?"

"Hmm, most unusual…" As Ivy contemplated the question, she sucked a bit of sour cream from her finger. Her lush lips kissing away the spot made him fixate on her mouth all over again. "Corned beef tacos. It was a St. Patrick's Day thing at a friend's house, though, not a restaurant. What about you?"

"Me?" It took a few seconds for him to pull his attention from her mouth and get his thoughts back on track. "Full disclaimer, a couple of years ago, I used to work at a restaurant in San Diego that specialized in tacos. Twenty-seven of them. Supposedly that's a lucky number."

Ivy released a half laugh, half cough.

"You okay?"

"Yes…a spicy jalapeño got to me." After taking a sip

of soda, she added, "Twenty-seven—I've heard something about that being a lucky number, too."

"Not with that place. They should have stopped experimenting after they created the pumpkin spice taco."

"Oh no." Horror and amusement filled her face. "Did they really take pumpkin spice everything to *that* level?"

"They did. And trust me, they shouldn't have. There are some places where pumpkin spice should be outlawed."

"Don't tell that to Amelia. She adores pumpkin spice anything. This afternoon she found pumpkin spice bubble bath in one of the bargain bins at a store. We spent at least fifteen minutes digging out every bottle we could find. Carrying them around wasn't fun, either. Luckily we didn't have to walk too far."

"Where are you and Amelia staying?"

"At a town house on the beach." Ivy mentioned the location.

"That's only a few blocks away from the apartment I'm subletting. A friend of mine is working in Dallas for a few months and he's letting me stay there."

"So you mentioned San Diego. Is that where you're from?"

"No, I grew up on the East Coast."

As Ivy took a sip of soda, Jaxon waited, practically bracing for the questions that usually came next. Ones about family.

He couldn't fault her if she asked. It was a perfectly natural thing to wonder about—it just happened to be his least favorite topic. Talking about his family always took him back to what he'd left behind close to three years ago. He'd rather focus on the present moment, here with Ivy, than his past.

That was hard for some people to understand, his younger sister being one of them. The other day she'd sent him a text about attending some award ceremony for his father. Yeah, not happening. He loved his sister, but he didn't care if he ever saw his dad again.

Jaxon pushed the unhappy memories of his father back into the mental box he'd reserved for them and decided to make a topic switch. He pointed to her almost empty container. "Did Milo win your vote?"

"Absolutely." She wiped her hands on a napkin. "Everything was excellent. I'm sure he's getting a lot of votes today."

"But you haven't tasted Flavor Fusion's spicy salmon ramen. It's pretty good."

"You're advertising for the competition *again*?" Teasing shadowed her face.

"I'm just being fair. If you want to try some, we still have time to get a bowl."

"I can't eat another bite." Liveliness reflected in her eyes. "Or maybe that was your strategy all along. Feed me an abundance of tacos so I wouldn't have room for ramen."

"Damn." He shook his head in mock disappointment and sighed. "You figured me out."

Pointing at him, she laughed. "I knew it. But seriously, thanks for the invite. I'm glad I didn't miss this. Amelia will be jealous."

He closed one of the now empty containers. "Why didn't she come with you?"

"She didn't want to feel like she was intruding." Ivy suddenly became fascinated with the side of her soda can, tracing her finger over the logo design. "I told her it wasn't a big deal. That your invite wasn't exclusive to just me. You did ask both of us."

Jaxon picked up on the unspoken question. "Amelia wasn't excluded, but it was you I wanted to see."

Chapter Four

Ivy studied Jaxon's face, searching for insincerity. It was a habit. For years, she'd had to be mindful of who she let into her life because it wasn't just about her. Protecting her nieces and the bee farm had been her priorities. Now she was on her own. She only had herself to consider. Not having that crutch of responsibility holding her back was a tad unnerving. And so was being drawn to Jaxon.

He was almost too attractive. He had to know he was the equivalent of catnip for women, but he didn't seem to be caught up in his looks. He barely seemed to notice people staring at him with interest. For her part, she'd had to keep stuffing food in her mouth just to prevent herself from staring at him. But her attraction to Jaxon wasn't just about his looks. Curiosity played a part in it, too. He'd just confessed to wanting to see her again. Was it a game or a challenge to see if he could get her to go out with him? Or maybe he just hit on tourists because it was an easy come, easy go scenario?

Jaxon gave her a quizzical look. "What's your question?"

"I didn't say I had a question."

"But you have one." He pointed to her face. "I can see it." As he rested his hand on the table near hers, he gently nudged her fingers. "What do you want to know?"

The slight brush of his hand left tingles on her skin. She almost nudged him back just to feel it again. Instead, she put her elbow on the table and propped her chin on her hand. "Am I your usual type?"

"By type, do you mean beautiful?"

She laughed. "Oh, that's a slick answer."

He feigned innocence. "I'm sorry. Is that *not* what you meant?"

The expression on his face was a mix of teasing and honesty. She couldn't resist smiling back at him. "You know exactly what I meant. I'm older than you. I'm thirty-nine." *Soon to be forty.*

When it came to her age, she'd never been one to get hung up on a number, but sometimes, it did feel like her twenties and most of her thirties had just slipped by without her noticing. Turning forty felt like some tangible dividing point in her life. The first half would be over, and she still had no idea what was next for her in the second half.

"If you're asking me if I have a thing for older women, I don't," he said frankly. "You're interesting, and I'm happy that I'm getting the chance to spend time with you. I also don't mind that you're beautiful."

"You're really good at this."

"If you think I'm just blowin' smoke, I'm not. I'm telling you the truth. I wanted to meet you the minute you walked into the restaurant. Honestly, I thought you weren't going to show up this afternoon, and that really disappointed me. I was afraid I wouldn't get the chance to see you again."

He almost didn't. Deep diving in a store bargain bin with Amelia hadn't been the only thing that had delayed Ivy. When they'd returned to the town house, she'd sat on the bed in her room wondering if she should show up or if maybe she'd misread his interest. "I'm sorry I made you wait."

"You're worth it." As he reached toward her, he turned his hand palm up. "I'm glad you came."

Ivy laid her palm on his, and as he loosely interlaced his fingers with hers, warmth radiated into her skin. Holding his hand felt easy, right. No pressure involved.

"Are you in the mood for something sweet?" he asked.

"Depends on what it is."

Jaxon's gaze briefly dropped to her mouth. The vision of him leaning in and feeling his firm, kissable lips on hers made Ivy's breathing grow a little shallower.

Clearing his throat, he looked away and pointed to the booths. "Why don't we take a walk over there and decide what we want for dessert?"

Dessert was probably a lot safer than what she'd just imagined, but she did have one question. "That depends. How old are you?"

A small smile curved up his mouth. He stared at her face as if pondering the outcome his answer might bring. "I'm twenty-nine."

He was two years past the magic age. What did it mean? Would it make being with him even more interesting? A part of her hoped so, but unfortunately, she wouldn't get the chance to find out. She was leaving Hilton Head tomorrow. This afternoon was the only time she'd get to spend with him.

Jaxon leaned in a little. "So are you interested in dessert?"

His mouth was so tempting. A few inches more and she could definitely sample another version of dessert. Or maybe she could leave now with pleasant memories of an enjoyable afternoon, but what if she stayed? Magic age or not, she liked talking to Jaxon, holding his hand, and the possibility of maybe kissing him felt exciting and new. And Amelia was right that it was a safe bet he wouldn't ruin the afternoon by proposing marriage.

Meeting his gaze, she replied, "I'd love some."

Moments later, they were still holding hands and navigating the crowd. After casting their votes for Milo's food truck at the voting tent, they checked out the stalls with dessert offerings. Something light and cool appealed to them both. Shaved ice treats—blue raspberry for him and a mix of grape and strawberry for her.

Strolling down the wood planks of the narrow boardwalk near the beach, they seemed to gravitate toward each other naturally. A part of her eagerly anticipated the next brush of his arm against hers.

To distract herself from it, Ivy scooped flavored ice from her cup. "I haven't had one of these in ages. It reminds me of the thrills Grandma Jean made for my sister and I when we were kids visiting her in Georgia for the summer." She was surprised to hear herself recall the memory aloud. She usually didn't reminisce like this, especially with someone she'd just met. Feeling out of step with herself, she averted her gaze from him. "Thrills—you probably have no idea what I'm talking about."

"Actually, I do. It's a homemade popsicle in a plastic cup. I heard they're kind of a Savannah thing. I used to work at a restaurant there and they served them to customers after dinner. You look surprised that I know that."

"Most people don't. It's so specific."

He gave a small shrug. "Maybe it is, but they seemed to bring back a lot of good memories for all of the people at the restaurant. The neighborhoods they lived in. Family. Friends. Sounds like it's the same for you."

"It is." Ivy paused with him shoulder to shoulder on the walkway near the railing. As they overlooked the ocean, she let more of her own pleasant recollections float in. "My sister and I used to argue over what flavor to make. She liked strawberry. I wanted grape." Remembering the innocent intensity of her and Lexy's childhood squabbles, she laughed.

"Who usually won?"

"She usually did, but only because she was five years older than me and tall enough to reach the drink packets on the shelf. I had to use a chair, so she always beat me to it." Still, at least half of the time, Lexy did play fair and she'd choose a grape-flavored packet.

The memory of her five- or six-year-old self sporting twin braids, enjoying her frozen treat and showing off her purple tongue to Lexy sprang into her mind.

He pointed to her cup. "Did you learn to like strawberry or is that a compromise?"

Ivy glanced at the mix of strawberry and grape flavored ice. When she'd ordered both flavors earlier, she hadn't registered they were her and Lexy's childhood favorites.

The image of her and Lexy as children faded to one of the last times she and her sister had been together as adults. It had been at the bee farm. Lexy had been the one with braids, looking youthful and happy as they'd walked around Bishop Honey Bee Farm. The farm had been Lexy's dream, and she'd been so excited about the future. But by the end of that year...

Swallowing hard, Ivy blinked the image away. Undoubtedly sadness was written on her face, and she didn't want to explain it. Instead, she focused on swirling her spoon through the melting ice in the cup and pulled herself together.

Forcing a smile, she looked at him. "The flavors just bring back good memories. Speaking of flavor, when will we know who won the food competition?"

From the understanding look in his eyes, Jaxon wasn't fooled by her sudden topic switch, but he was kind enough to go along with it. "They'll probably make the announcement in an hour or so, but Milo will have to call me with the news. I have to get back to the Wavefront."

Disappointment unexpectedly flooded her tone. "Oh? You're working a split shift today?"

"Sort of." Jaxon set his cup on the railing. He slipped hers from her grasp and set it next to his before taking hold of her hands. "I really want to see you again. Go out with me tomorrow. It's my day off. We can hang out at the beach. Do the tourist thing. Whatever you want. Just spend the day with me."

Ivy dropped her head a moment and prepared to deliver the bad news. "I can't. I'm leaving tomorrow afternoon."

"Leaving?" Surprise mixed with disappointment took over his face. "I thought you were going to be around longer."

"I wish I was. Spending the day with you would have been nice."

As Jaxon tugged her closer, he released a heavy sigh. "I wish we didn't have to end things like this."

"So do I." If only she had one more day, but Brooke and Harper were expecting her to come home.

Jaxon hung his head a moment then looked at her. "I really need to go."

Ivy released a heavy sigh. "I understand."

As the sun magnified the color of his eyes, it came to her which paint hue she would need to fully capture them. *Gold.* Just a hint to bring out their true rich color. Ivy cataloged his face in her mind. It would stay there along with the wonderful memory of this afternoon with him, but one thing was missing.

As if he'd read her mind, Jaxon leaned in. His hesitation was a silent question, asking her if she was on board with what he was about to do next.

She was.

He brushed his mouth over hers. The firmness of his lips delivering slow, soft kisses had a drugging effect on Ivy. As she slid her hands up his chest and around his neck, he settled his in the curves of her waist. Jaxon gently sucked her bottom lip until she opened her mouth with a small sigh, allowing him to glide in past her lips. As his tongue caressed hers, she was lost in a rush of delicious heat. She rose on her toes for more as he explored her mouth.

A long moment later, the kiss reluctantly came to an end. Ivy's heart bumped in her chest. He rested his forehead to hers, and she closed her eyes, soaking in the wonderful aftereffect as they both breathed unsteadily. And there were those electric-like sparks of desire she'd wondered if she would ever experience again. She'd felt them, all right, but with someone she wasn't going to see again. The unfairness of it all hit with a bittersweetness that turned into sad disappointment.

"Come to the Wavefront tonight," he said.

She pictured herself sitting at the end of the bar at the restaurant, watching Jaxon work and waiting for scraps of time she could get with him. The image wasn't appealing at all. In fact, it seemed a little desperate.

"You have to work," she reasoned. "I need to pack."

"I'm actually not on the clock tonight. I'm volunteering. One of the servers is leaving and the boss is letting us throw a party in the outdoor dining area. I'm pitching in with the rest of the staff that are off, bartending, taking care of the food, cleaning up, that sort of thing."

More time with Jaxon. It was so tempting. "I don't know..."

"What time are you leaving tomorrow?"

"I have to be at the airport by three o'clock."

"So, it sounds like you could pack in the morning, then?"

As she started to answer him, Jaxon intercepted her response with a soft teasing kiss. "I could…but I…" A final lingering kiss chipped away at her resolve.

Jaxon lifted his mouth a hairsbreadth from hers. "Say yes."

Chapter Five

Ivy strode down the sidewalk to the Wavefront Bistro. A few yards from the entrance, she reached up and adjusted the halter strap on her fitted paisley dress. It just didn't want to stay put. One minute it felt like it was nearly strangling her, the next, it felt too loose. Or maybe the strap wasn't the real problem and she was just agitated…though she wasn't sure why that would be the case. She'd been fine when she left the town house a half hour ago. Okay, maybe she hadn't been 100 percent fine. Her thoughts were almost consumed by Jaxon, which was ridiculous. She was a grown woman, not a girl with a crush.

Once again, the memory of the passionate kisses they'd shared that afternoon flitted through her mind. Remembering the sparks ignited a full body flush. Experiencing that feeling after so many years of not having it with anyone had been unexpected and wonderful. But that didn't mean anything. Maybe she'd gone through an affection drought and Jaxon had satisfied it with a really great kiss. Why was she losing her head over it?

Not coming up with an answer to that question

brought Ivy to an abrupt halt. Amelia slammed into her, and they both teetered in their stilettos.

"Ow, my foot," Amelia hissed. "Why did you stop like that?"

"Coming here was a mistake." Ivy started to reverse her steps.

Looking slightly confused and all kinds of cute in a green long-sleeve minidress, Amelia stood in her way. "We can't leave. We're already here, and isn't Jaxon expecting you?"

"Yes, but if we go now, he'll never know I was here."

Ivy propped a hand on her hip. "So just like that, you're going to ghost him?"

"I didn't say that."

"Then what are you saying?"

Ivy grabbed Amelia's arm and tugged her out of the flow of pedestrian traffic. "I'm saying that I'll text him an excuse when we get back to the town house. I'll tell him I'm really tired or that I had more stuff to pack than I realized before catching my flight tomorrow."

Amelia blankly stared at her. "Those are the saddest chickening out excuses I've ever heard, and as your friend I refuse to let you use them."

"Seriously, for once, can you not be such a good friend?"

"No, I can't. What's really going on?"

"Fine." Ivy threw up her hands in surrender. "Meeting Jaxon here at the restaurant feels more like a date than meeting him at the food competition. What are we going to talk about?"

"You talked this afternoon, didn't you?"

"Sure, but it was small talk. Nothing deep."

"And apparently that wasn't a problem. You came home with a dazed, kiss-drunk look on your face. An hour ago, you couldn't wait to see him. What's changed?"

Ivy opened her mouth to deny she wanted to see Jaxon again, but she knew Amelia wouldn't let her get away with such a blatant lie. She released a breath of defeat. "I'm attracted to him. No, I'm *too* attracted to him. What if seeing him tonight turns out to be a disappointment?"

"Okay, now I'm confused." Amelia frowned. "Are you worried about not liking him as much as you did or liking him too much?"

"Both, maybe." Ivy honestly couldn't decide. "What if things aren't the same as they were this afternoon? I'll feel like being with him today was a waste of time."

"You're overthinking it. Get out of your head." Empathy shone in Amelia's eyes as she gave Ivy's hand a squeeze. "What if you walk in there and he is the same, and you're not disappointed?"

"But I just met him—and I'm leaving tomorrow. Where can this go?"

"It could lead to a lot of fun, and it could be the highlight of your trip." Humor came into Amelia's eyes. "Well, one of the highlights after me, of course. Anyway, we have to go in. You owe me at least one drink since you made me give up my date with a hot tub."

She actually did owe Amelia. Her friend had been comfortable in her bathing suit, planning to call her husband, when Ivy had convinced her to abandon her hot date.

Amelia nudged Ivy. "Come on, what's one drink going to hurt?"

Ivy glanced at the restaurant again. One drink and a chance to say goodbye. What was the harm in that? She looped her arm through Amelia's. "Okay, one drink, and we're only staying for thirty minutes." That was plenty of time to tell Jaxon how sorry she was she couldn't stay without resorting to the sad excuses Amelia had vetoed.

Inside the lobby of the Wavefront Bistro, two couples the same age or younger than them walked away from the host stand with expressions of disappointment.

One of the women leaving the restaurant looked at them and said, "Don't even bother unless you have a reservation. It's a two-hour wait."

The young brunette standing behind the podium regarded Ivy and Amelia with polite detachment. Her reserved, almost snooty demeanor didn't quite fit the relaxed atmosphere of the restaurant. "Hello, do you have a reservation with us tonight?"

"No," Ivy said. "We're here for the party."

"Which party?"

The staff member who was leaving—what was her name? Ivy couldn't remember. "Jaxon invited us."

As the young woman's brows rose to meet her straight bangs, something Ivy couldn't decipher flashed through her eyes. "Jaxon is busy. You'll have to wait—"

"No, he's not," announced a tall, brown-skinned woman with a runway model-like flair, and the name Piper on her name tag. "I can take them back." She met the hostess's frown with an all too pleased smile before turning back to Ivy and Amelia. "Follow me, please."

As they trailed after the younger woman, Amelia whispered with interest, "Ooh, that looked messy. I wonder what that was about?"

Ivy raised her brow and shrugged. Who knew when it came to workplace interactions?

At the back of the restaurant, the server pointed to a glass door. "The party is out there. Jaxon's behind the bar. Have fun."

Ivy and Amelia thanked her then walked out the door. The notes of an upbeat pop song waved over them from the speakers set up front.

Small lantern centerpieces on the tables along with bright café lights strung along the trellises helped illuminate the space. Food was set up on a table off to the right. The permanent bar was on the opposite side.

It wasn't a huge party, but there were just enough people for Ivy and Amelia to blend in as part of the crowd. The way everyone easily chatted, laughed, and lived it up on the dance floor, it was clear everyone was comfortable with each other.

Ivy glanced over at the bar then around the area. "I don't see him."

"Maybe he just stepped away for a second." Amelia pointed. "Let's go to the bar. We can ask the guy working there if he knows where Jaxon is."

Striding over, they spotted two available stools and headed straight for them.

Soon after they sat down, the linebacker-sized dark-haired bartender with a beard and a goatee came over.

"Hey," he greeted them both, but his gaze lingered on Amelia. Leaning in on the counter in front of her, his smile widened into a flirty, slightly cocky grin. "Are you ordering from the menu or can I offer you something else?"

As Amelia pointed down the bar counter, the impressive diamond and emerald wedding ring on her left hand almost clipped his nose. "Just the menu, please. Have you seen Jaxon?"

Taking her rejection in stride, the younger man leaned away and smiled. "Last time I saw him he was headed inside. If I see him, I'll let him know you're here." He slid the plastic holder with the drink menu in front of her. "Let me know when you're ready. My name is Drew." He ambled away, laughing as he greeted people waiting at the other end of the bar.

Amelia released a breezy laugh. "That was cute."

"Cute? It was a near tragedy. You almost put his eye out with your ring."

Amelia waved off the accusation. "I'm not heartless. I would never mess up a pretty face, but I would have swatted him on the nose if he got too close."

From the amusement on Amelia's face, she'd enjoyed the bartender flirting with her, but they both knew she would never cheat on her husband. Since they'd been in Hilton Head, the couple had talked every day. As recollections of Amelia's soft, dreamy smile whenever she was on the phone with her husband flickered through Ivy's mind, a pang of wistfulness struck. Would she ever be that happy with someone special?

Clearing the thought away, Ivy leaned over and looked at the drink menu. "What are we getting?"

Amelia tapped one of her soap manicured nails on the menu. "A frozen cocktail maybe? But I haven't had a maple old-fashioned in a while. Oh, check out these mocktails. A berry basil pineapple slide. I've never had one of those before."

"Neither have I."

Loops and horn sound effects blended into the music track. As they recognized the beat and lyrics from the song, Amelia looked to Ivy, and both of them grinned as they bopped in their seats.

It was sung by the rapper and singer Eve. They'd danced to it along with Amelia's bridesmaids at her bachelorette party six years ago.

Amelia dropped the menu on the bar and grabbed her hand. "We have to dance to this."

"What about Jaxon?"

"He'll find you." Amelia pulled her to the dance floor, and they joined the crowd.

With every drop and sway of her hips, Ivy let the beat take the lead. She embraced the good memories of Amelia's bachelorette party, along with the freedom to let loose now and just be herself. She and Amelia whooped and sang the lyrics as they danced with each other, and Ivy laughed for no reason other than her own happiness at being with her friend. Who gave a damn what anyone thought about her? Other than Amelia, she didn't know these people. It wasn't like she was going to see any of them again.

Smiling widely, Amelia took hold of one of Ivy's hands and twirled her around.

Ivy released a combination of a laugh and a shout. In the middle of the spin, Amelia let her go…

…and Jaxon took hold of her hand. Ivy stumbled into him. Her heart jumped wildly in her chest as he drew her closer.

He used his free hand to take hold of her waist. As he held her gaze, one of his slow sexy smiles tipped up his mouth. Gliding his hand to her lower back, he leaned in close. She was overwhelmed by the graze of his lightly stubbled cheek along hers. The solid strength of his chest pressing against the peaks of her breasts. The wonderful scent of leather, amber, and spice wafting from him. It all made her a bit lightheaded.

He murmured something, and Ivy tilted her head a little as the warmth along with his words feathered over the shell of her ear. "You made it," he said.

She leaned back to look up at him. "I did."

It was a repeat of how they'd greeted each other that afternoon. From his widening smile, he'd picked up on that, too.

People jostled them, and the message was clear— dance or get out of the way. They let go of each other and stepped apart. As they moved to the beat of the music, they easily complemented each other's steps.

Ivy let her gaze wander over him, shamelessly appreciating the view of him in an untucked navy button- down and jeans that hugged his thighs.

The DJ transitioned to a new song.

Jaxon leaned toward her. "Do you want to grab a drink?" He tipped his head toward the bar.

"Yes." The sight of Jaxon dancing had made her feel heated and thirsty, and she needed to cool off.

He took her hand and was leading her from the dance floor when a thought hit Ivy and she stopped. *Amelia!* She'd been so into Jaxon, she'd forgotten all about her. Ivy looked back at the people dancing, but Amelia wasn't in the crowd.

"What's wrong?" Jaxon asked.

"Amelia was with me. I don't see her."

He pointed. "Isn't that her over there?"

Amelia sat on a stool at the end of the bar, engrossed in a lively conversation with Drew.

As they reached them, Ivy caught part of their conversation.

"Peppermint?" Drew asked. "Are you serious?"

"Absolutely." Amelia nodded. "Just put a few drops of peppermint oil in a spray bottle with water and spritz some on the window sill. Your spider problem will go away."

"I'll try anything at this point." Drew made a face and shuddered. "Spiders are the worst."

Ivy smiled to herself. It wasn't surprising that Amelia had somehow flipped the script, turning the big flirty guy into a teddy bear eager for practical advice.

As Amelia looked in her direction, Ivy caught a flash of "I told you so" on her face. "Hey, Jaxon."

"Hi, Amelia." He pointed at her half-full glass. Based on the small waffle garnish, she'd gone with the maple old-fashioned. "Would you like another one?"

She shook her head. "No, I'm good."

"What can I get you?" As he looked at Ivy, he rested his hand just below her exposed back and shoulders. Immediately, her bare skin started tingling, scattering the rest of her thoughts. Yeah, she'd better forget the alcohol and keep a clear head. "I'll have the berry basil pineapple slide."

"Got it." Drew looked to Jaxon. "Beer?"

"Yeah, thanks."

"Oh, and someone's waiting for you." Drew pointed to the other end of the long counter.

Ivy followed Jaxon's gaze. It was the hostess.

"Wendy said she needs to talk to you about bar service," Drew added. "Something about the wedding reception this coming weekend. She wants an opinion about changes she made to the setup diagram."

Jaxon frowned. "I'm off the clock. Can't you talk to her?"

"Nope, according to her, one of the managers said she should talk to you."

Drew gave Jaxon a loaded look that Ivy didn't know how to interpret.

Jaxon's frown dissipated as he looked to Ivy. "I have to handle this, but it won't take long."

He slipped through the crowd. As soon as he reached Wendy, she smiled eagerly and handed him a piece of paper. As he read over it, the hostess stared longingly up at him.

Amelia huffed a chuckle. "That explains the tart expression on her face when you said Jaxon invited us. Poor thing. Did we ever crush that hard on a guy?"

Drew delivered the drinks, and Ivy picked up hers. "Back in the day, I'm sure we did."

Amelia laughed. "I definitely don't miss that kind of chaos in my life."

As the hostess pointed something out on the paper, she stepped closer to Jaxon and he moved a step away. Maybe they'd gone out at some point? That wouldn't be unusual. A lot of people dated their coworkers. If they had, and the hostess wasn't completely over him, it was probably hard to see him interested in someone else.

"I agree." Ivy turned away and took a sip of the chilled drink made with pineapple juice, ginger beer, and muddled strawberries. Dancing with Jaxon had made her forget the plan—say hello and then good-bye to him in short order. Yes, she'd had fun dancing with Jaxon, but it wasn't worth staying to watch other women chase after him. As appealing as Jaxon was, she wasn't interested in a competition where he was the prize. Amelia was right. Who needed that kind of chaos? She didn't.

As Amelia set her empty tumbler on the bar counter, she put her half-full glass beside it. "Are you calling a Lyft or am I?" Ivy asked. "If we leave now, we'll still have plenty of time for our date with the hot tub."

"What? No." Amelia pointed to herself then Ivy. "*I* have a date with the hot tub. *You* have a date with Jaxon."

"Jaxon and I danced and now we're done. It's time to say goodbye, like I planned on doing when I got here. Don't give me that look."

Amelia tilted her head with a questioning stare. "Why are you running from him?"

"I'm not. It's just time to go. You said it yourself about crushes and chaos. He's clearly a drama magnet, and I don't have time for it." Ivy nudged her glass farther up on the bar. "One drink, thirty minutes. That was the plan, remember?"

"Do me a favor. Turn around and look at him."

"Why?"

Sighing, Amelia gave her a long-suffering look. "Just do it."

Ivy glanced to the other side of the bar counter and fell straight into Jaxon's gaze. The hostess was still talking and pointing to the paper, but his attention remained on Ivy. Longing and hints of frustration were on his face.

"Does Jaxon look like a guy who's interested in chaos or drama, or does he look like he's interested in nothing but you?"

As he continued to gaze at her, Ivy's mouth dried out. She picked up her glass and took a long sip of her drink. Maybe Jaxon was interested in her, and she couldn't deny her attraction to him. But was he worth staying for?

Chapter Six

Jaxon mentally kicked himself as he listened to Wendy's convoluted explanation about what seemed to be an unnecessary change. He shouldn't have left Ivy. Honestly, he hadn't thought the issue would take this long. Management always seemed to support pointless, last-minute decisions, and it was a headache for the staff.

He'd transferred from the Wavefront's sister restaurant in Florida a couple of months ago and had been expecting a chill place to work. Instead, he'd walked into the middle of a potential dumpster fire. Luckily, he had another job lined up. His friend Nate had called him about the opportunity a little over two weeks ago.

He and Nate had worked together at the restaurant in Jacksonville. Nate had ended up leaving to open a wine bar with his girlfriend. Then he and the girlfriend had broken up. Now his friend needed a hand running things, and Jaxon had gladly accepted Nate's offer of a temporary job.

He'd already given the Wavefront his notice. Soon, he wouldn't have to deal with this mess. Still, he couldn't help thinking that the restaurant's issues would be so easy to fix.

Jaxon mentally ticked off several improvements. It was so obvious to him.

Like father, like son...

The jarring, uncomfortable thought leaped into his mind. It was something he'd heard many times—that he was just like his father when it came to business strategy. He hated hearing it every time. No. He was nothing like the man who'd raised him. His father was a vulture in an expensive suit, a dismantler of people's dreams, including Jaxon's.

Rolling his shoulders, Jaxon refocused on Ivy, and pure longing moved through him. He wanted to kiss her again and hold her for as long as he possibly could tonight.

"So what do you think?" Wendy asked, smiling at him. "Do you have any suggestions?"

Many of the staff believed the dark-haired woman had an agenda and was sucking up to management to get a promotion. And there was also a rumor going around the restaurant that she had a thing for him. If she did, he didn't want her forming any ideas about them being together. He was with Ivy, and he really wanted to get back to her.

"Hate to interrupt." Drew stood in front of them on the other side of the counter. He looked to Jaxon. "But don't you really need to discuss that *thing* you mentioned with Amelia and her friend? Isn't that why they stopped by tonight?"

Drew was throwing him a lifeline, and Jaxon grabbed onto it like a drowning man. "Yeah, that *thing* we need to discuss is important." He looked to Wendy, whose eager smile had turned into a scowl. "I really have to go. Why don't you run your ideas by Drew?" Jaxon handed him the diagram. "You are one of the lead bartenders."

"Sure, I'll take a look." Drew gave Jaxon a "you owe me" look.

Within seconds, Jaxon was back at Ivy's side. He picked up the bottle of beer that was waiting for him. "Sorry. That took longer than I expected."

Amelia stood. "It's getting late. Time for me to go."

Stricken, Jaxon looked to Ivy. "You're not leaving, are you?" He set down his beer and took her hand.

She glanced down to where he'd loosely linked their fingers together, a small frown of uncertainty tugging at her brow.

If only he could erase whatever she was debating in her mind. "It's just us for the rest of the night. I promise." He gave her hand a gentle squeeze.

After a long moment, she met his gaze. "I'll stay as long as you're totally off the clock."

Relief poured through him. "Totally. I'm done."

"Then I guess I'm leaving on my own." Amelia picked up her purse from the bar counter then pinned him with a stare. "I'm trusting you to get her home. If you don't, I will hunt you down and make you wish you lived on another planet. Are we clear?"

He gave her a nod. "Crystal."

"Really, Amelia?" Ivy gave her friend a bemused look. "I'm a grown woman."

"And I'm your friend."

The looks of slight exasperation and amusement the two women exchanged almost made Jaxon chuckle, but he glanced away and swallowed it along with a sip of beer. Based on the feistiness in Amelia's eyes, he was completely certain she would hurt him if he didn't honor his promise to make sure Ivy made it home okay.

"See you later." Amelia gave Ivy a quick peck on the cheek and then whispered something in her ear. Whatever she said made Ivy's brows rise with a quiet laugh.

As Amelia walked away, Jaxon released the chuckle he'd been holding in.

Ivy gave him an apologetic look. "I know she's a lot."

"I'm okay with it. It's good that you have a friend who cares about you that much."

"It is, and I love her for it." Ivy smiled. "At least 99 percent of the time."

Jaxon sensed he had Amelia to thank for why Ivy was still there. Not wanting to let go of her, he pointed with his beer in his other hand. "There's a free table over there. Let's grab it."

The table was off to the side, and once they took their seats, they were finally alone.

He looked to her. "So what do you—"

"Coming in hot." Drew walked up carrying another mocktail for Ivy and two beers.

After handing off a beer to Jaxon, Drew turned one of the empty chairs around and dropped down on it. "I'm done. Now I can join the party."

Before Jaxon could subtly suggest he should join the party elsewhere, more people walked up.

"Yay. We're all together now." Piper sauntered over with Lori, the guest of honor. Each of them balanced trays of wings, cupcakes and loaded potato skins in their hands.

As soon as the food was on the table, Drew snagged a drumette. "You read my mind. I'm starving."

Apparently so was everyone sitting around them. Soon more people dragged over tables and chairs with an eye on the food.

Jaxon inwardly groaned. A crowd at their table was not what he'd had in mind. He glanced at Ivy, expecting to see disappointment on her face, but she smiled as someone handed her a cupcake.

"Service has been wild tonight," Piper said.

That opened the door to gripes about customers and last-minute changes to the menu—common topics of conversation with any group of restaurant staff. Someone else asked Ivy about her coin-shaped silver earrings. She'd gotten them during a cruise to Aruba, Bonaire, and Curaçao.

The group conversation expanded to vacations. The Caribbean, Canada, Italy, and destinations in the States.

Ivy had been to some of those places and so had Jaxon. Apparently, they both liked to travel. From the way she talked about wishing she had a chance to take up hiking again, she might have enjoyed the trip he'd taken to Colorado last year. He'd hiked but also done some rock climbing.

A vision of Ivy outfitted in the appropriate gear as they hiked together came clearly into his mind. She looked just as good in it as she did in the dress she was wearing. Jaxon washed the image away as he drank his beer. That was weird. It had been a long time since he'd envisioned going somewhere specific with someone.

It wasn't because of the "nonstick" claim Milo had made about him when it came to relationships. It was just that since he'd left New York three years ago, he hadn't stayed in one place long enough for a relationship to have a place *to* stick in his life.

He was good with the short term, usually. But something about Ivy made him wish she could have stuck around a little longer. If only he could have had more than one night with her.

Ivy sipped her mocktail. Caught up in the swirl of conversation with Jaxon's friends hadn't been what she'd expected tonight. Not that she was mad at it. The group was lively and friendly as they ate, teasing each other and reminiscing about their escapades at the restaurant.

She'd sensed from Jaxon that he wanted to be alone with her, and honestly, she'd felt the same way. But maybe it was good to have a bit of a buffer between her and Jaxon for a minute, especially after what Amelia had planted in her mind before she'd gone back to the town house.

Catch and release. You've already caught him. Don't be afraid to enjoy it.

It was pretty clear Amelia was talking about having a one-night stand with Jaxon. Was that what she wanted? Admittedly, she hadn't fully thought out how tonight with Jaxon might end. What had she expected when she decided not to leave with Amelia? That they'd just have a few drinks, talk and make plans for him to visit her in Maryland or for her to come back to South Carolina to hang out with him? Or had she really wanted to explore where more of his kisses might lead?

As Ivy glanced at Jaxon, he took a sip of beer then dipped his tongue along his lower lip. Her mouth dried out as undeniable want expanded inside of her. At the same time, part of her felt she should be cautious. Sleep with him? That wouldn't be a sensible thing to do.

But you don't have to be just sensible anymore... do you?

Raucous laughter pulled Ivy from her thoughts. Staff members were talking about some of Lori's "oops" moments.

The young woman laughed and buried her face in her hands.

"Oh, we can't forget the best one. Remember that time she walked out here and thought a kid's sparkly stick toy was a snake?"

"Hey, you didn't see it." Mirth was in Lori's eyes. "It moved like one."

Jaxon spoke up. "No, you were the only thing moving, along with the tray of food you threw in the air. You vaulted over the bar so fast, I thought I was seeing things."

"I couldn't see anything," Drew interjected. "I was blinded by the fettuccini Alfredo that smacked me in the face."

As Drew, a natural pot stirrer, added more to the story, peals of laughter erupted from the group. It was infectious, and Ivy's own laughter bubbled out. As she turned toward Jaxon and buried her face against his shoulder, her hand rested on his chest. Suddenly she was lost in his warmth and how good he smelled.

He took hold of her other hand resting on his leg near his thigh and intertwined their fingers. She raised her head. Jaxon had been laughing, too, but as they stared at each other, the expression on his face transformed into a look that made her crave the feel of his lips on hers. His gaze dropped to her mouth, and she sensed that he was feeling the same thing.

"Will you dance with me?" he asked.

A slow song played through the speakers. He stood and she took his hand. They left the friendly teasing and debate still happening at the table and went to the dance floor.

As he moved his hands from the curves of her waist to her lower back, she slid hers over his shoulders to rest at his nape.

With each gentle sway, they moved closer. He glided his hands to her lower back, tugging her even closer until finally she was pressed flush against him. She released a soft sigh and leaned into him. The way he held her, the way she fit against him, was perfection.

His shaky exhale feathered along her cheek, proving that he was just as affected as she was.

Ivy looked up at his face. Jaxon's gaze held hers as if only she existed. The laughter and conversation around them faded away until all that was left was the feel of him holding her. She soaked in his strength, his warmth radiating his appealing scent, and the want she saw in his eyes.

Giving in to her own want, Ivy rested her hands on his chest and kissed him. Jaxon wrapped an arm around her, deepening the kiss as they swayed together, lost in each other. They started to ease away with the final notes of the song, but like a magnet, desire pulled them back together.

As they kissed again, Ivy leaned more into him, and he tightened his hold. She felt his arousal pressing through his jeans against her belly, and heat flushed over her skin. She felt heady and grounded at the same time. She wanted more of this. She wanted more of him.

Jaxon lifted his mouth a fraction from hers. "Can I take you home?"

There wasn't a doubt in her mind as she said yes.

Standing in the open front door of the town house, the urgency to be with him grew stronger as one deep, delicious kiss flowed into the next.

Jaxon's breathing was ragged as he brushed open-mouthed kisses down her throat. "I want you so badly."

His voice was husky with need in a way that made her legs unsteady. "I want you, too. Come inside with me."

He looked into her eyes as if asking whether she was sure, or giving her time to back out. But her mind was made up. She only had this moment with Jaxon, and she wanted to have everything one night could give them.

She took his hand, leading him inside, then locking the door behind him.

From the quiet stillness surrounding them, Amelia had gone to bed, so she stepped out of her heels, trying to move quietly. It had been decades since she'd snuck into a house with a guy, but technically, she wasn't sneaking. Just being a respectful roommate.

The town house had a simple layout. A living room with a basic furniture, and a widescreen television on the wall. A breakfast bar counter separated the room from the kitchen. The hall to the left led to Amelia's room. The hallway on the right went to Ivy's bedroom.

Jaxon followed her down the hall. Desire and anticipation made her feel like a live wire ready to spark. He must have felt the same way. As soon as they were enclosed in the room, he met her for a heated kiss.

Frantically running her hand on the wall near the door, she found the light switch. The lamp on the bedside table turned on. Good—she wanted to see every inch of him.

Ivy tugged up his shirt, enjoying the feel of his skin underneath her fingertips. As he took it off, she followed it upward, gliding over his abs and solid pecs. They broke from the kiss long enough for him to toss the shirt aside.

Jaxon inched up the skirt of her dress to palm her butt and press her against him. The feel of his erection, pressing through his jeans, low on her belly heightened her need for him.

Ivy reached up and unclipped the strap at her nape. Holding her by the hips, he stepped back, allowing space for the fabric to fall to her waist, leaving her bare. Emboldened by the want flaring in his eyes, she moved back a few inches more and slipped from his grasp. She slowly shimmied the dress past her hips until it glided down her legs.

Her breasts grew full and heavy as his gaze traveled downward, pausing on the triangle of sheer blue lace between her thighs before rising back up again.

"Wow," he whispered faintly, shaking his head as if he was at a loss for words. The look in his eyes said everything. He desired her as much as she desired him.

Jaxon stepped forward and took hold of her hips. As he pressed his mouth to hers, the heat of his skin seeped into her. Soon, he lowered her to the bed. Unhurried, he brushed his lips along her brow, her cheeks, and down her neck to the peaks of her breasts. The intoxicating way he explored her body with kisses and gentle caresses made her tremble. Jaxon told her how beautiful she was. How much he wanted her. His words and his touch, along with the soft feel of lace gliding down her legs, fueled the ache growing inside of her. He satisfied it with more soft caresses between her thighs until she found ecstasy.

He left her on the bed long enough to take off the rest of his clothes and slip on protection, then he glided into her. They moved together, finding pleasure as he took her higher and higher, and she lost herself in Jaxon...and in the moment a part of her wished it would never end.

Chapter Seven

Ivy awakened the next morning to the sound of water running in the en suite bathroom.

As she stretched underneath the sheets, she turned and snuggled into the pillow next to her. It smelled like him. She breathed in his spicy scent and smiled.

Jaxon had planned to leave hours earlier, before dawn, but a lengthy toe-curling kiss at the bedroom door had made her drag him back to bed—and he'd come willingly. Eagerly, even. Her smile widened and her cheeks flushed as she remembered all that happened next. Last night had been nothing short of amazing.

The bathroom door opened, and Jaxon walked out dressed in nothing but his jeans. Jaxon shirtless should have been against the law.

With a lazy, self-assured, panther-like grace, he came to her side of the bed and dropped down on the mattress beside her.

He smiled. "Good morning." Bracing hands on each side of her, he leaned in and pressed his mouth to hers.

He smelled clean like soap and tasted of mint. She'd told him he could use whatever he needed in the bathroom, including the prepasted toothbrushes in the amenity basket.

He sat up straight and took one of her hands. "So, I was thinking. There's a bakery that makes a fruit Danish that you really need to try. You should have some with me."

"I should, huh?" She smiled up at him. "But only with you and no one else?"

"They won't taste the same without me." He leaned in and kissed her. "And I need to be there to lick the filling off your lips when you take a bite."

"Oh, so just because you saw me drop tacos on my lap once, you think I'm a messy eater?"

As he hovered over her, the slow smile curling up his mouth made her heart stutter. "If it means I get to lick you clean, then I'm certainly hoping you are."

The low sexy growl in his voice went straight to her core. Heat flushed through her breasts and her nipples tightened. *Down, girl.* If she went out with him for Danish pastries, that would be all they would have time for, nothing else...and then she'd have to tell him goodbye.

Sadness pinged in her chest, surprising her. She was supposed to be okay with this just being one night. Like she'd told herself at the party, they weren't going to keep in touch. The letting go part. The walking away. That was what catch and release meant. It was probably best for the release part to start now.

She laid her hand on his chest and dug deep to channel a sense of ease. "I wish I could, but I really need to pack, and Amelia would never let me hear the end of it if I didn't spend time with her before I leave. You understand, right?"

As if validating her excuse, sounds of Amelia moving around the town house echoed through the closed door.

Jaxon gave her a rueful smile. "Yeah, I understand." He got up and scooped his shirt up from the floor. At the same time, she snagged the peach sweat shorts and T-shirt she'd put on the first time he'd planned to leave.

He gave her time to take care of a few essentials in the bathroom and to do something with her hair. A ponytail would have to do.

Then, holding hands, they walked silently down the hall.

In the front entryway, he leaned down to put on his boots, not bothering to really tie them. He stood, and in the next instant, he caught her around the waist and captured her mouth. Their earlier almost-goodbye kiss had only been a warm-up compared to this one. Every stroke and glide of his tongue over hers had her rising on her toes for more as she held on to his shoulders. His taste, his touch. His strength. It felt as if the very essence of him was seeping into her, leaving an impression.

He ended the kiss, and as he looked deeply into her eyes, he said, "Goodbye, Ivy."

Before she could pull herself together to respond, he was gone.

Slightly breathless, Ivy rested back against the wall.

Amelia, dressed in a pair of silky red pajamas, stared at her from the kitchen over the breakfast bar counter. "Whatever happened last night, I want details."

Ivy sauntered over and took a seat in one of the chairs. She felt free, sexy, and wonderful. "I'll give you details, but only if I get that." She pointed to the mug of coffee in Amelia's hand.

"You don't ask for much, do you?"

Ivy laughed as Amelia handed over the mug. "Trust me. It'll be worth it."

Jaxon stepped inside the two-bedroom apartment he was subletting and locked the door. It was a comfortable enough place, stocked with everything he might need, including modern furnishings and an updated kitchen and baths. But right then, it felt disappointing to be there. He'd envisioned a different kind of morning with him and Ivy. One where they'd enjoy pastries and coffee at the bakery, maybe stroll around the neighborhood before he took her back to the town house.

He'd also been thinking about suggesting meeting up again. Nothing complicated. Just a weekend here or… Where did Ivy say she was from? Jaxon drew a blank. She'd talked about the places she'd traveled last night at the restaurant, but he'd never heard the word *home* mentioned. The fact that Ivy didn't volunteer personal details about herself possibly pointed to one thing. She hadn't been interested in seeing him again beyond last night.

It wasn't a pleasant thought, but he had to face it. He also had to face his growling stomach—he needed to eat. Jaxon went straight ahead through the living room to the kitchen. After tossing his things on the counter, he was pouring himself a bowl of cereal when his phone rang with a ring tone he recognized.

Jaxon released a heavy sigh. She wasn't going to give up until he talked to her. He snagged his phone and answered it on the way to the refrigerator to grab some milk. "Hello."

"He lives," his sister, Nicki, quipped wryly. "I was about to send a search party to… Where are you now?"

"I'm still in South Carolina. How's Isaiah?" Nicki and her husband worked for their father at Coffield Ventures in New York, even though they lived in Philadelphia.

"He's great. We're both good. Did you get the emailed invitation to the award banquet?" As a financial analyst, Nicki didn't like wasting time with small talk. She usually cut to the chase in a conversation.

"Yes." Jaxon poured milk over his cereal. "And I RSVP'd as requested."

"You checked no."

"I did." He had no intention whatsoever of attending anything involving his CEO father or the man's corporate investment firm.

"Jaxon…" Nicki's voice held traces of weary sadness. "I get why you're upset with him, but hasn't this thing between you two gone on long enough? Can't you try to find a way to get past it and reconcile with Dad?"

"When you say *thing*, are you referring to when Dad fucked me over? Yeah, kind of hard to get over that."

Six years ago, Jaxon had quit his job working at Coffield Ventures, his father's corporate investment firm, to pursue his own business interests. He and two of his friends started an online wine subscription service. Three years later, in the midst of their most profitable year, his father had convinced his partners to sell the company out from under him.

Bitterness gnawed away at Jaxon's appetite. The bite of his father's betrayal wasn't as fresh as it had been three years ago, but he still couldn't forgive him.

"I know it's hard," Nicki said, "but he regrets it." She paused. "He misses you."

Disbelief made Jaxon huff out a breath. "He said that?"

"Not in so many words, but you're his son. We're a family. You've kept us all at a distance for too long. I miss you, too. I miss my family being together."

A pang of guilt hit Jaxon as he thought of how little time he'd spent with his sister and brother-in-law since the split with his father. The biggest chunk of time he'd spent with them had been when he'd popped into town for their wedding two years ago. He and his father had barely spoken two words to each other on Nicki's wedding day. They'd smiled and filled their roles, proud father and brother of the bride, but they'd interacted as little as possible.

Nicki and Isaiah had met up with him last year at the airport for a quick meal when he'd had an extended layover at LaGuardia. He'd also driven to Charleston to have dinner with Isaiah a few months ago when his brother-in-law had been there for a conference.

He would have traveled to see them more often, but he knew that Nicki had a stubborn streak and that if he came to visit, she would try to stage a reunion/

intervention that would only lead to an even bigger blowout this time around.

Jaxon still remembered their last words to each other in his father's second high-rise office in Manhattan.

How could you do this? he'd asked James. *How could you screw over your own son?*

James had turned away from him to stand at the window, looking over the city as if he owned it. *If you didn't want to get screwed, you should have been watching your back.*

And now Nicki expected him to sit at some hundreds of dollars plate event to watch his father receive an award? It was too much to ask.

Frustration having ruined his appetite, Jaxon slid away the bowl. "Nicki, there is no getting past it. I know he's not sorry about what he did to me, and I have nothing to say to him. My answer is still no."

Chapter Eight

Ivy was still a little groggy from lack of sleep when she left her bedroom at Bishop Honey Bee Farm. Her flight from South Carolina to Maryland had turned out to be more eventful than anticipated. What should have been a short trip home had been extended by multiple delays at the airport. It started to feel like the plane would never get underway. She'd finally arrived late last night. Harper had picked her up, while Brooke had sent along the message that she'd see her at the bee farm.

She'd been looking forward to catching up on the latest news from Harper about everything during the drive home, but Ivy had been so mentally and physically exhausted from the long ordeal that she'd fallen asleep in the car. As soon as she walked in the door of the house, she said good-night to Harper, exchanged pecks on the cheek with Brooke, and gone straight to bed.

Surprisingly, waking up early had come naturally to her even without using an alarm. After she'd left the bee farm, it had taken weeks for her to finally be able to sleep in. She'd gotten used to it, but this morning, muscle memory had taken over, urging her to rise at six thirty and get ready for the day. Once she put on her standard uniform at the farm—button-down shirt, jeans, boots—a list of tasks had automatically clicked in her mind.

First she'd get an update from Brooke and Harper about farm business at their usual morning meeting. After that, she'd read over Brooke's notes about the health of the hives, and then she and Brooke would probably spend most of the afternoon checking on the bees.

The farm's major honey harvest was only a little over two months away. And so was the celebration they had planned for the third week in September during National Honey Month. The weeklong promotion would feature honey-themed menus at two restaurants and a bar in the area, tours of the farm's processing room at the bee shed, and fun activities at the greenhouse for kids. They were also offering a special Symphony line of honey products in the retail store. Brooke was putting together a booklet to hand out featuring honey-based recipes from the bar and restaurants participating in the promotion.

Just thinking about all the upcoming activities kicked Ivy's energy level up a notch, but she was still going to need a caffeine boost. After that, she would be ready to dive in and get some work done.

As Ivy walked down the staircase, she glided her hand over familiar grooves and scratches in the polished wood banister. That and the squeak in the fifth step from the bottom were like a welcome home greeting. The only thing missing was the smell of breakfast. She'd always gotten up early to make something hot for her, Brooke, and Harper to start the day. She could do that for them today. Scrambled eggs and toast, or maybe pancakes? Once she got a peek in the cabinets and refrigerator, she would decide what to make.

At the bottom of the stairs, she veered left into the living room. As she passed the salmon-colored sectional, something caught her eye and she paused. The room looked different. Throw pillows with a russet and navy design replaced the old beige ones, A navy ottoman sat where the side table used to be, and the brass lamp that had been on top of it was gone. She'd fallen in love with the lamp at an antique bazaar years ago and had bought it on the spot.

As she glanced around, she picked up more changes. Plants, a new rug, the bookcase had been shifted farther down the wall on the right. Everything looked nice, well put together…and it was a little jarring for her to see all of the changes. She mentally shook off the odd sensation of feeling like a stranger. The house fully belonged to her nieces now. They were free to change whatever they liked to make the house feel like their own.

She walked into the adjoining kitchen. A small sigh of relief slipped out of her after seeing the space looked just as it had a few months ago. Stainless steel appliances gleamed in the sunlight shining through the side windows, while flowers in mason jars decorated the windowsill. Vintage canisters that coordinated with the deep green cabinetry sat on the white quartz countertops.

Harper sat at the end of the rectangular kitchen table, drinking coffee from a mug and reading messages on her phone. Just like Ivy, she was dressed for work. Her dark hazelnut-colored curls were secured neatly in a ponytail.

As she looked up, Harper's expression reflected her surprise. "Good morning. I didn't expect to see you up so early."

"Why not? Did you think I got lazy since I've been away?" Ivy kissed her on the cheek before heading to the coffee maker on the counter.

"No, I just thought you might be taking it easy your first day back."

"Taking it easy? I can't do that when we have so much work to do." Ivy grabbed a mug from an upper cabinet then poured herself a cup of coffee. She opened another cabinet to get the sugar and found glass cookware instead. "Um…where's the sugar?"

"In the pantry."

The pantry? As Ivy went to retrieve the sugar, she tried to follow the logic of moving everything but couldn't. It was a lot easier to have the ingredients she used all of the time within easy reach, especially when she was cooking or baking.

As Ivy grabbed a carton of cream from the refrigerator, she peered inside. "I'm making breakfast. What are you in the mood for?"

"Nothing for me. I already ate."

Ivy spied the clean bowl and spoon on the drying pad on the counter. Harper had always been on the thin side, but she looked even smaller. *That child needs to eat something more than just cereal.* No, she wasn't a child. She was an adult capable of fixing meals for herself. But what had she been eating these days? And what about Brooke?

It took a huge effort for Ivy to hold back from expressing her thoughts. "Okay. I'll wait for Brooke to see what she wants. What time are we starting our meeting?"

"Oh." Harper's brow rose a fraction over her coppery-brown eyes. "Brooke and I already met. She's out running errands all day. I'm sorry. We really didn't expect you to jump into work this morning."

Ivy's mental checklist for the day dwindled to nothing. "It's fine." She forced a smile on her face. "I'll call Brooke a little later to see when she wants to catch me up with the apiary. We still have at least a day before she leaves on Wednesday."

"About that." Harper put down her phone.

More changes? Ivy tried to remain optimistic as she took a seat at the table. "What's going on?"

"Nothing too bad, just a little hiccup. Nellie asked me to help her plan a surprise for Brooke." Nellie was one of Brooke's good friends. "She arranged a girls' weekend for Brooke with a few of their friends to celebrate Brooke's engagement. But we scheduled it for this weekend. And then Brooke told me the other day she was going to see Gable."

Ivy paused taking a sip from her mug. "But Brooke asked me a week ago about coming here to fill in while she was gone. She didn't tell you about her trip?" *Oh no...* Had she just slipped up by mentioning that? Maybe communication hadn't improved between her nieces as much as she'd hoped.

To her surprise, Harper didn't seem upset. "She told me—but she gave me the wrong dates. Her head's been all over the place since Gable left. When I went over to see her at his house the other day, she'd put the sugar in the fridge and an open carton of milk in the plate cabinet." Her niece snickered. "I think she needs to get some, like, yesterday."

Ivy's night with Jaxon flashed in her mind. Well, sex *was* a good stress reliever. Smiling, she managed to hide her own laugh and not choke on her sip of coffee. She swallowed hard. "So, what's the plan now?"

"We had to tell her about the surprise. Everyone who's flying in had already bought their plane tickets. We booked the rooms and restaurant at Tillbridge Horse Stable and Guesthouse over a month ago. We even got a deal with the new spa in town to provide mani-pedis and hand and foot massages at a discount rate. Brooke agreed she *had* to push back her trip, and she's looking forward to catching up with her friends. Now she's not leaving until next Tuesday."

Brooke wasn't leaving right away? Did that mean she hadn't actually needed to rush home and could have spent yesterday with Jaxon? Ivy nudged the thought aside. No. What they'd shared was amazing, but catch and release had an expiration date, right? Theirs was one night. Nothing good would have come of dragging things out.

Harper glanced at her phone and stood. "Shoot. I better hurry. I have a meeting at the greenhouse. Sorry, I can only give you a quick update. Brooke checked the bees yesterday. Everything's good in the apiary and the hives at our other sites. The Symphony Honey order is done and will be here on time for National Honey Month, and so will the other things we ordered for the celebration. Everything is under control. Really, you should just sit back and relax. Brooke and I took care of everything." She blew Ivy a kiss as she hurried out of the kitchen. "See you later."

"Bye." A moment later the front door closed.

Silence engulfed Ivy. No breakfast. No morning meeting. Sit back and relax? What was she supposed to do? Wander around the house to see what else had changed since she'd left?

Ivy sipped coffee and tried not to feel too sorry for herself. She stared out the window at the white cottage across the side lawn that served as the farm's offices and retail space. Before she'd left, Harper had been re-designing the cottage. Nothing there would probably look familiar, either, and right then, another change was the last thing she wanted. She needed a bit of normalcy. There was *one* place she knew hadn't changed on the farm. It had existed in a similar form for well over a million years, created by some of the hardest working winged creatures she'd ever encountered—the beehives.

Later in the morning, she stood by the farm's UTV on the wide gravel path separating the apiary from the field of wildflowers. Instead of a full bee suit, she'd opted to wear a bee jacket, gloves, and a veiled helmet.

Without even thinking about it, she took a calming breath as she looked out at the grassy field with its multiple stacked, square, approximately waist-high light-colored wood boxes.

Each of the hives were comprised of a stand on the bottom holding a deep body brood box where the larvae were sheltered and cared for by worker bees. On top of the brood boxes sat shallower boxes, or honey supers, where the bees stored nectar in the frames of wax comb. Over time, the nectar ripened into honey that could be harvested, processed, and enjoyed.

Ivy walked to the back of the truck. Since Brooke had already checked the hives recently, this visit was strictly for her own enjoyment, so she would only look in one of the hives. Opening a hive too often could disturb the bees, interrupting their important work. In her mind, she envisioned what she expected to find in the hive she opened. Healthy, thriving bees and honey supers on their way to filling up with one of the best marvels of nature.

Honey production was a delicate balance that required time and healthy bees. Bad weather, disease, and lack of good food and water sources were just some of the things that could affect that health. As beekeepers, it was their job to protect the bees' environment and provide the right conditions for them to flourish. Actually, it was Brooke's job now—and from the number of supers Ivy counted stacked on the hives, Brooke was doing an excellent job. The farm could expect a good harvest.

It would be Brooke's first harvest as head beekeeper. Lexy would be so proud of her "little bee charmer," as her sister used to call Brooke.

Bittersweet nostalgia swelled in Ivy. Although she knew Lexy and Dion were looking down on it all, she was their physical witness to Brooke's and Harper's achievements. It felt like a sacred privilege to do so, and she never took it for granted.

Ivy opened a storage bin on the back of the UTV. It contained a full assortment of beekeeper tools. Grippers to safely remove the frames in the hive. Brushes for coaxing bees off of frames and back into the boxes. A hook and a scraper tool to help pry apart the frames and scrape off any excess wax. The smoker with pellets to manage the bees, if necessary.

In the apiary, she walked amongst the hives, just looking, not getting too close to agitate them by her presence. From a short distance, she could see the bees flying in and out of the bottom entrances of the hives.

The steady hum of the bees, caused by the rapid vibration of their wings, was soothing and familiar. The sound naturally slowed her pace as she continued walking through the field. Finally, she chose one of the smaller hives, comprised of a colony of bees they'd inherited from an amateur beekeeper. The man had moved out of state and couldn't take the hive with him.

According to Brooke's notes, which Ivy had skimmed earlier, the bees were healthy and had adjusted well to their new home.

Using the smoker, she released a fog of smoke that would prompt the bees to go inside and start gorging on honey. Their full bellies would make it hard for the bees to bend and sting.

She removed the one honey super and set it aside. Using her tools, she gently nudged out a frame from the brood box. The intricacy of the rainbow-like structure of pollen, honey and brood toward the middle of the frame never failed to delight her. Somewhere on another frame in the brood box, the queen bee was encircled by her court, which attended to her every need. As fun as it would be to find the queen, Ivy decided to resist the temptation. It wasn't necessary, and the queen bee and her court were kind of busy.

Ivy closed up the hive. She couldn't wait for her own full inspection of the apiary next week. She'd check the hives located on properties away from the bee farm, too. Some were on working concerns like the fruit and vegetable farm just outside of town. Others were at private homes.

It was a symbiotic relationship. Bishop Honey Bee Farm received access to diverse forage for the bees. The farmers and homeowners received the potential for increased yields in their crops and gardens. And most important of all, the arrangement supported a healthy ecosystem and that benefited everyone.

After finishing in the apiary, Ivy stowed her jacket and the rest of her gear in the back of the UTV then drove to the bee shed not far away. Everything was in order there, too.

One part of the tan brick building was used to store multiple racks of beekeeping and cleaning tools and parts for the hives. The other was a processing room with honey extraction equipment. If needed, the farm could process, bottle and label small batches of honey, but for larger harvests like the one coming up, it was more efficient to process the frames at a bigger commercial facility that served the whole area.

Outside the bee shed, Ivy looked around, taking in the apiary on the right, the wildflower field next to it, and the two large greenhouses in the distance on the left. To the left of that, across a narrow road, was Gable's house and property. Ahead of Ivy was home, a yellow house with white trim, but instead of feeling grounded by what she saw, she felt strangely apart from it all, like a visitor passing through a familiar place. She recognized everything but it was no longer truly hers. Where would she call home now?

She had enough in her savings to keep her going for a while without having to worry about making ends meet, but it wasn't about the money per se. She had an itch to stay busy, useful, and engaged with something that was important. She'd told Von that she was a retired beekeeper, but honestly, thinking more about it, she didn't see herself entirely giving up beekeeping. Maybe she would maintain a hive or two for her own enjoyment at her future home. But outside of that, what would she do with herself?

I would love to paint him...

The remembered thought popped into Ivy's mind—and with it came memories of being with Jaxon. Jaxon holding her. Kissing her. Her kissing him back. Her palms tingled as she replayed gliding them over his chest and along the ridges and valleys of his tight abdomen. She recalled the intense way he'd looked down at her as she'd traced over the lines and angles of his face.

She could probably draw him from memory. But of course, she had no intention of doing that. When she'd been thinking about painting him at the Wavefront Bistro, she really hadn't meant it. Even if she tried to draw or paint again, what if the skill and passion for it weren't there anymore?

After a stop by the greenhouses to see if Harper was interested in having lunch together—only to find that Harper had already left to tend to something else—Ivy returned to the house. As she walked up the steps to the porch, she released a heavy breath. Handing everything over to Brooke and Harper had been the right thing to do, and her plan to nudge them to reconcile their differences seemed to have worked. They were getting along better, otherwise, Harper wouldn't have been so involved in planning a surprise girls' weekend for Brooke to celebrate her engagement. All of that should have made her happy.

Still, what was that saying about expectation and reality not always matching up? When she'd made her plans, she hadn't expected this sense of aloneness. She didn't like not being needed as much. It left her feeling almost like she didn't belong anymore in this place that had been her sanctuary for so many years.

Her phone rang. Glancing at the screen, she was surprised to see the name on the caller ID. *Gibson Law Group.* Von was calling her?

Entering the house, she answered her phone. "Hello?"

"Hello, is this Ms. Daniels?" The woman's tone was polite and professional.

"Yes, it is." Noises came from the kitchen in the house, and Ivy glanced that direction. Was it Harper?

"My name is Kelly. I'm Mr. Gibson's assistant. He's hoping you're available for a little trip to celebrate your birthday…" She went on to explain that the "little" trip would be to London.

Von had remembered her birthday? Ivy was touched, but after she'd just told him that she wouldn't marry him, taking a trip like that alone with him felt…awkward. Was he trying to change her mind?

"That sounds wonderful," Ivy responded. "But I'm back in Maryland helping out at the farm. Based on my schedule right now, it'd be really difficult for me to get away, and I might already have plans." Why was she throwing in all of that extra information? She just needed to get to the point and say no. "Please tell him I appreciate the offer, but I can't."

"I'll tell him."

As she and the assistant said their goodbyes, Brooke and Harper swarmed out of the kitchen.

Brooke came across the living room, arms wide open. "Hey, Auntie!" A loose, cropped blue T-shirt and matching skirt fluttered around her lithe frame. Her natural face, dark shoulder-length curls, and the smile that reached her coppery brown eyes all radiated energy as she threw her arms around Ivy.

Her niece's enthusiasm and her own happiness at seeing Brooke fueled Ivy's smile. "Hi."

Harper joined them, and her two nieces sandwiched her in a hug and kissed her cheeks.

Surrounded by love, Ivy smiled even harder. "What's all this about?"

"We didn't really get a chance to welcome you home last night," Brooke said.

"And," Harper chimed in, "we wanted to apologize for not including you in the meeting this morning."

"Thank you, but I understand about the meeting." Ivy looked between them as she wrapped her arms around Brooke's and Harper's waists. "You're both busy living your lives and running this place. I can already see the work you've put into it." She gave them both a squeeze. "I'm proud of you."

"Thanks." Brooke grinned.

"We had a great teacher," Harper added.

Feeling herself getting a little misty eyed, Ivy focused on an appealing savory scent in the air. "Something smells good. What is it?"

"We made lunch." Brooke looped her arm through Ivy's as they all walked toward the kitchen. "Baked chicken, broccoli, and rice."

Harper snickered. "Made? Be honest. It's a take-out meal from Pasture Lane Restaurant."

Brooke shot her a look. "We had to heat it up. That counts."

Ivy looked between them and laughed. This was a refreshing switch from how they'd practically been at each other's throats before she'd left. She liked it. It really was good to be home, even if, technically, she didn't have a home…or a job…or a purpose of her own to focus on. As that thought ran through her mind, all of the unknowns in her life hit her at once.

Brooke glanced at Ivy, picking up on the shift in her mood. "What's wrong?"

Ivy felt like a deer caught in the headlights. She

didn't want Brooke or Harper worrying about her. "I'm… I just…"

Her phone chimed with a text. Grateful for the distraction, she broke eye contact. "I've been waiting for a message, and look, it's finally here." She pushed out a lighthearted laugh. "You go ahead. I'll be there in just a minute."

"Okay."

As Brooke went inside the kitchen, Ivy looked down at the screen.

It was from Von.

I'm sorry you're not available to join me in London. Should your plans change, call me.

Her plans weren't going to change, but she couldn't tell him that. Ivy tapped in her response as she walked into the kitchen.

Will do.

"Is everything okay?" Brooke looked down at Ivy's phone as the three of them sat down at the table.

"Great. It's just an old friend. He and I ran into each other, and he wanted to see if we could meet up again around my birthday."

"He who?" Harper's and Brooke's heads swiveled her direction as they said it at the same time.

"Von. You probably remember me mentioning him." As they filled their plates, Ivy told them about seeing him in Miami after her fake cruise, but didn't tell them about his marriage proposal or his current offer of a birthday trip to London.

While Harper was just pleased Ivy had a nice time, Brooke was excited over the news. "You and Von, that's amazing. It must have been fantastic connecting with him again and remembering all the great times you had together."

The way-too-happy look on Brooke's face was surprising. Maybe she was just so exuberant about love because she was in love, Ivy mused. Or was Brooke entertaining some idea that something more could happen with her and Von?

In case it was the latter, Ivy chose her words carefully. "It was good to see him. He and I getting a chance to catch up was really nice. We're happy as friends."

"But you are going to see him again?" Brooke said. "Soon?"

"What's the rush?" Harper asked as she paused before taking a bite of food.

"There isn't a rush," Brooke replied. "It's just they only had a few days to catch up." Brooke looked to Ivy. "You said he wanted to meet up for your birthday. Maybe you should consider spending it with him in New York."

Harper snorted a laugh. "You make it sound like Von's the only available guy in the world. Maybe she has plans to spend her birthday with someone else."

"Hold on." Ivy held up her hand, forestalling what sounded like a potential argument. "You two are making this more serious than it is. I saw Von. It was nice. I'm not seeing anyone else, and you don't have to worry

about my birthday plans. Now, let's change the subject."
She focused on Brooke. "Are you all packed for your
trip to see Gable? Oh, and do we need to check on anything at his place while you're gone?"

Brooke leaped on the topic bait. "Yes, I'm packed.
The only thing you could do maybe is check the mail."

As Brooke talked more about her plans with Gable,
Ivy's mind wandered. She had all the answers when
it came to her and Von, but what about her life? What
was next for her? Where was home? She honestly didn't
have a clue about any of that yet.

Chapter Nine

The weekend-long get-together to celebrate Brooke's engagement was in full swing.

One of the guest cottages at Tillbridge Horse Stable and Guesthouse had been cleared of furniture and set up with portable mani-pedi and hand and foot massage stations. Trays of appetizers as well as beverages were arranged on the kitchen counter. Staff from a local spa pampered attendees, including Ivy and Harper, who were rotating between services.

The relaxing mini-spa moment was the perfect follow-up to Friday's horse trail ride and barbecue dinner under the stars the day before on the property. Ivy hadn't gone with the group of women. She hadn't planned on being a part of the festivities at all, but one of the group had canceled at the last minute. Brooke and Harper had persuaded her to take the open slot for the mini-spa morning as well as join them for lunch that afternoon.

She checked out her nails, now painted in a sheer neutral color. They had a healthy-looking glow. "I could get used to this," she said.

Harper, seated beside her, wiggled her fingers, showing off her lavender-colored nails with a white floral design. "I know. I wish I could do this more often."

"You should."

"As much as I've been playing in the dirt lately at the greenhouse? Getting a manicure like this would be a waste."

"Not if you wear gloves and maybe not pick open staples on papers with your nails."

Harper chuckled. "Yeah, those are good points." She glanced at Brooke laughing with a few of her friends across the room.

Nellie, a pretty blonde with flawless tawny-brown skin, said something that made them all laugh, especially Brooke.

"Brooke looks really happy," Harper said. "And she and Gable are too cute when they're together. I can't tell whose smile is bigger, hers or his."

"That's a good sign, isn't it? I can't wait to meet Gable in person." He had just decided to move next door to the bee farm when Ivy had left almost three months ago. So far, she'd only interacted with him during video chats with Brooke. During those times, he'd been considerate and attentive to Brooke. She trusted what she saw and sensed in him. It was more than evident he loved Brooke, and as a couple, they looked to be a great match.

Ivy and Harper lifted their feet out of the soaking tubs and onto a towel-covered platform in preparation for their pedicures.

"You'll like Gable. He's actually okay for a cowboy."

"You still have a thing against cowboys?"

"You would, too, after the last one I dated. All he talked about was horses. He actually tried to include mucking stalls as an activity on one of our dates."

Ivy remembered the guy well. He was a trainer at Tillbridge Horse Stables, and he did seem a little horse obsessed. "Not all cowboys are like that." Ivy considered picking up her glass of sparkling water with lemon, but decided against it, not wanting to risk messing up her nails.

"I guess, but I'm still done with them. And right now, with all I have going on, I need someone who understands that work is my priority."

Ivy wanted to lecture Harper on balance, but it would have been hypocritical. She hadn't been the best role model when it came to that. She hadn't made time for a social life, spending all her attention on the farm and her nieces. But Harper's situation was different. She didn't have any dependents, and she had Brooke and a staff to share the load. She didn't have to bury herself under work. She could take time off and enjoy herself.

Ivy probably should have been encouraging her to relax and take more time for herself all along. She felt a flash of guilt as she recalled turning over key parts of the operation to Harper while her niece was still in college. Even though Harper had asked for the bigger responsibilities, she should have insisted Harper go out and enjoy herself more. Maybe Brooke and Gable's commitment to each other, while navigating their careers, would be a good example for Harper. Maybe she would see work didn't have to be everything.

After the mini-spa session ended, the women walked

up the tree-lined pathway. Short minutes later, they reached the back deck of Pasture Lane Restaurant at Tillbridge, located in the rear of the two-story, twenty-room guesthouse.

The restaurant, run by Chef Philippa Gayle Crawford and her celebrity chef husband, Dominic Crawford, was popular with the locals and tourists. Many of the episodes of his show, *Farm to Fork with Dominic Crawford*, were filmed at a kitchen studio near the couple's home.

Sliding glass doors enclosed the restaurant's wood deck except for two panels left open, providing access from the stairs. Servers welcomed them as they walked inside. A wall of glass separated the deck from the main restaurant. Four-top tables with white tablecloths were set up as well as one long table for ten. Off to the side was a black portable bar.

After claiming their seats, some of the women left to find the ladies' room.

Brooke was put at the head of the table. Ivy set her purse in a vacant seat at the corner on the other end but didn't sit down.

Nellie went to Harper, who stood nearby. Her voice was low but loud enough for Ivy to hear. "The restaurant let me organize a surprise for this afternoon. I brought in someone to do a wine tasting with our lunch."

"That sounds nice, especially since Brooke is already pulling together her dream menu for the wedding reception. Are they from Sommersby's?" Harper asked.

Sommersby Winery and Vineyard was located just

a few miles away. They were known locally for their wine as well as the wine tours on their property.

"No," Nellie replied. "They're from Charmed Vines, the wine bar in town."

"Are you sure whoever's coming is from there?" Harper exchanged a puzzled look with Ivy. "I've never heard of them doing tastings in the past."

"It's something the new owners have started," Nellie said.

That made sense. The wine bar that was more of a store had just been sold to new management before she'd left. It wasn't surprising that they'd be experimenting with new things to bring in more money.

Nellie leaned in, including Ivy in the conversation. "I just met the owner, Nate, yesterday. He's trying to get the word out and establish a connection with the restaurant, so he agreed to do it for practically nothing."

A tall guy with ginger-colored hair walked in through the glass door from the restaurant side carrying a wine box to the bar.

Nellie pointed at him. "That's Nate." The door opened again and her eyes widened. "Oh my gosh."

She rushed to the guy who'd just walked in, threw her arms around him and kissed him.

Ivy stared in shock. The guy looked a lot like Jaxon. No, actually, it *was* Jaxon.

"Aunt Ivy, what's wrong?" Harper asked.

It took a second for Ivy to find her voice. She forced a quick smile. "I left something back at the cottage. Go ahead and start lunch without me."

Ivy made a quick exit down the deck stairs.

At the bottom, she walked down the wide pathway, but instead of going straight toward the cottage where they'd had the spa session, she veered into a small circular paved area with a bench surrounded by trees.

Jaxon's last goodbye kiss at the town house in South Carolina blazed through her mind. As a flush ran over her, she pressed her hands to her heated cheeks. She'd had one night with him, and she'd enjoyed every minute of it. But now she should probably put those memories away. He'd obviously moved on…to Brooke's friend. How did they know each other? Nellie lived in Jacksonville. From the way she'd kissed him, they were obviously well acquainted with each other.

As possible scenarios about Nellie and Jaxon's relationship started to unfurl in her mind, Ivy gave herself a mental shake. It didn't matter. As far as her own connection with Jaxon, it hadn't been meant to last beyond that one night.

Ivy closed her eyes and allowed the image of her and Jaxon to fade. She replaced it with the one of Nellie a minute ago with her arms wrapped around him. They made a cute couple. With his outgoing nature and her fun-loving personality, they were probably a good fit for each other. Acknowledging that felt like a sharp bee sting, and just like a sting, it would be uncomfortable for a little while, but then the pain would fade. She had to pull herself together and focus on what was important. Brooke.

"Ivy…"

She'd hoped his voice was in her imagination, but the

sound of his heavy footfalls behind her, coming closer, confirmed he was really there.

Her heart sped up, fueled by dread but also a strange hint of excitement. Still, she took a moment to mask her feelings before she faced him. He was a little more dressed up than he had been in Hilton Head. He still looked good. The casual navy blazer, gray button-down shirt, and dark jeans suited him. "Jaxon, you're here… What a surprise."

"I'm surprised to see you, too." With his gaze holding hers, he walked closer. "Are you staying here at the guesthouse?"

"No, I live here. Are you visiting?"

"Yes, kind of. Nate, the owner of Charmed Vines, is a friend. I'm helping him out. I'll be here for about three weeks, maybe a month."

"That long? I haven't decided when I'm leaving yet."

His expression grew a tad confused. "So you're visiting?"

"Yes, kind of." She'd just repeated what he said. From his small smile, he'd noticed it, too. "I used to live here and help run our family's bee farm. My nieces, Brooke and Harper, are in charge of it now. I'll be helping out while Brooke is away for a couple of weeks, and after that, we'll see. I'm not sure what's next."

His brow rose. "You're related to Brooke?"

"Yes. So I guess you know her along with her friend Nellie?"

"I do—but with Nellie, it's not what you think."

Ivy tried to offer up a nonchalant shrug. "It doesn't matter what I think."

"It matters to me." Jaxon came closer. "I saw the look on your face."

She could smell his cologne. A few inches closer and she would feel his warmth. "I was surprised to see you."

"And you were surprised to see Nellie kiss me."

Ivy held up her hands to stop him. She didn't need to know about when and where he'd met Nellie or what their relationship was like. "I was, but you don't owe me an explanation."

Jaxon reached out and lightly clasped one of her hands. As he slowly lowered her hand with his, it reminded her of when he'd caught her mid-spin on the dance floor. "I *do* owe you an explanation, especially since I don't want you to read the wrong things into what you saw a minute ago."

"It was just a kiss."

"But you thought it was more than that. I saw it on your face."

He tugged her closer. An invisible gravitational pull did the rest, drawing her toward him. As she laid her hand on his arm near his shoulder, he cupped his other hand to her waist. A breath seeped out of her. She felt a rush of relief that he was holding her, along with a pulse of desire and a small bit of unease. This wasn't supposed to be happening. Jaxon wasn't supposed to be there.

"Okay, maybe it caught me off guard," she admitted. Finally giving into curiosity, she added, "So how do you know Brooke and Nellie?"

"They were regular customers at a restaurant I used to work at in Florida. Brooke and I went out for coffee a couple of times, but nothing happened. We realized we didn't have relationship chemistry, and she suggested that I ask Nellie out. She and I dated for a couple weeks, and then we broke up, but all of this happened months ago."

He'd gone out with Nellie *and* Brooke? Though it sounded like, technically, he'd only dated Nellie. "Now you and Nellie are friends like us?" Wait, did that sound like she was fishing? She wasn't. Okay, maybe just a little, but he hadn't actually explained his status with Nellie now.

"No, not like us." Jaxon's gaze didn't waver as he looked in her eyes. "I missed you after you left. I really wanted to spend more time with you. You've been on my mind ever since."

His confession made happiness zing inside of her. She might as well be honest with him, too. "I wish I could have stayed longer, and I've missed you, too."

Jaxon grinned. "I like the sound of that."

"I'm not sure I know what that means."

He put both hands on her waist, and as he brought her closer, she slid hers up to his shoulders. "It means I want to kiss you."

His soft husky tone automatically drew her attention to his mouth. As he leaned in, she met him halfway. Their lips touched, and she softly moaned into a deepening kiss. Like spark to flame, the need to reclaim, explore, to lose herself in the headiness of being this close to him again took over.

"Aunt Ivy?"

The familiar voice hit her like a splash of ice water.

Ivy quickly broke away from the kiss. She would have fallen on her butt if Jaxon hadn't held on to her.

Looking over his shoulder, she met Brooke's shocked stare.

"I… We…" Ivy stammered.

Clearly disturbed, Brooke shook her head. "I don't know what this is, but no."

As Brooke rushed off, Ivy's heart plummeted. "What just happened?" She dropped her head in her hands and covered her eyes. "Oh no, what have I just done?"

"I think we just caught her by surprise." Jaxon gently grasped her shoulders. "Everything will be okay. We'll just explain the situation and how we know each other."

But Brooke wasn't the type to get upset over nothing—nor was she the type to let things go. An explanation wouldn't matter. What she saw had clearly bothered her.

Ivy shook her head. "No."

As he studied her face, wariness came over his. "No? What are you saying?"

Even though every part of her wanted to move back into his arms, Ivy slipped from his hold. "Today was about celebrating her engagement, and I might have ruined it for her. Brooke was clearly upset about seeing us together. The why doesn't matter to me. I won't risk having a conversation that might make her even more unhappy. The safest way to handle this is to leave what happened with us in Hilton Head in the past."

Chapter Ten

Sauvignon blanc, merlot, cabernet. The varieties of wine they'd tasted so far with the salad and main course at lunch became one big blur for Ivy. The pan-seared chicken currently on her plate remained mostly untouched because her appetite was gone. All Ivy could see was Brooke's shocked expression after catching her kissing Jaxon earlier.

Every time Brooke looked at her now, there was something odd in her gaze. Questions? A hint of disappointment? Worry? Ivy couldn't decipher it.

The only thing that could have made it worse was if Jaxon were assisting with the tasting. He wasn't. Nate had mentioned his colleague had to return to the wine bar. Was that true or had he made an excuse to get out of there? He hadn't been happy when she'd left him to come back to the restaurant. He'd tried to talk her out of her decision to keep away from him, but when she wouldn't budge, Jaxon said he'd respect her decision.

Whatever the reason, she was glad she didn't have to face the awkwardness of Jaxon being in the room, too.

Time felt like it was standing still as Nate talked about the body, notes, and acidity of the wine in front of them. She just wanted to set things straight with Brooke, but there wouldn't be a chance for a real talk any time soon. The next outing planned for the weekend was pool, darts, dancing, and possibly karaoke at the bar connected to the Montecito Steakhouse, a local spot south of town.

Finally, the dessert course arrived—chocolate raspberry layer cake.

Nate, a thirtysomething guy with a slightly flirtatious smile, had already charmed Brooke's friends with his quick wit and appealing descriptions of the wine offerings.

He held up the next bottle. "This last pairing is my favorite. The bittersweetness of the chocolate plus the ripe, jammy fruit elements of this zinfandel could be compared to a nice hot bubble bath after a long day."

"Um…can I get two bottles of that?" one of the women asked.

Easy laughter reverberated in the room, but concern about what was on Brooke's mind dimmed the moment for Ivy.

Ivy didn't bother to taste dessert. The plan had always been for her to only join the group for the spa session and lunch. If she left now, maybe her niece could still salvage her joy in the day with her friends.

The women began to take photos with each other and with Brooke. It seemed more like a girlfriends' moment anyway from here on out. She wouldn't be missed.

Harper was the only one who noticed her about to leave, catching Ivy's eye from across the room.

Forcing a smile, she mouthed, "I've got to go." Ivy

waved, pointed to the door leading from the deck to the main part of the restaurant, and left.

Pasture Lane Restaurant had a light green decor with pale wood floors and lots of natural light. It gave the space an inviting, open feel.

They were busy for lunch. She quickly wove through the tables occupied by patrons, ducking her head to avoid making eye contact with anyone she knew. It worked until she made it into the restaurant's foyer. There, she ran into a familiar face.

"Hey, Ivy." Zurie Tillbridge, a petite Black woman with straight, shoulder-length hair, greeted her with a smile.

She was the co-owner of Tillbridge, along with her sister Rina and her cousin Tristan. Twelve years ago, she'd been the first person to welcome Ivy to her first town hall business meeting in Bolan. Over the years, they'd become good friends. She'd also been the one discreetly keeping an eye on Brooke and Harper while Ivy was away.

As they both moved in for a hug, Zurie paused and her smile faded. "Is everything all right?"

Ivy wanted to say that she was fine, but the other woman's empathetic expression got to her. She shook her head. "Not really."

Zurie's expression morphed to concern as she gripped Ivy's hand. "Did something happen with Brooke's event?"

"Oh no." Ivy gave Zurie's hand a quick squeeze. "It's…" She wasn't sure how to explain.

"Come on. We can talk in my office."

"But you're working. Aren't you busy?"

Judging by her navy pantsuit, Zurie was clearly on the clock. "I have time for coffee." She flashed a small conspiratorial smile. "And we haven't had time to catch up on things since you've been back."

Not taking no for an answer, Zurie nudged her out of the foyer and down a long, wide, light-tiled corridor toward her office. Along the way, they passed the gold tiered literature stand that held tourist information.

Ivy caught a glimpse of a brochure for Bishop Honey Bee Farm. She'd never seen that one before, but she knew who must be responsible for it. Brooke had a degree in marketing and had worked in the profession for a couple years. Aside from beekeeping, Brooke had also started handling most of the marketing and promotion for the farm.

Her niece's shocked face from a little more than an hour ago played in her mind. Concern rose in Ivy all over again. She and Brooke had to talk so she could straighten things out with her.

In Zurie's office, a laptop and full, stacked in-and-out boxes sat on an otherwise tidy desk. Behind it sat a large leather chair. Its rich brown color shone with the patina of time. It had belonged to Zurie's father, who'd built and run the stable along with his brother.

Zurie had been in her twenties when her father passed away over a decade ago. Like Ivy, she'd had to unexpectedly take on a lot of responsibility, practically running the family business on her own until a few years ago.

Zurie pointed to a round meeting table on the right.

"Have a seat." She went to a corner beverage station and got the coffeepot going. "You take cream and sugar, right?"

"Please." Ivy took a seat and put her purse in the chair beside her.

As the coffee brewed, Zurie dropped off a caddie with sugar, cream, and spoons on the table. "So everything is going well for Brooke and her friends this weekend?"

"Today has been perfect, and from what I heard, everyone enjoyed themselves on the trail ride yesterday."

"Oh good. Brooke looks so happy. Any idea when they're planning to tie the knot?"

"I haven't heard anything. Maybe they'll talk about it while Brooke's visiting him. She leaves on Tuesday."

Zurie came to the table with two full mugs of coffee. As she sat down next to Ivy, she handed one of them to her. "How long will she be gone?"

"Two weeks." Ivy added sugar to her coffee along with a little cream. "The way those two look at each other, I don't think they'll be able to hold off getting married for too long."

Zurie stirred her coffee. "Everyone's happy. Things are good at the bee farm. It sounds like everything is going the way you wanted with Brooke and Harper's reconciliation."

"It is."

"So why did you have a world-ending look on your face a minute ago?"

Ivy sighed, still trying to process what happened

before lunch. "Did you see the guy that was with Nate, the new owner of the wine bar in town?"

"I haven't seen him, but I heard people on my staff talking about him. Apparently, he's cute. What about him?"

No surprise that the staff had noticed him. "When I was in South Carolina last week, I met him at the restaurant where he worked. His name is Jaxon. We really hit it off, and before I left, he and I slept together."

Zurie laughed. "Is that all? Girl, the way you looked, I thought something bad had happened. You met someone. Good for you."

"No, it's not good. He and Brooke met when they both lived in Florida, and they went out on a couple of coffee dates. When they didn't hit it off, he took her suggestion and asked her friend Nellie out. They dated for a couple of weeks."

Zurie paused in taking a drink from her mug. "Was he dating her when you two got together?"

"No, he said it was months ago, and they broke it off as friends. Maybe that's not a big deal but being with the same guy that Brooke went out with is the real issue. She caught me and him kissing this afternoon. She was upset when she rushed off."

"Ahh, okay. So Brooke was caught off guard because she didn't know."

"Exactly. And I was just as surprised to run into him. We didn't plan on meeting up again. He was a cute younger guy. We had fun for the night. You know, catch and release."

"And you're still feeling caught because you like him."

Ivy fiddled with the handle of her mug. "No...maybe." The lies almost stuck in her throat but the truth came out easier. "Yes, but I can't see him while I'm here."

Zurie put down her mug. "Please tell me the age difference isn't a problem. It really is just a number. Mace and I are proof of that. It's about whether or not you have a connection with Jaxon. *Do* you have a connection with him?"

Zurie and her husband had known each other for years growing up in the area. He'd been friends with her cousin Tristan in high school. There was at least a nine-year age difference between them.

Ivy responded, "We connected physically, and there might be some sort of a connection beyond that, but Jaxon and I didn't spend enough time together to find out."

"And?" Zurie pointed. "There's something else. I can see it in your face."

Jaxon had said almost the exact same thing. The memory of that made Ivy smile. "I don't know. It's like when you've gone to a new restaurant and the food is so good. You can't wait to go back." Laughing, she shook her head. "That's a really bad example."

"Bad example or not, I can tell that it makes sense to you because of how your eyes lit up just now when you said it. Look, you left Bolan to encourage Brooke and Harper to step up at the farm, and they have. You should start focusing on what you want. If it's Jaxon, I think you should go for it."

As Zurie continued, she leaned in. "You made so many sacrifices for Brooke and Harper. Shouldn't you be allowed to enjoy something you want, just because it makes you happy? I can tell that he makes you happy. If you tell Brooke that, she might understand. It's not like you're taking her best friend's man. He's free and single and so are you."

But what if she talked to Brooke and she didn't understand? Ivy couldn't risk endangering the family peace that had just been restored. "No, I already told Jaxon we won't be able to pick up where we left off in South Carolina. He's only here for a short time. I promised my sister that in her absence, I would nurture and take care of her children as my own. That I would keep them together and make sure they had a happy life. That's a forever promise." A promise that meant to her that she would put their needs over her own, even in a situation like this.

As Ivy drank another sip of coffee, the decision she'd had to make went down hard with it. "I'll get over Jaxon. Not seeing him again is the right choice for everyone involved."

Done with the tasting.

Jaxon read the text from Nate as he walked down a pathway on the Tillbridge Stable property.

On either side of him, horses were in the distance, grazing in pastures surrounded by a low white ladder fence.

Coming to the parking lot in front of the guesthouse, he headed for the steps leading to the entrance. He'd have to explain to Nate why he'd bailed on the wine tasting, but hopefully his friend would understand that it had been the best thing to do under the circumstances. His presence at lunch would have probably caused even more tension between Ivy and Brooke. He also didn't want to get in the way of Nate's agenda. He was hoping the wine tasting would make a good impression on the chef owners of the restaurant and open the door to doing business with them. Ruining lunch for Brooke definitely wouldn't have made the right impression.

If only he'd run into Ivy someplace else in town. Maybe they could have talked and fully reconnected before it came up that he knew Brooke. Maybe they could have figured out a way to iron out the situation. Maybe right now, he and Ivy would have been making plans to see each other instead of the opposite—not spending time together at all.

The memory of Ivy's expression changing from happiness to sadness when Brooke ran filled him with regret and frustration. He'd been so glad to see her. When she'd confessed that she'd been happy to see him, too, he'd just known they'd pick up from where they left off. Then one kiss later, that possibility had evaporated. Ivy didn't want to see him again. He understood her concerns about not wanting to upset Brooke, but it didn't seem right that she had to give up her own happiness to do it. Or maybe he was just being selfish because he wanted to be with Ivy again.

In the guesthouse, he went through the lobby and strode to the back corridor where Pasture Lane Restaurant was located. From there, he headed out to the enclosed deck to find Nate with a couple of waitstaff.

His friend was chatting with one of the servers, and from the looks of things, he was getting her phone number. Nate had been moping a little over the breakup with his girlfriend. Maybe he'd decided to move on.

Jaxon picked up a closed box from the top of the portable bar and loaded it onto a nearby hand truck.

Nate strolled over to him. "I think that's all our stuff." He tilted his head toward the server he'd been talking to, who was now bussing tables. "If we've left anything behind, I'm sure Mandy will call me. She has restaurant supervisory experience. She could be a good candidate for your position."

Jaxon chuckled. "You do know that stealing the restaurant's staff to work at the wine bar will shut down any opportunity to do business with them."

"I wasn't." Though judging from Nate's smile, he'd thought about it. "I just thought I should take her to coffee as a thank you for jumping in and taking your place for the wine tasting."

Jaxon grimaced. "Yeah, sorry about that."

"So I'm guessing your disappearing act had to do with the threesome between you, the bride-to-be, and her friend Nellie?"

"Threesome? What are you talking about?"

"Seriously?" Nate shot him a skeptical look. "Nellie kissed you as soon as you walked in the door. You left, and then a couple of minutes after that the bride-to-be followed you. When she came back into the restaurant, she didn't look happy."

That was what it had looked like? Jaxon shook his head. "You got it wrong, and it doesn't matter. The problem is resolved."

Nate looked over Jaxon's shoulder. "I don't think so."

Jaxon looked behind him.

Nellie's stride was determined as she walked through the restaurant toward the deck.

Nate clapped Jaxon on the arm. "Good luck with that. Meet me in the car when you're done." As he left the deck with the hand truck, Nellie approached and went up to Jaxon.

"I think we need to talk."

As Jaxon started to answer, something caught his attention. Was it his imagination or had the two servers cleaning up suddenly moved closer to them?

Nellie must have noticed the same thing. She tilted her head toward the courtyard. "We should go out there."

After clearing the stairs outside, they walked to the small grove where Brooke found him and Ivy.

As he and Nellie faced each other, he said, "I guess Brooke filled you in on some things."

"She did. You got involved with Ivy? You and Brooke aren't best friends, but you know her. What were you thinking?"

"First of all, Ivy and I met in South Carolina. We were together for less than a day, and family didn't come up a lot in our conversation. I didn't know Ivy and Brooke were related. Second of all, why is Brooke so concerned? She and I didn't work out, and you and I aren't dating anymore, plus we broke up on good terms."

Nellie opened her mouth to speak then paused. "Then I guess you don't know what happened to Brooke's parents."

From the look on her face, it wasn't a happy story. "No, I don't."

"She lost her mom and dad in a car accident when she was in high school. Ivy is her mom's sister, and she moved here to raise Brooke and her sister, Harper. As far as close family, Ivy is all they have. She's like their second mom."

From the "second mom" perspective, he could see where Brooke might be especially protective of Ivy. "So is the problem the age gap between me and Ivy?"

Nellie held her hands up in defense. "Brooke didn't say that. She did say, she didn't want her aunt getting hung up on a guy who was going to be gone tomorrow, especially since she lives in a town where stuff is remembered forever. According to Brooke, it's easy to get spun up in the hot gossip mill around here just because people are bored."

Jaxon released a long breath. He had no idea what it was like to live in a small town. If the locals did like to gossip, and Ivy got involved with him—a guy ten years younger who was in town for only a couple of weeks—it might raise speculation and cause people in town to talk about her after he left. If Ivy would be bothered by the gossip, he wouldn't want that for her, but he had gotten the sense that her main concern had been about keeping Brooke happy.

Nellie added, "Also, Ivy has a chance to get back with her former fiancé."

"She was engaged?" The news caught him by surprise.

"It was a while ago. From what Brooke said, he and Ivy broke up mainly because of distance. She had to move here to raise Brooke and Harper, and he worked in another state. A few weeks ago, Ivy ran into him again in Miami and they're staying in touch. Brooke's really hoping things work out for them this time. The two of them randomly running into each other again just seems like they're meant to have a second chance. You get that, right?"

"Yeah, I get it." Jaxon glanced toward the grove. Holding and kissing Ivy earlier, he'd started to believe it was *his* second chance with Ivy. In that short moment, it had felt like they were meant to pick up where they'd left off. But it seemed like he'd been wrong.

Chapter Eleven

Ivy stood at the window in the kitchen, watching the early morning rays from the sun eclipse the predawn shadows on the grass. She'd come downstairs early just to make sure she didn't miss her chance to talk to Brooke again.

Yesterday, Brooke and Harper had spent most of late Sunday afternoon ferrying people to three different airports in Baltimore and DC. Nellie's flight didn't leave until nine o'clock last night. She and Brooke had hung out by the harbor until it was time for her to go to the airport. Brooke had gotten back late.

As the kitchen grew more illuminated by sunlight, Ivy thought about what she had to say to Brooke, as well as Harper, running it over in her head several times. She'd waited to tell them together. Once it was resolved, they could all move on.

Harper trudged into the kitchen. "Good morning."

"Good morning." Ivy glanced at Harper's face, searching for signs she knew about what happened Saturday afternoon in the courtyard. All she could see was the zombie-like need for caffeine as she approached the coffeemaker. After their busy long weekend and playing chauffeur yesterday, she could probably use a break. Ivy took a seat at the table. "Maybe you should take the day off. I can pitch in where you need me."

"No, you don't need to do that." After getting coffee, Harper took a chocolate croissant from a pastry box on the counter and put it on a saucer. Various things Brooke's friends couldn't take with them on the plane, including food, had ended up at the house. "I've got it covered. I'm mainly reviewing financials today. The silence of working with numbers by myself will actually feel like a break after the last few days."

They used to work on the financials together. Ivy held back on mentioning that. Harper wanted to work on her own. She needed to accept that things had changed. "You looked like you were having a good time this weekend."

"I was." Harper sat down across from Ivy with her coffee and croissant. "But Nellie and I had to rush around to get a lot of things done. Nellie seems to like chaos. I don't. Brooke asked Nellie and me if we would be her co-maids of honor. We said yes, of course, but I hope Nellie isn't like this the entire time we're planning things for the wedding."

"Sometimes chaos is a part of life, and that's why we need celebrations. I know the farm is important to you, but as hard as you work, you have to take time off, especially to celebrate Brooke getting married."

"I know, and I plan on taking time off and celebrating with her, trust me." Harper sat back in the chair. "But honestly, this weekend seemed to be more about Brooke hanging with her friends than anything else. I don't mean that in a bad way, but at times, it felt like I was just along for the ride."

Was Brooke aware of this? Maybe Brooke didn't realize Harper felt left out. Ivy bit the inside of her cheek, stopping herself from commenting. Brooke and Harper had made so much progress in mending their relationship, but it had to be up to them where it went from here. As much as she wanted them to hang out with each other and be as close as they had been when they were younger, that might never happen again. She'd have to add it to the list of things she had to accept, along with Harper not being interested in a hot breakfast and not needing her help with the financials, and her not seeing Jaxon again.

The memory of the disappointment she'd felt from Jaxon as she'd left him in the courtyard sank into her now. In that moment, a part of her had honestly wished she could have wound back the clock to minutes earlier when they'd been so happy to see each other. The other part of her, the mom part of her, had just wanted to make sure Brooke was all right.

Brooke came into the kitchen and walked straight to the coffeemaker. "Good morning."

"Morning," Harper replied before taking a bite of croissant.

"Good morning," Ivy said.

An awkward silence hung in the air—though thankfully, Harper didn't seem to notice as she remained absorbed with her phone.

Ivy released a quiet sigh then took a sip of coffee. She needed to resolve things before Brooke left tomorrow. The best way to do that was head-on. As she set down her mug, she cleared her throat. "I need to talk to you both about something that Brooke discovered on Saturday."

Harper looked up, her expression quizzical. Brooke's remained neutral as she joined them at the table and sat down.

Ivy looked to Harper. "The guy who came in with Nate, the manager of Charmed Vines, before our lunch started—I know him. We met each other in South Carolina." As she looked to Harper and Brooke, she released a breath and let candor lead the way. "He and I spent a night together. We had fun. Our personal lives didn't come up, which was why we didn't know he knew Brooke and Nellie. We weren't expecting to see each other again. Running into him was a total coincidence."

Harper's mouth dropped open. "You hooked up with someone while you were away? Good for you."

Talking and laughing with Amelia about hooking up with Jaxon had made her feel fun and carefree. Hearing Harper say "hook up" felt weird, especially since she'd been the one to help educate Brooke and Harper about having sex. Now they were all on par as adult women in the dating world, even if Brooke was no longer on the dating scene. But right now, her discomfort wasn't the issue. Brooke's unease about her having been with Jaxon was.

Ivy shook her head. "Unfortunately, it's not good. He and I got a little carried away in the courtyard at the guesthouse." She met Brooke's gaze. "I'm sorry seeing Jaxon and I kissing was how you found out about us. I didn't mean to ruin your day. As soon as I discovered he knew you and that he'd dated Nellie, I should have kept him at arm's length. I'm sorry I didn't."

"Oh." A new understanding dawned on Harper's face. Her brow rose as she looked between Brooke and Ivy.

"You didn't ruin my day." Tension seeped out of Ivy as Brooke gave her a small smile. "I was just surprised by it…and concerned. I like Jaxon, but he isn't someone who's into commitment. He goes from place to place. He doesn't have a stable career. He's not settled."

Harper shot her sister a quizzical look. "So you think the guy's shady because he moves around a lot? Didn't you used to do the same thing?"

That was the very question Ivy was asking in her mind.

"Yes, I did, and I know it sounds judgy, but I didn't call him shady. Honestly, he's a nice guy. I just don't think he's boyfriend material." She looked to Ivy. "I don't want you to get burned your first time back out in the dating world, with a guy whose motto seems to be 'here today, gone tomorrow,' especially since you potentially have a chance with Von. Maybe you two finding each other again after all this time means you're meant to have a second chance. We just want the best for you. Right, Harper?"

Harper paused, looking from Ivy to Brooke. "Yes, I do want the best for Aunt Ivy based on what makes her happy."

"And that's what I want, too," Brooke interjected. "But I really believe the chances of that are slim with Jaxon. He can be closed off, like he's holding something back. I don't know. Maybe he has trust issues."

Harper sighed. "Everyone has issues. No one's perfect."

Ivy considered mentioning she didn't care if Jaxon

wasn't the stick-around-for-long type. As far as trust issues, that could be complicated. If he didn't stay in one place for long, maybe he just never made it to the trust stage with people he'd met. It didn't mean he wasn't capable of it.

But right now, she had to focus on Brooke and Harper. It sounded like they had differing opinions about her and Jaxon, and she didn't want to introduce anything that could inadvertently nudge them apart even just a few millimeters. Not seeing Jaxon was a small sacrifice to keep them happy and keep the peace, wasn't it?

Ivy looked at Harper and Brooke. "I appreciate you both telling me how you feel, but there's nothing to talk about. Jaxon and I have decided to leave our past in the past. We're over." As she swallowed her unhappiness, it almost stuck in her throat. She forced a smile. "Now that we've got that straightened out, we can move on. Brooke, I know you're ready to go, and I'm sure Gable can't wait to see you. Is he meeting you at the airport when you arrive?"

The topic of Gable was an obvious low-hanging fruit for a change of subject. From Brooke's expression, she knew what Ivy was doing, but she still went for it. "Yes, he's meeting me. And you're right, he called first thing this morning to tell me he can't wait to see me."

"Ugh, I can't believe you guys." Harper feigned exasperation. "The way you and Gable are acting, it's like you're each other's first major crush."

"We're not that bad." Brooke tried to look offended, but her lips twitched with a smile. "Okay, maybe just a little, but just wait until you fall in love."

"I definitely won't be as bad as you."

Ivy chuckled at them both. Harper was right. Brooke and Gable were kind of acting like teens with a crush, but it was cute. And hopefully Brooke was right. It would be wonderful to see Harper find someone who loved her just as much as Brooke and Gable loved each other. Ivy let her mind wander into the future.

Brooke and Harper both married to great people. Harper and her husband at the farm and Brooke and Gable living next door. They would teach their children about bees at a young age just like their mom had done with them.

Ivy breathed against the well of feelings building inside of her. Those moments needed to be captured, treasured.

You could do that if you started painting again…

The thought raised goose bumps on Ivy's arms. It distracted her as they discussed Brooke's wedding plans.

"Tillbridge is definitely the perfect venue… Most, if not all, of the flowers should come from our nursery… Layla at Buttons & Lace Boutique has already come up with designs for the dresses…"

Ivy nodded along to what was being said, even as her thoughts wandered elsewhere. *Start painting again? I'm too rusty.*

Later on, after the three of them went their separate ways, thoughts about painting the bees and the farm continued to pester her. Ivy went to the bee shed, hoping to distract herself by inventorying supplies, but she couldn't concentrate. She messed up counting the hive tools and frames multiple times because she kept thinking about what color or technique she would use to capture the form of this or that. Finally she gave up, drove back to the house, and marched to the spare room downstairs.

The room had become more of a storage space for office supplies. It held a long wood table that had once been in the retail store, and other furnishings, like the table and lamp from the living room, sitting in the corner.

She opened the sliding door closet. Pushing back the old clothes that should have been given away a while ago, she finally found tools of the trade from her painting days sitting on a built-in shelf. An open box of paintbrushes. Old sketch pads. An unopened box of acrylic paint colors. The collection used to include easels and blank canvases, but she'd donated them twelve years ago to the community center a few towns over that offered painting courses.

As Ivy picked up a small box to read the label— charcoal sketching pencils—she recalled the conversation she and the manager of the center had gotten into about art. After finding out her background, and that she had worked in an art gallery, the woman had asked her if maybe she'd like to teach a beginners art appreciation course or even help with a beginner sketching class. It had been tempting to say yes, but she'd felt she had to decline. She'd needed to devote her time to learning the skills of a beekeeper and how to be the best guardian she could for Brooke and Harper.

When she'd first moved into the house, she felt like a mix of aunt, caretaker, and intruder, diving into a role she didn't know how to define. In the midst of that struggle, on what had felt like her worst day, the accusation she'd been dreading had come out of Harper's mouth.

You're not my mom!

Hearing those words had felt like shards of glass digging into her heart. No, she wasn't Harper and Brooke's mom. She didn't know how to be a mom or do things like their mom. She didn't *want* to be their mom. She wanted to roll back time and bring back their parents. She wanted to take away the grief she saw in Brooke's and Harper's eyes. The same grief that met her every day she woke up to face the task as an inadequate replacement for what the girls had lost.

It had been such a balancing act—cooking healthy meals, tackling the weekday school hustle, navigating the schedules for after-school activities, helping with homework and learning to disguise her own dislike of math. It had taken months for her to figure out the best way to delegate chores and how to hunt down clothes that just seemed to disappear somewhere between the hamper, washer, and dryer, and she'd done it while learning how to run the apiary.

And then it happened one afternoon on a snow day. They'd been camped out on the couch watching movies, eating bowls of ice cream loaded with so many toppings, it should have been a crime. As she'd thrown a blanket over the three of them, teen bravado and angst had somehow slipped away and Harper then Brooke had snuggled in on either side of her.

Feeling them pressed so closely to her had raised a myriad emotions she'd never felt before. She'd held them close as new understanding as clear as a finished canvas had washed over her. She realized in that moment that she would give her last breath to protect them. She would keep them safe. She would work hard every day to make sure they had everything they needed, and most of all, she would make sure they knew they were loved and that she would always choose them first over everything or anyone else.

Now they were resilient, capable, and compassionate young women, but she still felt the same way. She probably always would to some extent, even as she tried to define her new role in their lives now that they were all grown up.

Ivy put down the box of brushes, and her hand gravitated toward a box of unopened pencils still sealed in plastic. Years ago, whenever she'd needed to think through something, sketching would help calm her mind.

She grabbed a blank sketch pad and the box of pencils then walked over to the table. As she opened the pad, a feeling of excitement waved through her as if she was about to start a new adventure. She opened the box and removed one of the pencils. What would she draw? The lamp? The room itself? Maybe she could tackle the view of the tree outside the front facing window? Or should she freestyle it and see what came up?

Taking a deep breath, she started drawing lines on the blank page. Abstracts were what she'd done the most in the past. The combination of shapes and lines had their own unique movement, inspiring individual interpretation. The meaning of it changed from artist to viewer, person to person. But unlike years ago, the pencil didn't feel like a comfortable extension of her hand. She felt clumsy. Lines and shapes that should have been light and refined were heavy and almost messy. It was naive to think she could just pick up where she left off over a decade ago. She'd completely lost her touch.

"Are you hiding out in here?"

Startled by Harper in the doorway, Ivy's pencil stroke went askew. "Hey, I didn't hear you come in."

"I needed a break so I grabbed a snack in the kitchen." Harper went to the table beside Ivy and leaned back against the edge. "You know, what we were talking about this morning, about you and Jaxon…"

"Yes, what about it?"

Harper paused for a long moment, then breathed. "I get how Brooke feels about it, but I don't agree with her. If you and Jaxon hit it off in South Carolina, and he's here now, why shouldn't you see him if you want? That's what I believe."

Hearing how Harper felt pleased Ivy, but she was still resolved to avoid a situation where Brooke and Harper felt like they had to take sides. Better to just close the door on the matter once and for all. "I appreciate how you feel about me seeing Jaxon, and I can understand how Brooke feels, too. I love that both of you want me to be happy. But like I said, I'm happy on my own right now."

Her phone buzzed with a text. Pulling it out, she saw that a message alert bubble with Von's name had popped up on the screen.

Ivy didn't unlock her phone to respond. She had an

inkling she knew what his message was about. Her birthday was just a few days away.

Harper glanced at it and said, "You know you can go out with Von and someone else at the same time. You are single. As long as they know you're not exclusive, it's fine."

Ivy chuckled to herself in her mind. When Harper had been old enough to date, Ivy had given her the facts of life talk about dating boys. Hearing Harper give her dating advice now felt like an odd, comical full circle moment. "Yes, I do know, but really, I'm fine being on my own."

"Okay. I was just making sure. Hey, what's that?" Harper pointed to the sketch pad.

"Oh nothing. I was just looking in the closet, and I saw the sketch pad and pencils. I thought I'd draw something. It's just a bunch of random lines."

Harper frowned pensively as she stared at the pad. "From here, it kind of looks like the start of a face."

I would love to paint him.

The thought that had gone through her mind that afternoon at the Wavefront Bistro resurfaced. Ivy peered at the sketch. Now that she took a closer look, those random lines *did* seem like the beginnings of a familiar face. It wasn't a painting, but had she just been making a sketch of Jaxon?

Chapter Twelve

Ivy checked out her reflection in the full-length mirror in her bedroom. The dress she had on was a shade too close to neon pink for her taste, but it was a gift from Von for her birthday. Apparently, he'd mixed up the dresses she'd been admiring on mannequins in a boutique window in Miami during their day together.

The one that had caught her eye had been the aqua-colored sheath dress, but she'd feel guilty if she didn't wear the dress, especially since he was flying in from New York tonight just to take her to dinner.

The text he'd sent her that afternoon when she'd been in the spare room with Harper really had been him asking her out for her birthday again. But this time, he'd offered to come to Bolan and suggested dinner at Pasture Lane Restaurant.

Turning him down had been the plan until she'd overheard a call on speakerphone a couple of days later between Harper and Brooke discussing her upcoming birthday.

Harper had felt terrible because she didn't have time to plan anything special, while Brooke had mentioned feeling guilty about not being there to help celebrate.

Without further hesitation, Ivy had accepted Von's invitation. Then she'd gone to Harper and pretended she'd just remembered to tell her about her big birthday plans, apologizing for not doing it sooner.

Ivy turned in front of the mirror, taking in different angles, but instead of the dress she had on, she imagined the form-fitting, aqua-colored sheath clinging lovingly to her breasts and hips. Yeah, she would have looked good in it, but the boutique was known to be expensive. She couldn't imagine spending that kind of money on herself.

She put on the gold heart-shaped earrings Amelia had given her as an early birthday present. They actually made the outfit a little cuter. Too bad she couldn't tell Amelia where she was about to wear them for the first time. Her friend would tell her she needed her head examined for going out again with Von. *Nope, not telling her...* And it wasn't as if Amelia was going to call her out of the blue just to ask her about the earrings.

Ivy's phone chimed on the dresser. Someone had sent her a message. Amelia? No, it couldn't be. Right? She picked up her phone.

It was only a text from Von. *Whew.* She released her paranoia in a single breath and read his message.

Just landed at BWI. I'll probably be late.

Before responding, Ivy ran a quick mental calculation of time and distance from Baltimore/Washington International airport to the restaurant.

Head straight to the restaurant. I'll be there on time to claim our reservation.

A moment later another text bubble from him chimed in.

Our reservation is solid. I took care of it.

Solid? That was mighty confident of him. Pasture Lane Restaurant at Tillbridge was the hottest restaurant in town, especially when Philippa and Dominic Crawford were in residence. The policy was if you didn't make it by a certain time, you forfeited your reservation.

Or by taking care of it, did Von mean he'd used his financial influence in some way? The thought of him flashing his wealth around made her cringe a little. In Bolan, doing that just got you talked about and not always in a good way. She'd be sure to get there on time.

Later on that evening, Ivy got out of her blue two-door sedan in the main parking lot of Tillbridge.

Muted shades of orange and red radiated from the sun, hovering just above the horizon in front of the guesthouse. The white building and the surrounding pastures had an ethereal glow. The earthy scents of grass and horses drifted in the air. Even though people mingled on the porch, there was a sense of stillness, as if everyone were mesmerized by the sight and had paused with her to take it all in.

The time between sunset and nightfall had always been her favorite. At the bee farm, whenever she'd started obsessing over everywhere she'd fallen short, watching the sunset helped her regain perspective. Maybe this beautiful birthday sunset was her reminder to fully embrace her current fresh start. If only she could get a glimpse of what that should be, starting with if she should stay in Bolan or relocate. She had big decisions to make, but not tonight. Dinner, wine, and good company were on her immediate agenda.

She went inside the guesthouse and headed to the restaurant.

In the foyer, a young Black woman in a dark dress with white trim stood behind the host podium. She smiled. "Good evening. Welcome to Pasture Lane Restaurant. Do you have a reservation with us tonight?"

"Yes."

Ivy gave Von's name, and the woman's eyes sparked with recognition. "You must be Ivy Daniels."

"I am."

"Please, come this way."

Ivy followed her into the dining area.

Instead of leading Ivy to a table inside, the hostess led her to the enclosed deck.

None of the tables with white cloths were set except for one in the middle. The four-top was adorned with two gleaming place settings with intricately folded pale green napkins. A huge mixed bouquet with white roses and pink hydrangeas was in a clear vase off to the side. Smooth, soulful jazz played softly through hidden speakers.

"Oh." Ivy gasped. She put her small chain clutch beside her on the table as she sat down. "This is beautiful."

The woman's pleased expression made Ivy wonder if she'd played a part in setting it up. "Mr. Gibson wanted everything to be perfect for you, all the way down to your favorite flowers."

Roses and hydrangeas weren't her favorites, but that was hardly this woman's fault, so Ivy held back the comment and smiled. "Everything is lovely, thank you. But are we the only ones in here tonight?"

"Yes, he reserved the entire deck."

No wonder Von had said their reservation was solid.

As the hostess left, a dark-haired server came in carrying a pitcher of ice water.

Dominic Crawford walked in behind her, dressed in a navy chef's jacket and dark gray pants. Ivy had known his wife, Philippa, for several years, but had only become acquainted with him last year when he'd started attending the business council meetings.

As the tall good-looking Black man approached the table, he greeted her warmly. "Ivy. It's good to see you. Happy birthday."

"Thank you." She smiled back at him as the server filled her water glass. "It's good to see you, too."

"I hope you're ready to eat."

"I am." She pointed to the empty chair across from her. "As soon as my date gets here."

"No problem. Mr. Gibson's assistant called to let me know things would be running late tonight, but I'm prepared. The grilled sea bass is going to be perfection, I promise, and so will the aged rib eye."

"That sounds amazing. I've been away so long I missed the menu change."

He shook his head. "These items were brought in just for you two tonight."

Von had reserved the entire deck, arranged a special menu, and he'd sent her a dress. It was a lot. Maybe too much. In the past when it came to gifts, go big and expensive had practically been his middle name. Obviously, that hadn't changed, but did he truly understand they were just friends?

Dominic added, "But if something else is more to your liking, just let me know."

The concerned look on his face made her realize she was frowning. "Oh no, I just don't know which to choose. The steak or the seabass."

"You don't have to. It's your birthday. Have a little of each."

They chatted about the rest of the menu for the night. Variety with balance was the theme. As soon as Von arrived, they would start their meal with spicy edamame and calamari with an assortment of sauces.

"I can't wait. I already know it's going to be beyond delicious." Ivy's mouth had actually started to water in anticipation. Pasture Lane was known for taking simple dishes up a notch through unique flavors and beautiful plated presentations.

Dominic tipped his head in appreciation. "Have a glass of wine, relax, and let us know if you need anything."

"I will."

The server brought over two bottles of wine. "Mr. Gibson has chosen a pinot grigio and a cabernet for you tonight."

As the woman went on to explain the highlights of each wine, Ivy's thoughts strayed to that fateful lunch when she'd first seen Jaxon walk on the deck. It had been a total shock. What if he'd never met Brooke or Nellie and no one had known who he was but her? How would they have greeted each other? Would they have acknowledged each other at all in that moment?

The young woman finished her explanation, and Ivy made her selection. "I'll take the cabernet, please."

Moments later, Ivy was drinking her wine totally alone on the deck. She felt like she was in a fishbowl on display for the entire restaurant. Thankfully, the flower arrangement blocked most of her view of the main dining area. She couldn't blame anyone for staring or being curious about what was happening on the deck. If she looked hard enough, she would probably see a few people she knew.

Wanting to distract herself, she looked toward the pleasant view of the trees, manicured shrubs, and lights in the grass lining the sides of the pathway. The pathway that had led to where Jaxon had found her. He hadn't smelled sweet like the flowers. His scent had been clean with a hint of spice. In her mind, she relived the moment of catching whiffs of his cologne as he'd leaned in, and how his chest had felt even more solid than she'd remembered underneath her palms. The way his hands had tightened a bit more around her waist as he kissed her. The remembered feeling of being desired, missed. The rush of something like relief at being back in his arms.

No, you have to stop thinking about him. She faced forward and focused on being in the present, but the sitting-in-a-fishbowl feeling grew even stronger. Why couldn't Von have just gotten them a table in the main dining area instead of putting them on display? And where was he? He should have been there by now.

Agitated, she leaned forward and pushed back the buds and fronds in the bouquet to get a better look at the front of the dining room. Servers attended to their sections. No one was walking in with the hostess. As she started to glance away, she saw him.

Jaxon sat at a table with Nate. They were deep in conversation. As Nate said something to him, Jaxon glanced in her direction.

Ivy snatched her hand from the bouquet and sat back quickly in the chair. What was he doing there? Silly question—he was eating, of course. She'd just seen that with her own eyes. Had he been there the entire time and she'd missed him?

Her phone rang and she dug it out of her purse. She recognized the number.

Releasing a sigh of relief, she answered. "Von, I was starting to get worried. Are you almost here?"

"I'm in the parking lot."

"Okay, good. See you in a bit."

"No, wait. I'm sorry. I just got a call about a major client emergency. I have to fly to London tonight."

"Dinner will be a lot shorter than expected." Ivy wrestled down disappointment. With a laugh, she added, "Then I guess we better order dessert with our entrées. Maybe we should have it first. I am allowed since it's my birthday."

Von remained silent.

Her laughter died in her throat as realization sunk in. "You're not coming in at all?"

"I can't. My driver has already turned us around. I'm heading back to the airport now."

He'd gotten all the way to the parking lot, and he just turned around without even coming inside to see me? Ivy tried to reconcile in her mind how on earth it had made sense.

"Again, I'm sorry about this," he added, not sounding fully repentant. "But millions of dollars are at stake. I know you understand. I'll make it up to you."

How can you still be so generous when it comes to his lack of support or consideration for your situation?

Amelia's remembered words hit Ivy like a slap to the face. She'd ended her engagement with Von back then because he wasn't willing to go the distance with her. The fact that he wouldn't even get out the car for her now and take a few minutes to acknowledge her birthday proved he still couldn't. And that wasn't a surprise. The part of her that already innately understood his character was speaking loud and clear to her now. She'd always given him a pass for not showing up for her, but she wasn't going to do that anymore.

The beautiful sunset she'd witnessed before walking inside the building filled Ivy's mind. She deserved nothing short of wonderful on her birthday and in her life.

"Yes, I do understand," she said.

"I'll call you when I get back."

"Don't bother. I won't answer the phone. Have a good trip to London." Ivy ended the call. After tossing back the rest of the cabernet in her glass, she asked the server to find Dominic.

Moments later, the chef came in. Smiling, he said,

"I was just about to check in with you. Have you heard from Mr. Gibson?"

She nodded apologetically. "Yes, he just called. He can't make it. I'm sorry we kept you waiting for nothing."

Dominic's expression grew empathetic. "I'm sorry to hear that, but it's not for nothing. You're here, and I'm your chef for the night."

It was a fantastic gesture. Who wouldn't want a celebrity chef cooking for them on their birthday? But that was an experience meant to be shared. It just felt awkward when she was sitting at a table all alone. Funny thing, she'd told Harper she was happy on her own. Right then, she was far from it.

A solution to part of her problem came to her, and she managed a small smile for Dominic. "If you don't mind, I would really like to make someone else's night a little more special. Are there any reservations for a couple celebrating a birthday, anniversary, or some occasion? Maybe I can give the meal you planned for me as an anonymous gift. Give them the whole experience—private reservation, the flowers, everything Von had planned, if it's appropriate."

Dominic's face reflected understanding. "I believe we have an engagement happening later tonight. If not them, I'm sure there's someone, but are you sure?"

"Yes, I'm sure." After Ivy stood and picked up her things, she and Dominic exchanged a quick hug.

"Dinner's on the house the next time you come in," he said.

"I'd love that."

Walking through the restaurant, it felt like everyone's attention swiveled in her direction. Her face grew a little hot, but she reminded herself that no one knew that Von had practically stood her up. Of course, if her server liked to gab, maybe *some* people knew, but not the entire room. If she thought everyone's expressions looked knowing, it was all in her mind.

Head high, but not in the mood to chat, she acknowledged a member of the business council sitting at a nearby table with a quick smile and a wave and kept going—or rather, she tried to.

Waitstaff were setting up stands with food near a table, blocking her from passing that way. She took a detour…which brought her closer to Jaxon and Nate's table. Crap. Ivy focused on the exit.

Maybe it was cowardly, but she just couldn't look at him, especially since her birthday was starting to feel like one of those three choice questions. *A celebrity chef, an unreliable ex-fiancé, and a guy you had a fantastic time with are in the same place on your birthday. Keep, Kiss, or Kill. Gee, that's tough.*

Ivy was still spinning combinations of the answer in her head when she got to the parking lot. *A platonic kiss on the cheek for the chef. Kill all possible contact with Von. Keep my hands off Jaxon.*

That one made her laugh to herself, but why? Because it was cute and maybe truthful to a point? But what other option was there? They had already kissed—and it wasn't like she could keep Jaxon.

"Ivy…wait."

Jaxon's voice brought her to a halt.

Chapter Thirteen

Jaxon paused a few steps behind Ivy. She'd stopped walking but didn't turn around.

He'd overheard snippets of a conversation between two of the waitstaff and had an idea of why she'd abruptly left the restaurant.

Some rich guy stood her up...

Seriously?

Yep, and the worst part is, it's her birthday.

Irritation on Ivy's behalf rumbled through him, but as she turned to face him, he pushed it all aside. Right now wasn't about him or whoever stood her up. It was about Ivy.

"I heard your dinner plans were canceled," he said. "I'm sorry. Especially since I also heard that tonight's your birthday. You should be celebrating."

Suprise briefly flared across her face. "I guess a few stories about me being stood up are already starting to spread. When you go back inside, do me a favor and tell whoever's truly concerned that I'm fine."

"If anyone wants to know how you are, they can ask you themselves." He walked over to Ivy. "Did the guy have a good reason for not showing up?"

"He had a million of them but none of them were good." Ivy looked away, but not before he saw the hurt in her eyes.

"What are your plans for the rest of the night?"

"I'm going home." She adjusted the chain shoulder strap of her purse. "I've got a nice bottle of champagne waiting for me."

"It'll have to wait a little longer."

Puzzlement came into her eyes. "Why?"

"I'm taking you out."

"No." She waved away his invitation and shook her head. "I don't need pity. I'm fine. I've done plenty of birthdays alone."

"So have I. But that's not how you planned to spend this one. You'll realize that after the third or fourth glass of champagne, and that's when you'll call whoever ruined your night and cuss him out."

A small smile tugged at her mouth. "That actually sounds like a good plan."

"Mine is a better one."

"You sound really confident about that." Her smile grew, and there was a hint of amusement in her eyes. "And if I were to go with you, what would we do?"

"Well…" Jaxon rubbed his chin, pretending to ponder the question. "I would answer that but according to the rule book of birthdays, I can't."

"You can't?" She laughed. "How convenient."

"You know what else is convenient?" He slipped his keys from the front pocket of his dark green cargo pants. "We're almost next to my car." His navy crossover SUV beeped as he unlocked it with his key fob. "All you have to do is walk over and get in."

She laughed. "And just ride away with you without knowing where we're going?"

"It's a surprise, but I promise it'll be a good one."

"That's tempting." Her smile dimmed. "But I told Brooke and Harper that we were over."

Not if he had anything to say about it. But Jaxon held back on voicing the objection. "We're not picking up where we left off. This is about you enjoying your birthday. We're just going out as friends. Don't worry about anyone seeing us. Where we're going is out of town."

Ivy still didn't look convinced as she glanced down at her clothes and then to him. Her gaze moved down and up as if taking in his black T-shirt, cargos, and high-tops. "Am I dressed for it?"

"You're good, but do you happen to have a different pair of shoes with you?"

"I have flats in my car."

"Great. You should put them on."

Moments later, they were heading away from Bolan down a long stretch of a two-lane highway.

Anticipation rippled through him. Ivy had remained on his mind since that day in the courtyard. When he'd awakened this morning, the last thing he'd expected was being able to spend time with her. Jaxon felt bad that she'd been stood up, but a part of him was thanking the guy for messing up and giving him this opportunity.

On the radio, a commercial about pest control ended, and a song that was a mix of country, hip-hop, and soul came on.

Ivy's face lit up. "That's Gable's song. I mean Dell's. Sometimes, I forget he has a different stage name."

Jaxon made the connection to Brooke's fiancé. "So how does it feel to have a celebrity coming into the family?"

"In my mind, he's just Gable, until moments like this." She pointed to the radio. "I'm glad his career is going well, but what matters to me is that they're happy together."

He and Ivy had been happy together in Hilton Head, and they'd been happy to see each other again. Didn't that matter, too? Jaxon wanted to ask the question so badly, but she'd already made it clear that what happened between them belonged firmly in the past. He was lucky to be with her now, and it was her birthday. He just wanted her to enjoy herself.

"So from bartender in Hilton Head to helping run a wine bar in a small town," Ivy said. "What prompted that move?"

Jaxon went with the short version of the story. "I needed a change and Nate needed an assist. I'm helping him analyze the books and acting as assistant manager while he finds someone to take that role permanently."

Ivy adjusted her seat belt and sat more comfortably in the seat. "And after this, where are you going?"

"I'm considering a job in Tennessee. One of Drew's friends actually turned me on to it. A couple who lives there owns a farm. They want to turn it into a bed and breakfast type setup, and they need a handyman to make repairs and basically serve as a property manager for a few months."

"So you're really comfortable moving place to place like Brooke used to."

"I am." Jaxon checked his side mirror for oncoming cars, before changing lanes and speeding past the truck ahead them. "I like connecting with new people. Mixing up my skill set. Trying things I haven't done before."

"Developing skills, learning new ones—that sounds like it could be fun, as long as I got to visit my family in between. How often do you make it home? And where are you from, by the way?"

Home. That word settled like a lead weight in his stomach. Simply put, he considered his home to be wherever he happened to be at the time, as long as it was nowhere near his father. But that wasn't a fun topic. And he didn't want to talk about his family. He wanted to just enjoy what little time they had together tonight. But Ivy was waiting for his answer.

Jaxon realized he was tightly gripping the steering wheel and forced himself to loosen his hold. Clearing his throat, he left one hand at the top of wheel and rested the other on his thigh. "I was born in New York. My father lives there—upstate. My sister and her husband live in Philadelphia. I don't make it home often, but they understand."

That wasn't a lie. His father and sister were well aware of why he didn't visit them.

"What about you?" he asked. "Last time we talked, you said you were here to fill in while Brooke was gone, but you weren't sure what was next." The kiss they'd shared while they were talking popped into his mind along with all he'd felt holding her in his arms again. As he rubbed his hand along his jean-clad thigh, he pushed the memory aside. "Have you decided yet?"

"No, I haven't." She sat back in the seat and looked ahead. "At times like this, I really envy the bees."

"Why?"

"Because in the hive, every bee knows what they're supposed to do. They don't have any doubts. Forager bees are basically suppliers, and they know their main job is to bring back pollen to the hive. The worker bees know what they have to do…"

As Ivy talked, Jaxon had to stop himself from just looking at her instead of the road. Explaining the life of bees didn't diminish the sultriness of her voice or her natural glow of confidence. Her lips looked even more kissable than usual, and a part of him wanted to pull over to explore the soft lushness of her mouth.

He refocused his mind in time to hear the last of what she said. "And, well, the queen's and drones' roles are pretty straightforward."

He released a huffed chuckle. "Yeah, the queen assassinates the drones, doesn't she?"

Ivy laughed. "Well, you could see it that way. I prefer to view it as more of a noble sacrifice."

As Jaxon drove past a dense section of trees, the colorful lights of a Ferris wheel became visible a short distance away on the left.

Looking to Ivy, he said, "We're here."

Ivy and Jaxon drifted in through the entrance of the roadside carnival. A kaleidoscope of lights flashed around them from the game booths, and food trucks lined up on either side of them.

Carnival sounds surrounded them, ranging from the patter of the carnival barkers, to music, to the distant clacking from a roller coaster followed by screams from its riders as the cars hurdled down the slope on the track. The sweet aromas of cotton candy and caramel corn were mixed with the savory smells of hot dogs, boiled peanuts, french fries, and other food being deep-fried in oil.

The sights, smells, and sounds took her back to so many places. Bishop Honey Bee Farm often had a booth selling honey at crossover flea market/carnivals, but she also had a wonderful childhood memory of visiting a carnival purely for fun. She and Lexy went with Grandma Jean and other families in their grandmother's neighborhood.

This was the second time Jaxon had taken her back to a really good memory. Happiness, disbelief, and wonder bubbled out of her in a laugh. "This was not on the list of places where I thought we might end up."

Jaxon's smile held adorable uncertainty. "Do you hate it?"

"No, I love it." Her stomach growled. The giddiness she felt wasn't just from excitement.

Jaxon glanced at her hand on her stomach. "Hot dog? Pizza? Fried Oreos?"

He was speaking her language. "Hot dogs."

They found a truck serving foot-long dogs and decided to split one along with a boat of curly fries. Once they'd split the hot dog in half, they quickly mastered the skill of walking, eating, and checking out the booths.

The carnival was busy but not so full of people as to feel claustrophobically crowded. Ivy also noticed that there were more couples, young and old, and not a lot of younger school-age children. Maybe because it was a weekday?

She glanced over at him as she cleaned mustard from her hands with a paper napkin. "How did you find out about this? Did you see a flyer in town?"

"No, I saw it when I was driving to Bolan. I needed to stretch my legs. This looked interesting so I stopped." He offered her the fries.

She took one. As she munched on it, Ivy tried to imagine guys she'd gone out with in the past making a spur-of-the-moment decision to roll into the parking lot of a carnival just to check it out. She couldn't picture it for any of them. Especially Von. In Miami, he'd been a little reluctant to walk around the flea market until she'd talked him into it.

With Jaxon, she could easily see it. She sensed he wasn't afraid to explore or share the good things he discovered with other people. Did that quality come from someone in his family? Ivy wanted to ask, but remembering what Brooke had said about him avoiding his past halted her question. She ate fries instead. Brooke, Harper, Lexy, even her Grandma Jean had been mentioned by her in their conversations. He'd never mentioned anyone in his family except for when she'd specifically asked where he was from—and even then, all he did was say where his sister and father lived. He hadn't shared anything else about them, or about his relationship with them. Was his past that painful?

Soon her question was forgotten as they played games, tried to win prizes, and walked away empty-handed. The claw machine was a last-ditch effort. Jaxon went first. She tried next. He went again, but each time, the toy slipped from the claw's grasp before they could get it to the metal chute.

As Ivy took the controls to try a second time, Jaxon hyped her up. "Come on, birthday girl, you got this."

A kiss for luck. She almost said it, but the entire time they'd been at the carnival, he hadn't touched her. He'd clearly meant it when he said they were going out for her birthday strictly as friends.

"You got it!" Jaxon pointed at the glass case of stuffed toys. "Just lift it up. Don't rush."

She'd been aiming for the cute teddy bear with a bow tie, but the fate of the claw chose a stuffed bee wearing a polka dot tutu almost the same color as her dress.

Ivy sunk her teeth into her bottom lip as she slowly used the stick controls to maneuver the unwieldy metal claw upward. No sudden movements, just like when she carefully removed frames with bees from a hive. "Oh, please, please, please. Don't fall."

The prize seemed to barely hang on. Ivy held her breath as she steered the metal claw to the metal bin off to the side. She used the button on the controls to release the toy, and it fell into the bin with a soft thump.

"Yes!" Ivy turned to him as she threw her hands in the air.

"You did it!" Jaxon picked her up in a hug and spun her around.

She was still flush against him as he lowered her back down. It felt like every cell in her body had suddenly come alive, messaging her brain about the muscles in his broad shoulders, the hardness of his chest, abs and thighs. Images of them in bed together followed. Ivy closed her eyes and breathed.

When she opened them, her gaze landed on his mouth. *One kiss.*

But just as she started rising on her toes, Jaxon let go of her and stepped back. "We better grab your prize." Turning away from her, he opened the bin, took out the stuffed bee, and handed it to her.

"Thanks."

An energy filled with awareness and awkwardness hung between them.

He glanced to the midway. "Are you up for the Ferris wheel or the roller coaster?"

Sitting beside him, slowly circling round and round and pretending she wasn't still super attracted to him sounded like torture. "Roller coaster."

Moments later, the two of them sat side by side in the dual seat with shoulder harness restraints holding them in. All of her things were stowed securely in the side pockets of Jaxon's cargos. As they started to move, Ivy's heart thumped harder, and a part of her started to second-guess her idea.

Doubt must have been written on her face because Jaxon reached over and gave her hands, clenched in her lap, a squeeze. "It'll be over before you know it. Sit back and enjoy the ride."

Ivy couldn't figure out which accelerated her heart more—Jaxon's sexy grin and wink or the roller coaster starting to move. The anticipation of the upward climb raised goose bumps of excitement as her body grew heavier and heavier, and then it came. The fall. Wind whipped past her face as the momentum made her feel lighter and lighter. Just when it started to feel like it wouldn't end, they zipped into turns that moved them side to side. As the ride continued, sometimes it felt as if they were barreling out of control. At other times, she felt like an acrobat gliding through the air. She shouted. She laughed. She screamed at the top of her lungs just because she could. No worries. No consequences. Only her own unaltered joy.

Just like Jaxon had predicted, the ride came to an end. Her legs still felt a little rubbery on the way to the parking lot.

"Did you have fun?" Jaxon asked as they reached his SUV.

She smiled. "I did. It was the birthday present I didn't know I wanted. Thank you."

"Damn." He came to an abrupt halt. "I forgot something."

"What?"

He handed her the keys before he jogged off. "Get in. I'll be right back."

Ivy took a seat in the car. Floodlights partially illuminated the dark lot. While she waited, she responded to Happy Birthday texts from her friends, including one from Amelia. Ivy almost mentioned she was with Jaxon, but she knew that if she did, Amelia would call her.

Jaxon returned carrying a paper plate covered by a paper napkin.

Smiling, he got in and handed it to her.

"What's this?" She laughed. From the warm sugary scent, she had an idea.

"Take a look."

She lifted the napkins. "Funnel cake?"

"While we were walking around, I looked for cup-cakes or some kind of cake, but I didn't see any. This is the best I could do. I don't have any candles, but some-one was nice enough to give me these." Jaxon took a box of matches from his pocket. "So, make a wish." He lit a match.

"Wait, I wasn't ready."

The flame flickered.

He chuckled. "I'm about to get burned so think of something."

I want more roller coasters. The unexpected wish popped into Ivy's mind. Closing her eyes, she blew out the match. But what did that wish even mean?

Opening her eyes, she looked at Jaxon's face. Giv-ing in to impulse, she kissed him.

Jaxon remained still at first, but then he murmured, "Damn—I tried, but I can't." Cupping the side of her face with his hand, he pressed his mouth fully to hers.

Ivy grasped his shirt, holding on to him, kissing Jaxon like a drowning woman who'd suddenly discov-ered air to breathe. She couldn't get enough of him.

A long moment later, they broke apart because they actually did need to breathe.

Jaxon leaned his forehead to hers. "What are we doing?"

Ivy closed her eyes. "Honestly, I don't know. But I do know I can't just be friends with you."

Jaxon released a heavy sigh. "I feel the same way. I can't be around you without wanting to be with you again."

Ivy looked at him as multicolored lights played over his face. Ignoring how they felt wasn't playful or fun like rides at the carnival. It felt frustrating and wrong, and she needed a break from it. She needed Jaxon.

Ivy met his gaze. "Then let's find someplace where we can be together."

He leaned away to look at her. "Be together like…?"

She leaned back in and kissed him again. Pulling a fraction away, she said, "I want us to be together like we were in South Carolina."

Chapter Fourteen

Anticipation and desire muted any lingering doubts for Ivy. Need had taken hold as soon as they'd shut the door to their motel room. A trail of their shoes and clothing led to where she waited for Jaxon in bed. Her body, already feverish from his caresses and kisses, burned with a renewed flame of desire as she watched him kneeling between her legs, stroking a condom down his length.

As he braced himself on top of her, his erection teased at her opening. Looking into his eyes, she felt lost and completely seen by him all at once. In his eyes, she wasn't being summed up as just a beekeeper or a business manager or her past as a guardian to two grieving teens. In that moment, Jaxon saw her as the woman he desired.

Leaning in, he kissed her softly, slowly. As she glided her hands to his back, she widened her legs and wrapped them around his waist. She was eager to feel him inside of her, but Jaxon kept her hovering on the brink of anticipated pleasure. He swept his lips down her cheek and the side of her neck. His open-mouthed kisses bathed her breasts. Finally, Jaxon took hold of her hips, and in one continuous glide, he entered her.

Need swiftly uncoiled as she met the roll of his hips, letting their joining fill her with pleasure she wished would never end. But the rush of an ecstasy washing over her was too much, too wonderful. She had to let go and let her orgasm take her away. Jaxon soon followed.

Moments later, sated by pleasure, she lay with her head on his shoulder and her hand to his chest. Reveling in his warmth and skin-to-skin contact, she snuggled closer and could feel it when his heart beat a little harder underneath her palm.

As she closed her eyes, her phone rang. She recognized the ringtone. It was the one she'd set for Brooke. She was probably calling to wish her happy birthday.

Ivy debated about getting up. She wasn't ashamed about being with Jaxon, but she'd feel awkward talking to Brooke with him just a short distance away. In some ways it felt like some weird role reversal moment, where Brooke was the disapproving parent checking up on her, and she was the teenager, hanging out with some sketchy guy.

Jaxon stroked his hand up and down her arm. "Do you need to get that?"

"No. I'll call them back."

"Any regrets?" His voice, rumbling into her palm from his chest, held concern.

"About this?" She raised her head to meet his gaze. "No, I don't have any regrets, at least not about being here with you."

"I'm glad you're not regretting this." He studied her face. "So what *are* you regretting?"

"I don't know. I don't know why I said that."

"But you did. No one should have regrets on their birthday." Before she could rest her head back down on his shoulder, he eased away and propped himself up on his elbow. "Tell me about it."

Ivy lay back down on the pillow, avoiding his eyes. "It was just a random thought."

He remained silent and just looked at her.

Amelia's truth serum stare was powerful, but his immediately penetrated to a place where she'd hidden her secrets and dreams. Like a chest of treasures waiting to be revealed, she opened up to him.

"It's just that sometimes, I feel as if my twenties and thirties flew by without me." Pausing, Ivy let herself wade through thoughts she hadn't let herself fully examine before. "I guess I'm wondering if there are things I've missed out on, or things I stopped doing and should do again, now that I can."

He smiled. "Can I be added to the list of things you want to do again?"

Ivy laughed. "Who said I had a list?"

As she playfully swatted his chest, he caught her hand and kissed the back of it. "Maybe you should start one."

"You mean a bucket list? Do people even make those anymore? I thought it was just a trend."

"They do, even if they just don't call it that. Adventure Agenda, Life's Must Do's—same thing. So what's on your list?"

Not knowing how to answer, she laughed. "Like I said, I don't have a list. What am I supposed to say? Axe throwing? Goat yoga?"

"You should do all of that if they're things you would like to do."

"Oh, I should, huh? So when are we taking a goat yoga class, then?"

"You tell me. I've done it before. A friend persuaded me to go. The whole human and baby goat interaction thing—it's actually relaxing."

His gaze didn't waver, and there wasn't a hint of teasing in his eyes. "You're serious."

"About goat yoga or doing it with you?"

"Both."

"I'm very serious. Since I've run into you here, all I've heard you talk about is everyone else's happiness. What about what makes *you* happy? You just said you felt like years of your life have just flown by. You can't ignore how you feel. Maybe starting a list of things you want to do, and actually doing them, might help you catch back up again. And if you want me along for the ride, I'm here for you."

What Jaxon proposed sounded like it could actually be fun, especially if he was along for the ride.

She nodded. "Okay. Goat yoga is on the list."

"And what else? Back in South Carolina, you mentioned wanting to get back into hiking or trying something a little more challenging. Is that still something you want to do?"

"You remembered that?"

"Yes. You seemed excited about challenging yourself. You had a smile on your face when you said it."

"I did?" He really had paid attention to what she'd said that night. "Honestly, it wasn't thinking about the actual hike that made me smile." Ivy hesitated as she remembered what she'd been thinking about that night. In the past decade, other than Amelia, she hadn't shared this part of her past. "I used to be a painter. I was imagining myself capturing the view on a sketch pad or a canvas."

"Oh, I get it." He smiled. "So maybe your list should be more about doing the things that inspire your creativity as an artist?"

As she thought more about that, joy unfurled inside of her. "Yes, that's it." She didn't truly consider herself an artist anymore, but she still had a creative soul. Jaxon had picked up on that so clearly.

"So what else do you want to do? There has to be more."

"I don't know. This is something I really haven't thought about."

"If it helps, I could come up with some suggestions and you can decide if you want to try them out." Jaxon leaned in and gave her a lingering kiss that raised tingles on her skin.

Oh, he definitely had the top spot on her list.

"That would be helpful." As desire warmed inside of Ivy, she slid her hand up his chest to his nape, urging him back down. "Or you could inspire me now... It might help bring up a few good ideas."

As Jaxon curved his hand around her hip and leaned in, his need for her reflected in his eyes. He brushed a kiss against her earlobe and said, "I can do that, too." More kisses down her neck, along with his hand gliding from her hip to between her thighs, clouded her mind with anticipated pleasure.

Much later, lying beside him with his arms around her, their legs intertwined, Ivy realized that she had never felt so content. She wished they could stay in their own little bubble of happiness right then and never leave.

It wasn't just the physical side of being with Jaxon that was so appealing. He was so good at paying attention to the details. Bringing her club soda to get the stain out of her dress that day at the restaurant. Remembering what she'd said about hiking. Noticing she'd been stood up on her birthday and stepping in to give her a special night, sensing she needed to feed her creativity. He understood what she needed in the moment, and that felt incredibly special—like something she'd be a fool to give up. But on the other hand, she *had* told everyone she wasn't going to see him again.

She could just categorize what was happening now as a misstep and reset the clock on not seeing him again, but something he'd said a minute ago resonated. She couldn't ignore how she felt. When it came to her life right now, she felt…lost. Catching back up with herself again might get her past the fog of uncertainty so she could finally see a path forward.

As far as how she felt about Jaxon, she couldn't ignore that, either. She liked him and she liked being with him, and he was only in town for a few more weeks. She didn't want to stir up any discord in her family, but she wanted to see him, too. Was there a way she could do both?

* * *

The following afternoon, sitting at a back corner table at Charmed Vines, Jaxon smiled as he looked over Ivy's text. They'd decided where to go hiking that coming Friday. The area was an hour or so away and not only featured trails for hiking, but also mountain biking, horseback riding, and bird watching, all while providing lots of scenic views to inspire her creativity. He couldn't wait.

Nate walked up and dropped in the seat across from him.

Like Jaxon, he was dressed in dark gray pants and a black shirt. It was their low-key management uniform, slightly setting them apart from the staff that wore black pants, gray shirts, and aprons in the same coordinating colors.

He pointed to Jaxon's laptop that was open on the table. "Are you still working on the financials?"

"I am. What's up?"

"The usual worries about this place." Most of the time, Nate was happy-go-lucky, but, lately, he seemed more subdued. He looked around at the empty tables in the wine bar. The only patrons were three people sitting at the bar counter. "It's been dead in here this week. Maybe it'll pick up over the weekend."

"Yeah, that could happen." *Maybe* it would, but probably not enough to make a significant profit.

Currently, the place was set up more like a retail store than a wine bar. Nate was playing a tug-of-war between the objective he had in mind of people coming in to socialize and the bar's image of just being a wine store and not a place to hang out.

Nate sighed. "Hopefully. Hey—I got your message about not coming in until late Friday evening. Got plans?"

"I do. I'm going hiking."

"Really?" Nate perked up. "Where at?"

Jaxon pulled up the website on his phone and then handed his phone to Nate. "A place about an hour away."

"Hiking and biking trails? Let me know how you like it. I might check it out." He handed the phone back to Jaxon. "Are you going with someone or by yourself?"

"With someone."

Nate waited for him to elaborate during the extended pause, and then he smiled widely. "One of the women you were in a love triangle with? Or is it both of them?"

"It wasn't a love triangle. I'm only interested in one of them."

"Which one?"

Nate was just going to keep badgering him if he didn't say. "It's Ivy, but keep that detail to yourself." He wasn't crazy about the idea of hiding it, but this was the only way he and Ivy could see each other. "We're not telling anyone that we're together."

"Really?" Nate's brows rose as he chuckled. "You, Mr. Transparency, are keeping a secret?"

"Mr. Transparency? What are you talking about?"

"When we worked in Jacksonville at the restaurant, you were big on management being transparent with the staff. Since you've been here, you've reminded me to be transparent with the staff at least a half dozen times, and I get it. That whole thing with your former partners and your dad messed you up when it comes to trust."

Jaxon opened his mouth to protest then paused. Nate was one of the few friends who knew what had happened with his father and the business partners who went behind his back and betrayed him. Maybe he really did have a fixation on transparency now. For sure, after what happened with his father, the last place he ever wanted to be was in a place where there *wasn't* transparency.

He replied, "I don't remember harping on it that much, but it is a good idea, either way. Transparency in business employee relationships is important. But Ivy and I keeping our relationship a secret is a totally different thing. There are personal reasons as to why it's what she wants."

Nate sat back in the chair and crossed his arms over his chest. "And you're completely on board with it, too?"

"Am I happy I can't just walk down the street holding her hand? No, but I respect that she doesn't want to broadcast our relationship around town. The important thing is that she and I get to spend time together without any outside interference getting in the way."

Of course, Ivy mainly didn't want to risk creating a point of tension between Brooke and Harper, but Nate didn't need to know that. As for him, he hadn't forgotten what Nellie had mentioned about Bolan being a small, gossipy town. There probably were bored people who, if they cared to investigate, might want to churn up gossip about their age difference or her hooking up with the new guy for a few weeks or both. He didn't want Ivy to have to deal with even a hint of that BS.

Nate uncrossed his arms. "Sounds like you got your

mind made up. Don't get me wrong, keeping other people out of your relationship is a solid idea. But being straight up about things is important to you. I'm just checking in to make sure you're not compromising too much." Nate looked around the bar with a pensive expression. "My girlfriend and I made some compromises and look where we ended up. Now she's in California and I'm here. Hey, before I forget. The local online paper is doing a feature on the bar and they want some info on me and you for the article. They emailed me some questions."

"They don't need my info. You're the owner. I'm just the temporary help until you hire a permanent operations manager."

"I know, but the exposure will be good for the bar, and it's just a few questions." Nate stood. "I'll forward you the email. Answer the questions you want, and the rest, feel free to ignore."

"Okay, I'll take a look. Send it."

"Thanks. I'll be in the back office if you need me. I have some calls to make."

"I'm going to the Brewed Haven Café to pick up lunch. Do you want something? I'm buying."

"Sure. Pick me up a sandwich. Thanks."

If they closed off part of the large storeroom and remodeled it into a small kitchen, they could start serving their own food. A tapas-like menu with small sharable appetizers, including some sort of sandwich.

Charmed Vines needed balance. It needed to be redesigned into a place where people could unwind and have a glass of their favorite wine and possibly discover something new. If they loved the glass, they would buy the bottle. He'd mentioned the concept to Nate, but he was hesitant to sink more money into the business when it seemed on such shaky ground.

Jaxon left the bar and headed down the sidewalk toward the freestanding two-story light-colored brick building on the corner.

On the sidewalk, shoppers drifted in and out of the connected businesses lining the street—a book store, a florist shop, a clothing boutique.

Light traffic flowed up and down Main Street, a central thoroughfare split into two. In the center square, sun glistened off the water cascading from a stone fountain centerpiece. People sat on park benches or walked down the paths cutting through the grass that were lined with old-fashioned-style streetlamps.

Many of the people he saw on his way to Brewed Haven Café were clearly with a significant other.

Jaxon's gaze landed on a couple sitting on a park bench. They were eating ice cream, and the woman reached over with a napkin to dab at the man's mouth. As the guy leaned in and snuck in a thank-you kiss, Jaxon smiled. That's exactly what he would do if he and Ivy were the ones on that park bench eating ice cream together.

Longing opened up inside of him, and he found himself wondering—was agreeing to see Ivy only in secret too much of a compromise for him?

Chapter Fifteen

"I'm back together with Jaxon." Ivy smiled as she made the announcement to Amelia over the phone as she unpacked stacks of T-shirts in the cottage that doubled as an office/retail space.

The store was closed to customers for the day. Late morning sun highlighted the blond-wood floors, sunny yellow walls with white trim, and white shelving replicating a honeycomb pattern. Today, the bright interior of the space fit her mood.

Amelia's happy squeal upon hearing the latest news was also a perfect match to the sunny atmosphere surrounding Ivy. "What?" she said. "You're back with him? How? When?"

Ivy filled her in on the entire Jaxon situation, including the Nellie and Brooke involvement. She also waded into the deep end and told Amelia what happened on her birthday.

"Von—I'm not surprised." Ivy felt her friend's eye roll from miles away. "I don't know why you gave him a *third* chance. I hate that he nearly ruined your birthday, but at least now you know without a doubt Von's focus is himself. I'm glad you're done with him. Now your whole dating aura can get a total cleanse with Jaxon."

Ivy put a stack of shirts in one of the hexagonal-shaped nooks on the side wall. They were next to other bee-themed merchandise, including cute mugs with flowers and "Bee the Change" printed on them. "It honestly does feel like a cleanse. Jaxon is so different from Von. He listens. He pays attention to the details. He cares about what I want." Ivy filled her in on the adventure list. Jaxon had suggested something she was excited about. Skydiving.

"He pays attention and he's willing to do goat yoga and jump out of a perfectly good plane with you for the hell of it? I love that. Did you explain how amazing he is to Brooke?"

"No. Jaxon and I are seeing each other in secret. It's not worth potentially rocking the boat of Brooke and Harper's recently repaired relationship over something that's only happening for a few weeks."

"That's understandable. I'm glad you're exploring your secret adventurous side. I hope you're also taking that vibe into the bedroom."

Ivy couldn't help but laugh at her friend's enthusiasm. "I swear, for a married woman with kids, you have a one-track mind."

"I'm taking that as a compliment."

"Just to be clear, I'm not doing this to enhance my physical relationship with Jaxon, which is already great. I'm hoping it will help me see things more clearly." She laughed ruefully. "I'm a year older but I'm not much closer to understanding what's happening next for me, and I really need to.

"During the conversation I overheard between Brooke and Harper about my birthday, I also heard them talking about building me a cottage between the bee farm and Gable's property next door. That's not what I see for myself. I've decided to start looking at houses in case I want to stay here in Bolan. I have a call with the local real estate agent this afternoon. The cottage is probably their idea of the perfect failsafe in case I can't relaunch my life. I don't need a failsafe…at least I hope not." A tiny seed of worry remained inside of her.

"No, that's not it." Reassurance flooded Amelia's tone. "You took care of them growing up, and now they want to take care of you. That's probably what building you a cottage is all about. And as far as what's next, you'll know it when you see it. Give yourself permission to explore the options, like checking out a few houses there and elsewhere, because you never know, but have fun with it. Not many people get a chance or have the courage to relaunch at forty, and you have a cute guy around willing to help you do it. You're lucky. Stop worrying so much and just enjoy the moment."

As Ivy put more shirts on the shelf, optimism kicked in. "You're probably right."

Later that afternoon, she kept what Amelia had said in mind as she spoke with Peggy, the real estate agent. "I'm not ready to commit to renting or buying quite yet. I'm just curious about the options for places in the area."

"That's a smart thing to do. And there *are* options,

now and in the future. A couple new subdivisions are being built. I'm sure you heard about them."

She had, but Ivy had mixed feelings about the new construction cropping up. Expansion could equal progress, but it also meant less green space for wildlife to forage and thrive, and that included bees.

Over the years, she'd bought the land surrounding Bishop Honey Bee Farm to prevent the possibility of those land parcels being developed into homes or enterprises that could be detrimental to the hives.

Ivy responded. "Yes, I'm aware of the new homes being built, but I wouldn't mind an older house." The architecture, the history of people and events connected to them gave them character.

"I don't have any of those on my books at the moment, but I'll keep my ear to the ground. If anyone's ready to sell, I'll hear about it and can let you know." Peggy, who was born in Bolan and had lived there for decades, knew a lot of people. "Are you interested in a fixer-upper? I guess you'll have the time since Brooke is taking over for you at the farm. What do you plan on doing?"

Ivy wasn't fooled into thinking the woman was just making small talk. The older woman not only had a talent for finding out information, but she also loved sharing what she discovered with other people. Anything Ivy told her would make its way around town in no time.

"I'm still weighing my options," Ivy replied.

"Well, if you're looking to change up careers, I hear they're looking for an operations manager at the wine bar. Honestly, no one can figure out what's going on over there. First there was a couple running things. Did you ever meet them? His name is Nate. I don't know what the woman's name was, but anyway, now he's got a friend helping him out. I think his name is Jason or something."

"It's Jaxon."

"Oh, is it? I just know he's good-looking, and more than a few women in town want to know if he's single. Have you heard anything through the grapevine about him? Like maybe where he's from?"

"I have no idea." Ivy kicked herself for chiming in about Jaxon in the first place.

The last thing she wanted to be involved in was a gossip session with Peggy. She also wasn't going to share details about Jaxon's life, especially without his permission. She wouldn't do that to him.

"Well, I'm sure we'll find out more about both of them soon," Peggy said. "The newspaper is doing an article on them."

Ivy pressed her lips together and held back a laugh. The *Bolan Town Talk* might have claimed to be the local online newspaper, but it read more like a gossip blog. "Can't wait to read it."

After she and Peggy said their goodbyes, she couldn't help but wonder if Jaxon even knew the interview was coming. On the night of her birthday, she'd noticed how tense he got when she asked him about his family. After giving a few short answers, he'd changed the conversation back to her. She couldn't imagine him answering a reporter's questions. Maybe Brooke was right, and he was holding something back, but as long as it wasn't harmful to anyone, that was his right.

Still, it would be nice to know a few details about him. She didn't know when his birthday was or his favorite color. What type of music did he like? What did he do when he was bored?

Maybe, she'd get a chance to find out on their hike at the end of the week.

Jaxon paused on the rocky trail to adjust the straps of the small backpack on his shoulders containing a reusable bottle of water and energy snacks.

Ivy hiked ahead of him. The small waist pack she wore had sunscreen, bug spray and a small first aid kit. She also had a reusable bottle of water in the attached pocket.

Sun dappling through the trees created a pattern on her lightweight fitted khaki top. As she moved with a lithe grace, taking the most economical route, he couldn't help noticing the way her tan hiking leggings fit to her thighs and accentuated her backside.

Five minutes ago, he'd been staring so hard, he'd almost fallen off a single log bridge. It would have been damn embarrassing considering he'd been reminding her to watch her step.

She glanced back at him. A straw islander hat covered her head and sunglasses shaded her eyes, but her wide smile was on full display. It had been there since the beginning of their two-and-a-half-mile hike. "You're not slowing down on me?"

"Nope." He grinned back at her. "I'm just taking in the view."

From the way her smile widened, she obviously knew he wasn't just talking about the scenery around them. "Stop dawdling. We're almost at the end."

"Dawdling?" He laughed. "I don't think anyone's ever accused me of that before. I do not dawdle."

"Okay, how about pick up the pace then? I'm really looking forward to giving you a reward at the end of the trail."

"A reward? Really? What kind?"

"Stop dawdling so you can find out."

A chuckle shot out of him, joining her laughter and the sounds of chirping birds and rustling leaves.

They'd been on the same page about everything that morning. From what to pack to what precautions to take, including getting a paper map of the route at the park station even though they had it on their phones. The only area where they'd had a different expectation was with how Ivy planned to record the moment. He hadn't expected her to show up with a canvas and an easel, but he'd thought she would at least bring a sketch pad.

Amazing beauty was all around them. Every now and then, one of them would point out something—colorful flowers under a grouping of rocks, the odd curve in the trunk of a tree. As they took a short break to hydrate, a light breeze cooled them off.

After zigzagging through a narrow area in the tree, they made it to the end of the trail. It wasn't as epic as viewing the Grand Canyon, but the sweeping dip of the landscape covered with trees and foliage looked vibrant and alive. No one could claim Mother Nature was boring.

After a long moment, Ivy said, "More people should experience this."

"I agree." Jaxon stood behind her, resting his hands low on her waist. He was a little sweaty, so he kept space between them.

To his surprise, Ivy leaned into him, reached for his hands and brought them around in front of her in a full embrace.

Holding her close, he kissed her temple. "So how does it feel to check an item off of your list?"

"Satisfying. It's so peaceful here."

Jaxon's phone buzzed in his pocket with a text. He ignored it. A few seconds later, it buzzed again. Releasing a heavy sigh, he stepped back from her and took it out. "Sorry for ruining the moment. I should have turned this off." As he glanced at the screen, he couldn't stop a frown. It was someone from the *Bolan Town Talk*.

"What's wrong?"

"Nothing."

Ivy studied him. "That's not what your face says."

Jaxon almost waved off her question, but the reporter's persistence was annoying, and he didn't feel right griping to Nate about it when his friend was hoping the article would bring people into the bar. It would be great to just vent a little.

He put his phone back in his pocket. "One of the reporters from the local paper is doing an article on the wine bar. They sent over questions, and I answered the ones I felt were pertinent. The rest, I left blank. I'm leaving in a few weeks so no one really needs to get to know me. But they keep asking, and it's getting on my nerves. Especially since some of the questions they're asking are way too personal. It feels like they're trying to do a deep dive on my entire life. One of the questions was if I was enjoying the single life in Bolan. I'm sure people aren't that interested in knowing that."

Ivy chuckled as she faced him and laid her hand near his shoulder. "There's a saying about small towns. Everyone's always interested in everyone else's business. You and Nate are the new guys in town and people are curious. I was talking to the local real estate agent, and she asked me if I'd heard anything through the grapevine about you, like where you're from. I told her I didn't know anything."

A strange relief came over him. After he'd lost his company, everyone in his circle seemed to be speculating over what happened. They all had their own theories about it. It had given him a deep appreciation for women like Ivy, who seemed to have an understanding of the value of discretion. Still, he couldn't resist prodding. "Why didn't you tell her?"

"I don't participate in gossip. It's a waste of time. People think it's harmless, but it can actually be hurtful. I wouldn't do that to you."

Looking into Ivy's eyes, he could see her sincerity. He held her in a loose embrace. "Thank you."

"For what? Not being a gossip?"

"For a lot of things, mainly for today."

"I should be thanking you. I'm glad you encouraged me to do this."

He had to ask. "Why didn't you bring a sketch pad so you could capture the view? You mentioned you saw yourself doing that on a hike."

"I thought about it, but..." She shrugged. "I didn't know how challenging the hike would be, so I didn't want to carry around anything that wasn't necessary. And it's not like we have an entire day to do this, just a few hours. Trying to sketch something now just wouldn't have worked."

What she'd just said sounded like a bunch of excuses, but they were doing her adventure list. It was up to her how she wanted to shape the moment. Still, there was one thing she just had to do.

He took out his phone. "You need photos to remember this."

Jaxon took several candid photos of her with their surroundings as a backdrop.

On an impulse, he said, "Let's take one together." Once he said it, he wanted to reel it back in. With a secret relationship, there shouldn't be any photo evidence, right?

But Ivy stepped up beside him. "Okay."

They faced the camera.

Just as he took the picture, Ivy reached up, turned his face more toward her, and kissed him. She laughed. "Just thought I should give you your reward."

The smile on Ivy's face was more than a reward. Leaning in, he pressed his mouth to hers and captured that smile as his own.

Chapter Sixteen

Four days after the hike, Jaxon opened the front passenger seat door to his SUV in the parking lot of the airfield.

As Ivy got out, excitement and disbelief sparked inside of her. "Are you serious? We get to do this now?"

Jaxon shut the door and grinned. "Yeah, we're going skydiving."

When he'd called her early that morning and asked if she could free up her afternoon, she'd never imagined them doing this.

"What happened? Why are we doing it today?"

Jaxon took her hand as they walked toward the hanger. "I have an inside connection—a guy I met awhile back owns the business. They had a last-minute cancellation and wanted to fill some seats."

They walked into the entrance of Sky Rush East, and a tanned guy with shaggy dark hair standing in front of the station reception desk looked up and smiled. "Man, I can't believe it."

Jaxon clasped hands with him. Grinning, they came in for a bro hug and thumped each other on the back. "It's been way too long. Good to see you." He followed his friend's gaze. "Keith. This is Ivy."

"It's a pleasure to meet you." Keith shook her hand. "So, you're doing a tandem jump with us?"

"That's the plan." Despite her excitement, nervousness tinged Ivy's laugh.

"Well, let's get to it." Keith turned and pointed to a well-built blond guy standing behind the desk. "Ivy, this is Reese. He's your instructor and the one you'll be jumping with."

She had imagined herself safely tethered to Jaxon when she jumped from the plane, but maybe Jaxon wasn't trained for that. Ivy pushed the vision and rising anxiety aside. "Hello."

"Nice to meet you." Smiling, Reese shook hands with her and Jaxon then pointed to an open door to the left. "That's where orientation will be. You have time to grab coffee or a water from the beverage area before we start."

An hour later, the instruction video ended, and the people who'd been sitting with Ivy and Jaxon started rising from their seats. Anticipation buzzed in the air along with a few conversations between other soon-to-be skydivers and the instructors who would be tandem jumping with them.

Ivy still felt excited but also partly in a daze. *This is actually happening. I'm going skydiving!*

The video had gone over everything that would happen, and Reese had been thorough with his explanations. Before getting on the plane, she'd gear up in a jumpsuit, goggles, and a tandem skydiving harness. After takeoff, it would take fifteen to twenty minutes for them to be at the right altitude, and then… As Ivy recalled what she'd watched in the video, her heart beat a tad harder in her chest. *Can I actually do this?*

Jaxon laying his hands over hers on her lap pulled her out of her thoughts. As she grasped onto him, she was shocked to feel the tingles of blood flowing back into her fingers. She hadn't realized how tightly she'd been holding her hands together.

"You okay?" He smiled, but there was concern in his eyes.

Dryness had taken over her mouth. She managed to nod and smile.

A short time later, she, Jaxon, and the rest of the group were gearing up in the hanger.

Ivy checked the hair tie holding her ponytail. Low on her nape, it wouldn't interfere with the strap of her goggles.

Jaxon pulled her off to the side. After giving the tab on the closed front zipper of her blue jumpsuit a tug, he took her hand. "Are you sure about doing this? You don't have to. Just say the word and we can go."

From the understanding in his eyes, she was sure that if she did say she wanted to leave, he wouldn't hold it against her. But she *would* hold it against herself. Other than her own fears, she didn't have an excuse not to do this. No one was forcing her. She wanted this experience, and she was free to do it on her own. But she *wasn't* alone. Jaxon would be there making the skydive before her.

She gave his hand a squeeze. "I'm ready to do this."

He nodded. "You're in good hands. Reese has a lot of experience. Try to take it all in while you're up there."

"Okay." He loosened his grip on her hand, but instead of walking away, on impulse, she lifted up on her toes and laid her cheek to his. "Thank you for this."

Jaxon wrapped his arms around her. "You're welcome."

Ivy soaked in his warmth and breathed him in. It felt so good, so safe to be close to him.

As she moved away, his lips mere inches from hers lured her in for a kiss.

He tightened his hold and desire warmed her anxiety over her impending skydive into a heady mix of anticipation. Tension vibrated through Jaxon as they warred with the reality of where they were, teetering on the edge of an ever-deepening kiss.

He lifted his mouth a fraction away, then brushed his lips one last time over hers. "See you on the landing zone."

In what felt like only moments later, she rolled out of the plane tethered to Reese, speeding through the blue sky in a high-velocity freefall that took her breath away.

Ivy squeezed her eyes shut and screamed. Her jumpsuit plastered and rippled around her body. The sound of the wind whooshed in her ears, drowning out the sound of her heart beating double time in her chest. She shivered from the thrill and the cold.

Seconds ticked by. Life-changing seconds she'd never be able to get back. She shouldn't waste them.

Try to take it all in while you're up there...

Ivy latched on to what Jaxon had told her and a sense of peace, trust, and rightness washed over her. She opened her eyes, taking in the vastness of the sky.

The wind sweeping across her face. The beauty of land and trees below. It was all mesmerizing.

All too soon, Reese pulled the cord to the chute and as they soared, she released a loud whoop propelled by laughter and joy. Freedom embraced her.

As they made their slow, lazy ride toward the ground, Reese called to her, "Don't forget to lift your legs for landing."

Right! She still had a few instructions to remember. Ivy gave him a thumbs-up to let Reese know she'd heard him.

Seconds later, she slid home at the drop zone.

Jaxon was waiting for her.

As soon as Reese untethered the harness holding them together, she ran to Jaxon.

He grinned from ear to ear as she jumped straight into his arms. "You did it!"

"I did!" Laughter bubbled out of her as he lowered her back down.

Jaxon looked into her eyes. "How do you feel?"

"Happy, better than happy. I can't describe it." Still in awe of what she'd just accomplished, her smile almost hurt her cheeks. She rested her hands on his chest. "Did I thank you for this?"

"You did." He held her by the waist. "But I won't complain if you want to thank me again."

Jaxon leaned in and she met him halfway, winding her arms around his neck. He held her close as she kissed him hard and deep, not giving a damn who was around them.

The film she'd watched earlier had promised that

skydiving would be the thrill of her life, and it was in some ways, but it couldn't rival the thrill Jaxon made her feel in just an instant. If only she had the ability to capture that in a sketchbook or on a canvas.

A few days later, Ivy described the hiking trip and her skydiving experience with Jaxon in a video chat with Amelia. Her feet might have been on solid ground at the apiary, but a part of her still felt like she was soaring.

Having just finished checking the hives, Ivy was dressed in a white bee suit. She held her phone in one hand while she used the other to store the hood to the suit in the farm truck's storage bin. "Hiking was fun, but skydiving was amazing. I'm telling you, you should try it."

On screen, Amelia shook her head. "No, ma'am. I'll deplane the normal way, thank you. I'm living vicariously through you with the skydiving thing. So the ride up was good. What about the ride afterward?"

"Afterward? What are you talking about?"

"All that adrenaline coursing through your veins. I'm sure it needed to be *released*."

The memory of her and Jaxon tangling in motel room sheets after the skydive sizzled in Ivy's thoughts.

"Yes!" Amelia clapped her hands and laughed. "Get it, girl. Look at you. You're glowing."

Ivy couldn't hold back a smile. "I'm not glowing. I just got finished checking the beehives, and this suit is hot."

"I bet Jaxon's hotter. Bees have nothing to do with it. You are clearly stung. You're falling for him."

Ivy choked out a laugh. "No. I'm not falling for him. We're just having a good time. That's all."

"I don't know." Amelia's smile sobered a little. "You really seem to like him a lot. Are you sure you'll be ready to end things when it's time for him to leave?"

Ivy hesitated. Jaxon hadn't given her any indication he wanted something other than a few weeks together. "It's what we planned. When the time comes, we'll go our separate ways." The upcoming reality for her and Jaxon dimmed Ivy's happiness, but she did her best to shake off the sad feeling. "But we're having fun now. That's what my adventure list is all about. We might do goat yoga this weekend or go horseback riding. I haven't done that in a long time."

"Or you could just ride Jaxon."

Amelia's mischievous cackle made Ivy laugh. "Does Reggie know how sex obsessed you are? Don't answer that. I have to go."

"Have fun." Amelia blew her a kiss. "Bye."

Ivy hopped into the truck and drove to the bee shed. Just as she parked, her phone rang.

She picked it up from the cup holder in the middle console. It was Jaxon.

She answered. "Hi."

"Hey."

Happiness hummed inside of her at the sound of his voice. "Why are you calling me now? I thought we were talking tonight?"

"We were. We still can, but I've got some bad news."

Chapter Seventeen

"Thanks for suggesting we go out to dinner." Zurie stirred her frozen mojito with a straw. She took a quick sip then released a grateful sigh. "I really needed a break like this."

"I did, too. I'm glad you were free," Ivy said, before taking a sip of wine. As she sat back in the booth across the table from Zurie, she glanced around the Montecito Steakhouse.

The space with beige brick and chocolate brown walls was a hive of activity. Servers delivered plates of food as customers chatted at their tables.

Jaxon canceling their weekend plans had been a huge disappointment. Drew, Piper, and one other former co-worker from the Wavefront Bistro had unexpectedly popped in for a visit. Instead of trying to explain their situation to them, she and Jaxon had decided it was best to steer clear of each other while the others were around. He and his friends had plans to go somewhere away from Bolan that night.

For Ivy, taking Zurie up on her previous invitation to go out was the perfect distraction and definitely a better alternative than sitting at home missing him. On the good news side of things, Brooke was extending her stay with Gable, so she and Jaxon could make up their weekend later. The couple was battling a nasty cold virus and were cuddled up in Nashville taking care of each other or possibly just prolonging the germ swap.

Wait, had she actually thought that Brooke and Gable being sick was good news? What was wrong with her? Was she that caught up in Jaxon that seeing him had become *that* important?

Troubled by the question, she nudged it aside. She wasn't supposed to be thinking about him now, anyway. Tonight was about them both enjoying time apart with their friends.

Ivy focused on Zurie. "So how are things with you?"

"Busy. Between the stable, the guesthouse, the restaurant, and shows at the indoor arena, it's been nonstop." Zurie held up her hands in defense. "Don't get me wrong. I'm thankful everything is going so well, but it feels like a balancing act sometimes."

"Trust me, I get that. It was like that with me and the bee farm. Some days, it felt like everything was teetering on the edge of disaster."

"Exactly." Zurie nodded in wholehearted agreement. "Like today it seemed like everything mechanical decided to break all at once. I had to step away from my desk or I was going to lose it. I went to the stable to get away, and just as I was giving a very detailed rant to my horse, Belle, my new management intern walked up. The look on that poor girl's face…" Zurie shook her head and chuckled. "I have no idea what I'm going to say to her tomorrow. She's probably rethinking her career choices."

Ivy laughed with her. "Tell her it's called life. There isn't a manager alive who hasn't had a moment like that."

"But you don't have to deal with that anymore. I'm so envious. So have you come up with a plan for what's next for you?"

"I don't know yet. I'm still exploring my options." As Ivy fiddled with the stem of her wineglass, something she hadn't admitted before came to mind. "The farm was such a big part of my life, it's hard to imagine doing anything else, but I'm ready for something new. At the same time, I feel a little guilty. Like I'm abandoning Brooke and Harper."

"You're not. It just sounds like you're ready to make a pivot. That is healthy, and it's normal to feel confused or uncertain or even a little afraid. You're venturing into new territory."

As Ivy took a breath, part of the invisible weight she'd been carrying over her decision to leave the farm lifted. Amelia always had her back, but it was nice to have someone else in her corner who understood.

Ivy's phone dinged on the table and she glanced at the screen. It was a text from Jaxon.

I miss you.

Those three simple words made her heart swell a little.

Same

After she sent off her response, she hesitated. Maybe she should have said, "I miss you, too," or added, "Have a good time."

"Uh-oh. You're frowning. Is it bad news?"

"No, not even close." Ivy laughed as she set her phone back on the table. "It was…"

Not being able to share her secret about Jaxon was hard. Why not take advantage of the opportunity to tell the one person who understood the complications involved? "It was a text from Jaxon. He said he misses me."

"He misses you. Why…?" Zurie's eyes widened. "Wait, are you two back together?"

"Yes, but in secret."

"Wow, I thought you two were done. Good for you." Zurie's expression held genuine happiness and interest. She leaned in. "How? When? I want the whole story. Don't leave anything out."

Ivy launched into the tale of how Von stood her up and all that happened afterward, including the list.

The delivery of their steak entrées paused the conversation.

As soon as the server left, Zurie said, "He's willing to go skydiving and do goat yoga with you? That's amazing. I can barely talk Mace into going to the farmers market with me. It sounds like you're having fun."

Ivy cut into her steak. It was just the way she liked it, juicy and not too pink. "I am."

"But I'm sure seeing each other in secret is hard. Before Mace and I got together, we had to keep secrets about our real relationship status. It wasn't easy for either of us."

Ivy finished a bite of her perfect steak. "No, it isn't easy, but Brooke and Harper have opposite opinions about Jaxon and me being together. Harper was fine with it, but Brooke was concerned about me getting hurt. They were on the verge of really arguing about it. I don't want to do anything to upset their relationship. Making sure they landed on solid ground together with the farm was the point of me leaving to begin with."

"And you also left for yourself." Empathy showed on Zurie's face. "I get that you want Brooke and Harper to thrive and be happy, but you have to include yourself in that equation. If your relationship with Jaxon makes you happy, maybe you should find a way to help Brooke come to terms with that."

"I wouldn't call what Jaxon and I have a true relationship." As Ivy made the claim, it sounded…wrong. But how else could she describe it? "He's leaving in another week or so, and then we'll go our separate ways." Just like when she'd said something similar to Amelia the other day during their video chat, her happiness started to dim.

Zurie put down her fork. "Do you mind if I give you some advice?"

"Of course not. You don't even have to ask."

"I know the situation I had with Mace isn't exactly the same as yours, but when he and I got together, I thought I had everything figured out, and that I could keep it all compartmentalized. The feelings were clearly growing between us, but I thought I could control how things were supposed to turn out. I was wrong."

"So you think I might be getting in over my head with Jaxon?"

"No, not at all." Zurie paused as if searching for the right words. "I just think you have to remember that some things aren't that easy to compartmentalize. You can't put feelings in a box and expect them to stay there."

Just over Zurie's shoulder, a couple sat at a table holding hands and laughing as they enjoyed dinner. They were free to express how they felt about each other in public. They were probably going home together afterward. Of all the things she and Jaxon had done together, they really hadn't experienced that type of freedom.

Did she want that type of relationship with Jaxon? Maybe she didn't fully understand that yet, but she wished they had the time and space to figure themselves out. Or maybe she was the only one who wanted that. Maybe he was fine with moving on and never seeing her again.

Zurie's sigh pulled Ivy from her thoughts. "My little speech just ruined dinner. I'm sorry."

"No, you haven't. Honestly." Ivy laid her hand firmly on the table. "You've just made me think about a few things, that's all."

Their server stopped to check on them and ask about dessert.

After ordering cheesecake, Ivy excused herself and headed for the ladies' room.

The one in the lobby had a line.

The hostess pointed. "There's another restroom in the bar. As soon as you walk in, take a right then follow the sign pointing down the hallway."

"Thanks."

Business was brisk around the bar. Raucous laughter reverberated. Most of the stools at the bar counter were occupied, and so were the tables in the middle of the room. In the far corner, customers played pool and threw darts.

Ivy followed the signs down a long hallway. To the left, a glass door opened into an outdoor bar on a lit deck under the cloudy night sky. It was vacant, probably because the weather forecast predicted rain.

The dance floor near the deck reminded her of the one at the Wavefront Bistro and being there with Jaxon. The moment when Amelia had spun her around while they were dancing right into his arms flashed in her mind. Dancing. That was what he was probably doing right then. Jaxon had mentioned he and his friends might check out a club near D.C. Afterwards, they would spend the night at a hotel instead of driving back.

Tamping down the wish that she was with him, Ivy found the alcove where the restrooms were located. When she was done, she walked out. As she headed back down the hallway, a door opened behind her.

"Ivy..."

As she turned around, a smile she couldn't control took over her face. "Jaxon?"

She almost hurried to him but his long strides beat her to it. They stopped short of hugging each other.

Jaxon was dressed casually in black jeans and a long-sleeved, aqua-colored pullover that fit his solid torso in just the right way. He looked so good. The wonderful smell of his cologne lured her a step closer. "I thought you were going out of town?"

"We were, but then everyone got lazy. Then we heard there's supposed to be a bad rainstorm in the area tonight. With that, plus traffic, it didn't feel worth it to make the drive." He reached toward her then awkwardly dropped his arms to his side. "I didn't see you in the bar. I guess you're having dinner?"

She nodded. "With Zurie."

"That's good. I'm glad you didn't stay home." His gaze held hers. "I'm sorry we had to cancel our plans. We only have one more weekend after this before I leave."

"Actually, we have two."

"We do?"

"Brooke and Gable are both battling a cold virus. She's decided to stay with him until they're feeling better. They're at his place in Nashville, taking care of each other."

"Lucky them. I mean, not about being sick but being sick together." He chuckled. "That didn't come out right."

Ivy laughed with him. "Don't worry. I understand what you mean." She felt the same way. It was kind of funny and sad that they were wishing to be in Brooke and Gable's shoes right now. Probably more sad.

Her laughter faded away with that realization, and so did Jaxon's. From the hint of bleakness in his eyes, possibly he'd had a similar thought.

A man and two women entered the hallway. Instead of walking down they lingered, laughing and loudly talking with each other.

"Zurie is probably wondering where I am. I should go."

"Not yet. Let's go outside a minute." Jaxon took her hand and led her out the glass door.

Alone in the illuminated space, it felt like they were under a spotlight. Worried, she said, "Someone might walk by and see us."

He tugged her off to the side in a darkened corner near the bar. Standing close in front of her, he blocked out most of the view. "Better?"

"Almost." As she rested her palms on his chest, his quizzical look turned into a smile.

Following her lead, he slid his hands from her waist to her back and met her for a kiss.

The caress of his tongue along hers quickly took her desire from spark to flame. Needing more contact, she glided her hands around his neck and pressed herself against him.

His low groan rumbled into her as he backed her up against the wall. Every part of her felt molded to him. His solid torso. His muscular thighs. His hard length, rising and pressing to her belly. It was wonderful and tortuous at the same time.

Jaxon broke from the kiss. As he rested his forehead to hers, he released a long, ragged breath. "Damn. I wish I could be with you tonight. I wish we could be together the entire weekend. No interruptions."

Ivy slid her hands down his shoulders and laid her cheek to his chest. "So do I."

His chest rose and fell under her cheek with his inhale and exhale. "Then maybe we should."

She looked up at him. "You mean like go away together?"

"Exactly. For a long weekend."

That sounded idyllic, but… "I can't. What would I tell Harper?"

She'd explained away her first day trip with Jaxon by telling Harper she needed to go to the tractor and feed store in the next town over to price out supplies. The next trip, she'd told her she'd gone shopping somewhere else, stopped for a long lunch and just lost track of time. Luckily Harper hadn't questioned her about it.

"Couldn't you just say you were going away for a three-day weekend to see a friend?" Jaxon sighed. "I know it's a lot to ask. I just want to be able to be with you in public and not hide. We could go to a place where we can just enjoy ourselves."

The memory of the couple eating in the restaurant earlier, holding hands and smiling, came into Ivy's mind. It morphed into a vision of her with Jaxon. A moment like that with him. She wanted that experience so much.

"Where would we go? Someplace close?"

His eyes lit up, but then his brow rose a little as if he'd had a second thought. "Or I might have a better idea."

"Where are you thinking?"

Smiling, he briefly pressed his mouth to hers. "I don't want to say where yet."

"Another surprise?"

"Don't you like my surprises?"

"I've loved every one of them, but wherever we're going, you shouldn't have to pay for everything. I'm pitching in. No arguments."

He grinned. "Why would I argue when you just agreed to go away with me?"

She smiled as he brought his mouth back a hairsbreadth from hers. "Yeah, I guess I did say that."

Rain started pattering on the ground, and they both looked up as a small flash of lightning lit up the sky.

The overhang above them plus Jaxon in front of her shielded Ivy. "I think that's our cue to go inside," she said.

"Yeah, we should."

Neither of them seemed to be in hurry to let go.

"You go in first." He gave her waist a light squeeze then released her. "I'll text you with the plan for our weekend."

Chapter Eighteen

As Ivy hurried inside, Jaxon stayed behind, savoring her lingering warmth and the smell of her light floral perfume until it dissipated. Soon, he would be able to hold and kiss her in public. *Three whole days with Ivy.* Or as close as they could come to it. Either way, the weekend couldn't come soon enough, and he had a place in mind. Somewhere with privacy and a view.

As he thought of the plan, a slight push-pull of anxiety and anticipation tugged at him. He hadn't been to the house he owned in a while. Normally he wouldn't have considered it, but this trip was so last-minute, and going there would be the easiest to arrange. It was also far enough away to almost guarantee no one they knew would see them.

Ivy would enjoy the escape, plus it would give him the opportunity to find the right moment to ask her something important. It would mean taking their relationship beyond just the temporary. It had been a long time since he'd wanted that with someone. Since he'd trusted someone enough to even feel willing to take the risk. He felt that way with Ivy. Would she agree to what he wanted to ask her?

As he walked into the hallway of the restaurant, anticipation, hope, and urgency were helping to line up details in his mind. He had a travel agency hookup that could help with the plane tickets. He still wanted to keep the location a surprise for as long as he could. He'd have to tell Ivy what to pack. Casual stuff. Probably most of the same things she'd brought with her to Hilton Head. He hadn't seen Ivy in a bathing suit, but his mind easily conjured up the vision of her in one… along with him helping her to take it off.

He swept aside the vision and tamped down his need. As he entered the main area, Drew waved him over to the bar counter.

As Jaxon approached, he saw his friend corralling two frothy cocktails in glasses and two bottles of beer in his hands. "Do you want help carrying this?" he asked.

"Sure." Drew handed him half of the order. "The beer is for you and the drink is for Piper, but that's not why I called you over here. I just saw Ivy."

Jaxon didn't have to fake shock. "No, you probably just saw someone that looked like her."

"No. I'm sure it was her. She didn't look my way or I would have called her over here." He pointed with his chin toward the opening to the lobby. "I'm pretty sure she went into the restaurant. After we drop off these drinks we can check."

"Yeah, I don't think so." Jaxon faked a chuckle. "You're just seeing things with your beer goggles."

"Nah, dude, I'm way too sober to be seeing things. You don't believe me? Let's put ten—no, let's put twenty on it."

An f-bomb dropped into Jaxon's thoughts as he took

a drink from his beer. He hadn't even considered any-one might see her. And from the gleam in Drew's eyes, he was more than sure he would win the bet. He had to come clean. "I don't have to put a twenty on it. You saw her, but I need you to pretend that you didn't."

"Why?"

Jaxon put the drinks back on the bar. "I'm only going to say this once, so listen up. Ivy is from here, but I didn't know that when I came to work with Nate. Yes, I'm seeing her again but no one knows."

"So you're slippin' in then dippin' out?" Drew gave him a knowing grin. "I'm with you. All the benefits without the attachments."

"No, it's not like that. I really care about Ivy."

Drew's expression was slightly bemused as he took a sip from the frothy drink with a straw then said, "Cool. Your secret's still safe with me."

That was way too easy. "Hold on. What do I owe you to keep this to yourself?"

Drew chuckled. "Honestly, I can't even think of any-thing. I'm just shocked to hear you legit commit to Ivy. With the other women you've hooked up with, you made a point not to stick around."

Milo had almost said the exact same thing. Was that what people thought about him? Inwardly, Jaxon winced. Sure, he hadn't been in a relationship for a while, but that was only because they hadn't worked out. But was he committed to Ivy?

The question stuck with him for the entire night. He wasn't sure what label to put on their relationship. They couldn't call themselves a "one-time thing" since they'd ended up getting back together after South Carolina. Did he want to keep seeing her? Did she want to keep seeing him? But how would that work? Taking a single long weekend away from the farm was one thing, but she couldn't keep doing that on a regular basis, and then there was the whole Brooke situation.

Over the next few days, Jaxon pondered if he should even bring up what he'd considered asking her. Was he really planning on asking Ivy to be his girlfriend? The possibility of that felt unnerving and also right.

But Friday afternoon, waiting at the airport, he began to doubt if their trip might happen at all.

"I hit traffic." The anxious tone of Ivy's voice coming through his phone mirrored his level of concern. "I think there's been an accident. I should have left earlier. I'm so close."

People swarmed around him to check-in kiosks and airport security lines. He'd already checked them both in and gotten their tickets. The only thing missing was her.

If only they could have driven together, but taking their own cars had worked better for their work schedules and minimized the chance of someone seeing them together.

Jaxon wheeled his luggage to a nearby bench against the wall. "The important thing is you're not part of the accident. You're safe."

"I should have left earlier." She released a defeated sigh. "I was so worried about what to tell Harper, I wasn't thinking straight."

"Oh? Well, what did you end up saying?"

"I told her I was going away for a few days, and before I could even say with who, she said 'have a good time' and went off to answer a phone call. She really can run things on her own. That should make me happy."

"But?"

She chuckled ruefully. "It makes me feel unneeded. I guess once Brooke gets back, I'd better decide what I'm doing. Where I'm going."

Going? What did that mean?

Before he could ask, she exclaimed, "Traffic is moving again. I'll call you back when I get to the airport."

"See you when you get here." Hopefulness pushed a breath out of him, but time ticked by and she still didn't call.

Just as he was about to contact the travel agent to see if they could be rebooked on a later flight, Ivy rushed through the glass doors. She made skinny jeans, a simple T-shirt, and a jacket look fabulous.

Caught up in looking at her, he almost didn't meet her halfway.

"Can we make it?" Concern creased her brow.

Unable to resist, he briefly pressed his lips to hers. "If we hurry, we can."

Thankfully, they both had TSA pre-check. As they stood in the shorter line, he said, "You need this." He handed Ivy her ticket.

When they were done with security, Jaxon and Ivy grabbed their carry-ons from the conveyer belt and made a run for it. They arrived at the gate just in time to board their flight.

Moments later, buckling into their seats, they let out a breath of relief.

She smiled at him. "We're going to California, huh?"

A part of his surprise had been exposed. "Yeah, and that's all I'm saying."

Hours later, the second part of his surprise was revealed. From the rental car, Jaxon waved a card in the direction of the infrared reader at the entrance to a gated community.

It was after midnight, and Ivy had fallen asleep in the passenger seat shortly after they'd left the airport.

Jaxon let down the window next to him. A cool breeze carried the clean, briny smell of the ocean and the sound of crashing waves. Farther down the road, the same push-pull sensation of anxiety and anticipation he'd felt at the bar when he'd thought about bringing her there tugged harder in his gut.

Relax, Jaxon told himself. *You're getting twisted up over nothing.* Bringing Ivy to this place was what he wanted, and as far as the house itself, it was just a house. Walls filled with things that had at one time reflected his life, his ambition to make money and be recognized as someone powerful in business. Today, it didn't reflect who he was. These days, he was a man no longer influenced by his father. Someone who chose his own path and didn't need anyone's approval.

He let the thought settle in his mind as he parked the car, turned off the engine, and sat there for a few seconds more.

Ivy still slept peacefully beside him. Later that morning, he'd get to wake up with her in his arms. That along with the view and the privacy made being there worth it.

"Ivy…" He gave her a gentle nudge. "We're here."

She blinked awake and stifled a yawn. Mid-stretch, she paused and stared at the white split-level house through the windshield. "This is where we're staying? Where are we?"

"Laguna Beach."

Inside the house, they rolled their bags into the foyer bathed in a soft light. As she gasped, happiness sparkled in her eyes. He tried to see the room with its beige, gray, and white color scheme through her eyes.

One side of a wide sand-colored back-to-back sectional faced an electric fireplace. Above it was a wide-screen television with a continuous video of colorful fish swimming in the ocean. The other side of the sectional faced a nook with a tall café table next to a wall with a built-in wine rack.

On the opposite side of the room, a row of floor-to-ceiling sliding doors overlooked the ocean, reflecting the moon, stars, and night sky.

"This is amazing," Ivy said.

"You should see the view." Jaxon led her across the room. He opened the doors, and as she stood near the railing of the deck, she sighed.

He hugged her from behind and kissed the side of her neck. "Do you like it?"

"I love it." She rested her head back on his shoulder. As she looked at him, a wide smile was on her face. "This is perfect."

He'd made the right call.

"How did you find this place?"

He sorted through possible answers and landed on

the best one. "Through a friend. Do you want to see the rest of it?"

"I do." Ivy turned around in his arms. "Could I have a glass of water first?"

"Sure. Why don't you take a look around and I'll bring it to you."

"So, are the bedrooms upstairs?" As she slid her arms up his chest and around his neck, she pressed her body to his.

The feel of her soft curves against him made his heart beat faster. "They are."

She gave him a soft, all too brief kiss. "I'll start down here and wait for you to give me the rest of the tour."

Forget about the tour—carrying her to bed now sounded like a better plan. But he could be patient. "Sounds good."

While he went to the kitchen, outfitted with appliances and other features that were a chef's dream, Ivy wandered from the living room down a short hall. In that direction, she would find an office. A gym with an attached spa bath. A sitting area with windows facing the ocean.

After pouring a glass of water, he went to find Ivy.

She stood in the office, staring at framed pictures on the wall.

As he walked farther in, he got a clearer look at them. Recognizing the images, blood started draining from his face. His skin tingled.

She pointed. "This is you, isn't it?" He already knew what she was going to say next before she met his gaze. "Whose house is this?"

Chapter Nineteen

Jaxon placed the glasses on the desk before he responded. "It's mine."

Ivy tried to decipher the look on his face as he came to stand next to her. He appeared shocked, maybe even a little irritated as he stared at what appeared to be photos of happy moments of him at various ages along with a man, woman, and a young girl.

"Where did these come from?" he asked. "I don't recognize them."

Not understanding what his reaction meant, Ivy laid her hand on his arm. "Aren't they pictures of you and your family?"

"Yes, but they shouldn't be up. The property manager must have misunderstood when I told him I was coming to the house. The place has been under lease for the past three years. I'm planning to lease it again. None of this needs to be here. This wall should be a blank slate."

"Maybe they just wanted to make it more like home for you by putting up a few personal touches. Like this photo—it's beautiful." Ivy pointed to one that had captivated her as soon as she'd walked into the room.

It was a black-and-white picture of a pretty Black

woman sitting on the beach, cuddling a little boy who looked like Jaxon. In another color photo, the same woman stood in the arms of a tall man with lightly tanned skin and a neatly trimmed goatee. The man's smile reminded her of Jaxon's.

As Jaxon reached out toward the photo of the woman and the boy, some of the irritation left his expression. "That's me and my mom. I haven't seen this picture in a while. It's one of the few I have of us together. At one time, I was considering having it blown up to a larger size."

She could see why. Not only had the photographer succeeded in catching the right lighting, but they'd also managed to capture Jaxon and his mom laughing. Their smiles were infectious. And the way his mother looked at the person taking the photo, it was as if Ivy could feel the current running between them in that moment.

"A lot of love is in this photo, even behind the lens of the camera."

Jaxon's gruff chuckle drew her attention back to him. "That's just an optical illusion. The person who took that photo doesn't have a heart." He turned, went to the desk and picked up the glasses. As he came back to her, only a hint of his smile reached his eyes. "We should go upstairs. Like I said earlier, the view is even better from there."

Questions filled Ivy's mind, mainly about what had happened with him and his parents. But as they walked from the office, she could feel tension emanating from him. Those pictures, his family, were clearly an unwelcome subject.

Whether because of the photo incident, the time zone change, or both, the mood wasn't right for romance. After taking a shower, Ivy climbed into bed and fell asleep as soon as her head hit the pillow.

Later that morning, she woke up to the view Jaxon promised. Outside the large window, the crystal-blue ocean beckoned under a sunny, near cloudless sky. She wanted to enjoy it with Jaxon, but he wasn't with her. Where was he? Was he still upset by the photos? And why hadn't he told her this was his house from the start?

He's hiding something... Brooke's claim echoed in Ivy's mind.

If he was, maybe he had an explanation. One that he'd share with her now that he'd had time to process things.

Ivy took care of the essentials in the bathroom then grabbed her phone. Her battery was almost down to zero. She searched through her bag for a charging cord but couldn't find it. Still dressed in a comfy yellow fitted shirt and matching drawstring shorts, she went downstairs.

Jaxon was in the kitchen. He looked at home in a dark T-shirt and sweatpants. He walked over to her where she stood next to the wide marble-topped island. His demeanor was relaxed and as appealing as the sunlight filling the space through the sliding glass door overlooking the raised deck. The round table and chairs outside had a view of the water.

"Good morning." Holding her in a loose embrace, he kissed her. All traces of last night's irritation were gone. He was back to himself again.

He tasted faintly of minty toothpaste. Clean smells of soap and his spicy cologne wafted up her nose. Smiling against his lips, she said, "Good morning."

He leaned back a little. "I'd planned to wake you up with coffee and breakfast in bed, but the upside is, now I don't have to guess. How do you like your coffee?"

"I like it with two teaspoons of sugar and a splash of almond or oat milk, if you've got it."

"We have oat milk." He popped a coffee pod in the maker then retrieved the carton of oat milk from the refrigerator. After setting it on the counter, he rummaged around the shelves. "What do you want for breakfast? Pancakes? Scrambled eggs? We have stuff to make omelets, too."

"Omelets sound good. I'll help. Can I borrow your charging cord? I can't find mine."

"Sure. I'm charging my phone in the office. Just swap it with yours."

"Do you want me to bring back your phone?"

"If you don't mind. I saved a website with a list of places in the area you might want to check out." As he leaned down to take a carton of eggs from the refrigerator, her gaze automatically riveted on his firm-looking butt.

Exploring touristy spots might be nice but exploring a few attractions in the bedroom would be a lot more interesting.

Jaxon caught her staring. As he stood straight, he gave her a sexy, knowing smile. "Is there something else you want?"

He looked so good, she was tempted, but she was also

hungry. "Maybe after breakfast." Ivy left the kitchen before she changed her mind.

Walking through the living room and down the hall, she registered the furnishings, a couple sculptures in cutouts in the wall, and the multiple paintings. Everything about the house screamed high-end and expensive. Having wealth might have influenced how people saw him in the past. Maybe that's why Jaxon hadn't initially told her the house was his. Perhaps he was afraid it would change her perception of him. But the truth was, she didn't care about his money. What she valued most about him was that he was kind, adventurous, thoughtful. She loved Jaxon for who he was.

Love? She came to a halt in the hallway, trying to process the sudden realization and how she felt about it. She cared about Jaxon a lot. But she'd only known him for a short time. Still her feelings for him were real…and so right.

Ivy wavered between elation and anxiety as she considered what being in love with Jaxon meant for her. Happiness as well as challenges, even heartbreak. They were all a possibility. She knew that from her experience with Von. But Jaxon wasn't anything like her ex-fiancé.

Looking back to twelve years ago, a small part of her had remained guarded around Von. It was as if she'd expected him to fail her. In the short time she'd known Jaxon, she'd never felt that with him. She'd only felt safe, taken care of, even pampered around him, and most of all happy.

Reaching the threshold to his office, she spotted his

phone on the desk. In the midst of walking over to it, she did a double take. The pictures—all of them were gone.

She exchanged the phones and left hers to charge.

In the kitchen, he glanced over at her. "All set?"

"Yes." Troubled by the missing pictures, Ivy mulled over what to do. Should she bring it up or wait for him to mention it?

"I found some ripe avocados, olives, tomatoes and feta cheese to put in the omelets." He pointed to a knife and cutting board set up on the counter. "Do you want to start chopping things up while I crack the eggs?"

"That works for me." Ivy washed her hands at the sink then started dicing a tomato. Surely, he knew she'd notice. Did he just expect her to ignore he'd taken them down?

"Everything okay with the vegetables?" Jaxon cracked an egg open on the counter.

"Yeah, everything is fine." Was he even going to mention them at all? She'd just been thinking about the challenges that might come up with caring about Jaxon. Lack of communication wasn't what she wanted at the top of that list.

"Do you not like tomatoes?"

"Yes, I like tomatoes. What makes you think I don't?"

"Because you're murdering that one."

Ivy focused her full attention on the cutting board. The tomato was almost mush. "Oh…"

"You're upset about me taking down the photos, aren't you?"

A small bit of relief ran through her that he'd been

the one to bring it up. Ivy met his direct gaze. "I'm not upset, just confused. We came here to get away from secrets, but you owning this house, the photos…it all feels like one big secret."

"You're right." He wiped his hands on a towel then set it aside.

As he walked over to her, she set down the knife.

Jaxon leaned back against the counter, took her by the hand and pulled her closer. "I'm sorry. I didn't mean to be secretive, but those photos are misleading. My family situation is complicated." He closed his eyes a moment and took a long breath. "My mom died when I was eight. My sister, Nicki, was three."

The memory of how devastated Brooke and Harper had been when their parents died played in Ivy's mind. Jaxon and his sister had been even younger. Two children who'd lost one of the most important people in their lives. Her heart ached as she empathized with how they must have felt.

"I'm sorry." She laid her hand in the middle of his chest. "Losing her must have been hard."

He nodded. "It was for me and Nicki. It changed everything, and my dad…" Jaxon's expression hardened in the same way it had when he'd looked at some of the photos on the wall the night before. "Working at his company and making money became the center of everything for him."

His expression didn't change, but Ivy spotted the hurt in his eyes. She remembered how she'd struggled to process her grief over losing Lexy. She'd worked long hours, trying to hide her own pain from Brooke

and Harper until Amelia had called attention to her be-
havior. Had his father done the same?

Cautiously, she shared the possibility. "I don't know
your dad, but for me, after losing my sister and brother-
in-law, I tried to focus on work so I could repress how
sad I felt."

Jaxon didn't seem offended by her suggestion, but
the hurt remained in his eyes. "Maybe he did the same
thing, but that doesn't excuse who he became." A far-
away expression shadowed his face. "Why I wanted to
be like him, I have no idea. I pushed hard to graduate
high school and college early just so I could join our
family's investment firm. I did the grunt work for two
years, scored major deals.

"I should have taken the hint when he didn't notice.
Instead, I thought I'd prove myself by striking out and
building something on my own. I started a company
with two of my friends. We created a subscription service for wine that also featured eco-friendly, socially
conscious items for cooking and entertaining." A small
smile ghosted over his lips. "We collaborated with artisans and craftspeople, mainly small businesses and co-
ops here in the States and around the world."

"That sounds wonderful." She'd subscribed to a few
subscription boxes in the past, and Ivy wanted to ask the
name of his, but from the tone of his voice, she could
tell that something bad had happened with the business.

"It was for the first few years. We were ambitious
but we also got the chance to do some good. A larger
company wanted to buy us out, but I didn't want to sell.
Their ethics didn't match up with ours, in my opinion."

His gaze focused on her face. "My partners, my so-called friends, sold the company out from under me with the help of my father. He even helped facilitate the sale."

His own father did that to him? No wonder he took down the photos. They must have been a painful reminder of what he'd once had and lost. "Jaxon, I'm so sorry. And I'm sorry for making a big deal about you taking those photos down. I can't blame you."

"No. I'm glad you were honest with me when you were upset." Jaxon laid his hand over hers on his chest. "I brought you here so we could spend time together, but I also hoped we might get a chance to talk about our relationship. I don't want things to end between us when I leave Maryland."

A jolt of happiness made her blurt out, "Neither do I."

His expression morphed with a smile. "Really?"

"I had wanted to talk about the same thing. I just wasn't sure how you felt."

"And I'm sure that how I acted last night didn't help. The only other thing you need to know is that I'm not rich. This house and what's in it are mine, but they're leftover from back when I used to have a much bigger income. Most of the money I make leasing it out goes toward the mortgage, taxes, and the upkeep of the property. I really do make my living as a bartender and doing other temporary jobs."

"Like the caretaker gig in Tennessee?" Glumness she hadn't anticipated tinged her voice.

"About that..." He rubbed his hands up and down her arms then took her hands again. "They gave me a few more details about what's happening on the property. Not only is there a cow, a goat, and some chickens that have to be looked after, but there are also a couple of beehives that need to be reinvigorated. I can handle taking care of the livestock, but I don't have the experience to take care of bees, so they're looking for someone who can. I mentioned you."

"Me? Jaxon, why would you—"

He gripped her hands a little tighter. "Before you say anything else, hear me out. We just said that we wanted to spend time together beyond Maryland. The two of us taking on this job in Tennessee could be the perfect chance. For two months, we'd pretty much have the place to ourselves while we do or oversee the work. We could really spend quality time together instead of squeezing in a few hours here and there the way we have been up to now. I know I'm springing this on you out of nowhere, but beehives ending up being a part of this opportunity felt like a sign that it was meant for us. You don't have to give me your answer now. Will you just think about it?"

"Reinvigorated" probably meant the hives were in poor shape or possibly the bees had even created their own nests in places like the hollows of trees. Either way, she would be building an apiary almost from scratch. Giving the bees a fresh place to start. Wasn't that what she was doing in her own life? Going with Jaxon to Tennessee to help build something new for someone else might nudge her toward a better understanding of what she wanted for her own fresh start. And best of all, they would be together.

A part of her could see it. Her taking care of the

hives and building up an apiary. Jaxon putting his all into refurbishing the house and cabins. Spending their free time any way they pleased, but still...

"What happens if we get there and find out we don't get along as well as we thought we would?"

"I don't see that happening, but if you do decide to kick me out of the house, there are a couple cabins on the property I can move into." He tugged her closer then wrapped her in a loose embrace. "So will you think about it?"

His gaze held her so intensely during the pause as if his hopes were riding on her answer. She nodded. "I will."

Releasing a deep breath, he cupped her cheek. His smile sobered. "I know we've only known each other a short time, but I really care about you. I'm willing to take a chance on making this relationship work."

Hearing Jaxon say that he cared about her made Ivy's heart leap, but an unexpected sense of dread yanked it back down. She felt the same way about him, but for some reason she couldn't say it. Seconds expanded. Instead of trying to fill it with words, she rose on her toes and pressed her mouth firmly to his.

Need intensified and the kiss deepened.

Upstairs in bed, she used every kiss, every stroke of his skin, to convey her feelings for him. But why couldn't she just tell Jaxon how much she cared about him, too?

Chapter Twenty

Lying on the beach in a lounge chair under a wide beach umbrella, Ivy adjusted the halter tie to her aqua tankini and inhaled the cool, refreshing smell of the ocean. She and Jaxon had gone for an early morning walk at sunrise. Afterward, he'd decided to go for a swim while she relaxed and enjoyed the sunny day.

On her phone, she scrolled down internet results for recommended sights and destinations to see in and around Laguna Beach. For the first day and a half of their trip, she and Jaxon hadn't gone anywhere. Instead, they'd stayed in, hung out on the beach, eaten great food that they'd prepared side by side in the kitchen, and satisfied their need for each other in bed, as well as just talking.

He'd told her more about his mom and his younger sister, Nicki. She'd told him about growing up with her parents, about Lexy and Dion, and what it was like to become an instant parent to Brooke and Harper and an apiary full of bees. She loved the way he'd listened to her and asked questions as if he was recording it all in his mind for safekeeping. She'd felt seen, heard, and safe in their own world. But tomorrow evening they were leaving their own private bubble. Shouldn't she visit at least one place outside of the house before they left?

They'd just missed a major arts festival. The Laguna Art Museum was an option, but while strolling through exhibits for the rest of the day might be a blissful experience for her, it might not be as interesting to Jaxon. She could ask, but knowing him, he'd say yes just to please her. He'd said he wanted her to relax and enjoy herself, and she had. She'd also felt inspired.

More than once, when she'd come across him napping on the balcony, and he'd opened his eyes to look at her in a way that had sparked desire and made her heart race, she'd wished for a canvas and brush. And then there were moments like now, when the light was shimmering on the water with seagulls flying overhead, that she'd wished for the same. But even if she'd had them, she was so rusty, she probably wouldn't have been able to fully capture the beauty of it.

Skimming past the overloaded recommendation lists, she opened one boasting just four interesting things to check out. An offshore shipwreck…the second smallest cathedral in the world…*wings on a wall*. Ivy sat up a little straighter in the chair. She'd read about this before— an artist who painted murals of wings on walls all over the world. The online article about art, humanity, and togetherness had resonated.

Jaxon coming back from his swim pulled her attention. She tipped her sunglasses down her nose, hypnotized by the waves and him striding toward her wearing a pair of dark swim shorts. His gaze remained on her with every step. Just like when she'd first seen him that day at the restaurant, he moved confidently, easily, no second-guessing where he was headed.

He reached her, and as he leaned down to snag a towel to dry off, he gave her a quick kiss. His lips had a hint of saltiness from the ocean. "You know, a swim would be more fun than checking your emails."

"Probably, but I'm not checking emails. I was reading through suggestions about places to visit here and found this one."

He sat down beside her. "Show me."

She handed him her phone. Would he just see the wings as the same as graffiti on a wall?

Jaxon glanced through the information and nodded. "Photo spots in Laguna. I saw posts about this one on social media."

It's not about that... Ivy held in the comment. "In some ways, this reminds me of the artist's house back in Bolan." His curious expression urged her to continue. "It's a house near Bolan with murals painted on the interior walls. There's a story behind them. Decades ago, one of the locals was afraid to travel outside Bolan. He fell in love with a painter who came to town, and they started living together in his house. She used the walls of their home like a canvas and painted the places she'd visited so she could show him the world. The beauty of the murals helped him get over his fear. They left Bolan together to visit all of the places in the mural."

"Wow, that's a great story. Is it true?"

"The house exists. I haven't been to it. It's private property, but I've heard the murals are beautiful."

He handed back her phone and nodded. "I get it. The wings capture you as strictly an artist, not a photo op."

Jaxon understood. He got it. A rush of happiness made her smile. "Yes, they do."

In one fluid, rippling abs movement, he came to his feet and held his hand out to her. "Come on. Let's go."

After taking quick showers and throwing on casual clothes, they left.

A little later in the afternoon, she stood with Jaxon in front of the mural. It was located on the back wall of a neighborhood pizza restaurant. Hues of crimson, yellow, purple, and blue shaded and blended together and formed a pair of unfurled angel wings. When they'd arrived a few minutes ago, a few people had taken candid photos in front of it, turning themselves for just a moment into something angelic and wonderful.

She and Jaxon had already done the same. The violet color of her sundress had blended perfectly with the mural, creating a striking photo. In his photo, dressed in a dark shirt and shorts and wearing sunglasses, he'd looked like a tempting fallen angel.

Ivy briefly traced her finger over a small curve in one of the wings. As a painter, she'd once hoped her work would make room for someone to pause and feel something this powerful—maybe stir a sense of goodness that they'd pass on to someone else. One person inspiring just one other person was still significant. The artist's house was proof of that. Love and the power of art had broken down someone's fear and opened up the world to them.

A longing to be that painter again tugged in her

chest. "To transform a corner of the world like this, just by wielding a brush, is amazing."

He studied her face. "Is that something you wanted to do as an artist?"

"Yes, but… I didn't get to really deep dive into painting like I'd hoped to do. Life made other plans."

He took her by the hand and started leading her back toward the street. "Come on. We have one other stop to make before we go back to the house."

"Where?"

"The art supply store."

"Why do we need to go there?"

He stopped and faced her. "Because it's not too late for you to start transforming the world. You said you wanted to capture the moments on your list with art, and you never did. Hiking, skydiving, here on the beach."

"But I'm not the painter I used to be."

He cupped her face in his hands. "No, you're the painter you need to be today. Someone who has ideas and memories and dreams that need to be shared. You inspire me, Ivy, just by being with me. I can't even imagine what your art could do. What you could do."

Soft, happy emotions filled Ivy's chest. Jaxon believed in her that much? As she looked in his eyes, she saw a glimpse of herself sketching, painting, feeling that connection to herself as an artist again. But was she deluding herself? She wouldn't know until she tried.

They found an art store around the corner. Instead of questioning herself about what she was doing, she picked up a sketch pad and boxes of sketch pencils in black and in color.

Later on, Jaxon left her sitting in a chair on the deck off of the kitchen. "I'm going out for a bit so you can do your thing. I'll bring back some food."

"Thank you." She meant for everything he'd done for her. The adventure list, this trip, the sketch pad in her hand. But there was too much to say, and she didn't have the words yet.

"You're welcome."

Jaxon left, and Ivy stared out at the ocean, searching for inspiration. The birds in the sky? The people swimming in the ocean? Or maybe just the ocean itself? She began sketching the ocean, wanting to not only capture its form but also the energy and swell of the waves.

At first, she judged every line she made, but then, as she started to see what she wanted to convey through the drawing, she got lost in the moment.

The doorbell rang.

It wasn't Jaxon. He had his keys and he knew the key code to the lock.

Setting aside the pad and the pencils, Ivy went to the front foyer. She glanced through the narrow sidelight window next to the door before she opened it.

A young brown-skinned woman stood outside. She wore a sleeveless olive-colored shift dress. Something about her seemed familiar.

Ivy opened the door, and the young woman gave Ivy a puzzled smile. "Hello, I'm looking for Jaxon." She laid her hand over a small baby bump.

Curiosity piqued in Ivy's mind as she wondered who she was. "Jaxon stepped out for a minute. May I help you?"

A car pulled into the driveway. It was Jaxon.

"Oh good, he's back," the woman said. "I'm Nicki."

That's right. The family pictures. That's where she recognized her face. This was Jaxon's sister. "I'm Ivy, Jaxon's…friend."

Jaxon came up the walkway, carrying take-out food bags. As soon as he saw his sister he stopped in his tracks. "Nicki? Are you…?"

It took a moment for Jaxon to process that Nicki was there and was…was…

His sister grinned at him. "If the word you're thinking of is *pregnant*, then yes. I am."

Thrilled to see her and a little concerned, he strode over and gave Nicki a one-armed hug. "What are you doing here? Is everything okay?"

"Everything's fine. I'm in town on business." She hugged him back and kissed him on the cheek.

The same property manager who looked after this house also took care of the corporate apartments in LA that their father's company owned. They'd probably mentioned he was in California, and Nicki had viewed it as the perfect opportunity to pop in…and possibly ambush him.

Still, relief ran through him that nothing serious had happened. Feeling the extra padding between them, he stepped back and smiled. "You're pregnant. That's fantastic." Mentally shaking off surprise, he turned to make introductions. "Ivy, this is my sister, Nicki."

"I know. We introduced ourselves already." Ivy smiled at his sister. "It's nice to meet you."

"It's nice to meet you, too," said Nicki.

Jaxon followed his sister inside and shut the door behind them.

Nicki glanced at the bag in his hands. "I guess I'm interrupting lunch?"

"No, you're just in time," Ivy said.

Jaxon chimed in holding up the bags. "There's plenty of food. I picked up chicken parm and a salad. Why don't you join us?"

"Thank you, but I can't stay long. I have to get to the airport." Nicki's brown eyes, almost the same color as his own, pinned him with a direct look. "I was hoping we could have a minute to talk about something."

He didn't need a cipher to decode what "something" referred to—their father.

Ivy said, "I'll go upstairs so you two can talk. Just let me grab my things from the deck."

"You don't have to. You can hang out in the living room and eat or Nicki and I can go to another room." It didn't matter to him if Ivy overheard the conversation. She already knew what had happened between him and his dad.

"No, I need to start packing anyway. I can eat later." Ivy hurried toward the kitchen.

"She seems nice," Nicki said as they followed. "How long have you been together?"

"Not long."

A short moment later, from the friendly smile Ivy gave his sister as she headed for the stairs, she wasn't annoyed by the interruption.

As Ivy passed by him, empathy, caring and something akin to solidarity sat in her eyes. She was there for him, not just sexually, but in a deeper way. She hadn't said it, but he could sense it. He felt that way about her, too. That's why going to Tennessee together would be a good step for them to take so they could explore their relationship. Would she say yes?

Impatience to know her answer made the tense conversation he was bound to have with Nicki now even more frustrating. He just wanted to enjoy the rest of the day with Ivy.

In the kitchen Jaxon asked, "Are you sure you don't want something to eat?"

She laid her hand on her belly, and a look of interest flashed in her eyes. "Well, maybe a little. I don't want to eat too much before I get on the plane."

As he unpacked the food, she took a seat at the kitchen island. "Ivy must be pretty special if you brought her here."

"She is." He removed a plate from the cabinet. The food was still piping hot when he opened the foil-covered container and spooned some on a plate for Nicki.

As he put some salad in a bowl for her, he could feel his sister staring at his back. Was she wondering if he was annoyed that she showed up out of the blue? He was, because it felt like an ambush. How long was she going to dance around why she'd come?

He put the food in front of her with utensils and a napkin.

She ate a bite of chicken parmesan. "This is good. You know, I forgot how beautiful the view is here. Do you mind if we go outside?"

Moments later, they sat at the round table on the raised deck. He'd put salad in a bowl for himself, but he wanted to eat the main entrée with Ivy later.

Below, people walked on the beach and played in the waves.

In between bites of food, Nicki closed her eyes a moment and breathed. "Hmm, this really is phenomenal. Not just the food, but the entire experience."

Sitting across from her at the table, Jaxon crossed his arms over his chest and sat back in the chair with a weary sigh. "Nicki, just stop."

"Stop what?"

"Stop pretending this is a social visit. It's not. Just get to what you came here to say."

"Fine. You need to come home for Dad's awards ceremony." She took another bite of salad.

"New York isn't my home anymore, and I already answered that question."

"You need to change your mind. I get why you're upset at Dad, but like I said, he's sorry for what he did to you."

A harsh chuckle shot from his chest. "It's a little late for that."

"But it's not too late for you to forgive him."

"He's not interested in my forgiveness, trust me." And his father wasn't sorry. He knew that for a fact, too.

"But *I'm* interested in forgiveness."

"Nicki, what happened doesn't concern you. It's between me and Dad."

"No, it's between all of us, but you're too damn stubborn to see it." Just as he was about to respond, she waved him off. "I came here so we could have this out face-to-face. We lost our mom. Dad buried himself in work and we suffered an even bigger loss because of it. We grew up in a fractured family, but my baby won't experience the same. It's time to break the cycle of our family using separation to hide."

Reining in his own frustration, Jaxon held his hands out to his side. "I'm not hiding. I'm right here. You found me, didn't you?"

"You're physically here, but you haven't been present in our family for the past three years." She pointed at him with the fork. "You're hiding from what you don't want to face. You're also using it as an excuse for not trying again—starting another company, trusting people, being in relationships, engaging with life. You just escape to the next place. It makes it easier to just ignore you have a home and family, and feelings and fears you need to work out, but you can't keep running. I won't let you."

Realization hit him about how the photos had ended up on the wall. He pointed back. "You told the property manager to put those family photos on the wall in my office."

She lifted up her chin. "Yes, I did, and I know that was sneaky and probably unfair, but I won't give up on you. On us." Her eyes grew bright with tears. She'd called him stubborn, but knowing her, she was too damn stubborn to let the tears fall. "You needed a reminder, and I want to build a future for my child. One that includes all of my family."

The love and protectiveness in Nicki's eyes softened

him a little. She hadn't even had the kid yet and mama bear energy radiated from her. Not a surprise. She'd never hesitated to get in a scrap over the things and people she cared about, and that included him. But this time, she'd crossed a line and he couldn't let that go.

Jaxon leaned in. "I love you, and I understand you're passionate about family, especially because you're pregnant. But the last thing you get to do is invade my home with photos and come at me with demands. Did you really think I'd let you slide on this? You know me better than that."

"This isn't a demand. It's a plea. Damn you and damn these hormones." Nicki dropped her fork and it clattered on her plate. She got to her feet and walked from the table. Quickly swiping tears from her cheeks, she looked out at the ocean.

Shit. He'd made her cry. Jaxon picked up a paper napkin from the table and went over to her.

She weakly pushed him away before taking the napkin and letting him wrap her in a hug.

He rubbed her back. "I'm sorry. I didn't mean to snap at you so hard about the photos. But you had to suspect how I'd react when I saw them. It was more than just a little unexpected and it definitely wasn't right."

"I wasn't trying to make you angry. Honest. I just hoped seeing them would remind you that we had fun times, too." His sister dabbed her nose and sniffed as she moved out of his embrace. "Dad reacted the same way when I put the photos he'd taken down back up. You're just like him."

Jaxon rubbed the back of his neck. "Lucky me."

"But he's changing." Nicki's voice grew quieter as she rested her arms on the railing and stared back out at the ocean. "He's grown more introspective. The other day, he admitted to Isaiah that he regrets some of the times he was so ruthless at the bargaining table. The award he's receiving, CEO of the Decade, actually reflects that. He isn't even looking forward to the ceremony, because he knows half the people in the room will only be there because they want something from him. The other half will be people who are afraid of him or who hate him, but they'll all be there with smiles on their faces, pretending they love and admire him. When he mentions the ceremony, he just looks so defeated."

"Our dad, defeated?" Jaxon released a disbelieving chuckle.

"Don't get me wrong. He's still tough enough to negotiate the best of them under the table, but I think the reality of who's going to be in that room has reminded him just how alone he would be without me and Isaiah. He needs to see people in the audience who really care about him. That's why we have to be there. Why you have to be there, especially."

In the past few years, apparently Nicki had become quite the negotiator herself. He couldn't argue with her reasoning. Did he like his dad? No. But he honestly couldn't say he hated him. "Maybe, I'll think about it."

"Good."

"I said maybe," he warned. "I'm not promising I'll be there."

"You *maybe* thinking about it is a start and that's enough for me." A soft glow came over his sister's face.

In that moment, he saw glimpses of their mother in Nicki. Their mom's compassion. Her caring. The way she'd loved them.

Jaxon nudged Nicki's arm. "So when do I get to meet my niece or nephew?"

"A little less than four months."

"That soon, huh? Why did you wait so long to tell me?"

"I decided you didn't get to know until you agreed to see me face-to-face. Don't look at me like that. It's your fault. You kept avoiding me."

"And you say I'm stubborn? I can't wait to babysit. I'm going to teach that kid everything, from where to hide the vegetables they don't want to eat to how to set up a water balloon above a door for maximum impact."

"Okaaay." She laughed. "And while you're corrupting my innocent child, don't forget turnaround is fair play."

Kids of his own? That seemed so distant. Ivy had already been a surrogate mom to Brooke and Harper. Did she want kids of her own someday? Why was he even thinking about that? He shook off the thought.

Nicki bumped him with her hip. "So is Ivy someone I might see again in the future? Like in New York in a few weeks?"

Ivy as part of the future? He hoped so. The way they'd gotten along so well this weekend was an even stronger indicator that going to Tennessee together was going to work out. As far as attending his dad's ceremony, though…he was less certain.

Jaxon bumped Nicki back. "We'll see."

Chapter Twenty-One

As Ivy heard Jaxon and Nicki walking back inside the house, she pushed open the sliding door in the bedroom wider. She'd unlocked it as soon as she'd gone upstairs, welcoming in the sounds of the ocean, planning to sketch some more.

She hadn't anticipated Jaxon and his sister walking onto the deck below her. Instead of closing the door, she'd tried to tune out their conversation, but as their voices rose, she couldn't ignore it any longer, especially the part his sister had said about Jaxon not forgiving their dad.

Ivy slumped in the hammock chair outside on the bedroom deck. The remembered words she'd overheard played in her mind.

"You're hiding from what you don't want to face. You're also using it as an excuse for not trying again—starting another company, trusting people, being in relationships, engaging with life. You just escape to the next place. It makes it easier to just ignore you have a home and family, and feelings and fears you need to work out, but you can't keep running..."

Nicki's voice had sounded so heartfelt, but Jaxon

had just deflected. Hearing him refuse to acknowledge what his sister had said had made her hurt for him... and herself. Because Jaxon wasn't the only one ignoring feelings and fears.

She was, too.

Twelve years ago, Von may have trivialized her career as an artist, but she'd been the one to classify herself as a struggling painter instead of a talented one. She'd also used her engagement and his budding career as an excuse not to pursue her dream, all because she'd been secretly afraid to put herself out there as a painter and risk failure. And then, the accident had happened. Stepping into the role of guardian for Harper and Brooke and running the bee farm had made it even easier to let the dream slip away. But she didn't have those excuses anymore.

Jaxon walked outside. "I was wondering where you were." She made room for him in the hammock chair. He sat down and wrapped an arm behind her. "Are you packed?"

Ivy rested her head on his shoulder and swallowed against the tightening in her throat. "Uh-huh."

As the hammock swayed, he released a long breath. "I wish we didn't have to go back."

She wished more than anything they were both in a place where they had their lives figured out, but they didn't. One sketch in a sketch pad didn't mean her future was set. She still had work to do. And judging from the conversation with his sister, he did, too. The ache in her heart intensified, and Ivy closed her eyes.

"Hey, what's wrong?" Jaxon used his finger to wipe a tear from her cheek.

She hadn't even realized she'd started crying. "I don't want this to end."

"Neither do I. It's been a perfect three days, but it's not the end of us. We'll have more time together, especially if you come with me to Tennessee."

Ivy kept her eyes closed. Once she opened them, she wouldn't be able to stop him from seeing the misery tearing into her. She wanted to hold on to the daydream of them at the farm in Tennessee. Of her taking care of the beehives and building an apiary. Jaxon feeding the goat, cow, and chickens before he started his repair jobs for the day. Of them having lunch together on a blanket spread in the grass. Of him following her down on the blanket as he kissed her, the two of them making love…and avoiding the truth.

Jaxon tipped up her chin, and she finally opened her eyes. As he met her gaze, the happiness in his drained away. His expression morphed from concern to disappointment to disbelief. He shook his head. "Ivy, no. Don't say it."

She laid her hand to his chest. "Jaxon, I'm sorry, but I *have* to say it. I can't run away with you. Beekeeping isn't my passion anymore. I have to start painting again."

"So paint. I support you." Determination was in his eyes. "You can still do that and come with me."

"Going away with you would be the easy part, and being with you would make it even easier for me not to face what scares me—which is putting a paintbrush to a canvas again. I know you support me, but I have to do this on my own in the place where I'm meant to be."

"What about what's meant for us?" Hurt joined the determination in his gaze. "Or did you never see a future for us?"

"I did, and I wanted it more than anything." As she moved her hand closer to the middle of his chest, it felt as if his heart was close to bursting out of him. "But we have a life full of choices, and it would be a mistake for us to make one that allows us to lie to ourselves about what we're really doing. The truth is, you're running from your past, and I'm running from deciding what to do with my future."

She wasn't trying to cast judgment on the situation with him and his dad, but from his expression, her words hit close to home.

Ivy continued, wishing there was another way for them, but knowing that there wasn't. "Eventually, regret catches up with you. It nips at your heels until it wears you down and traps you in place. I know what that's like. It happened to my parents. They blamed each other for the chances they'd missed. I don't want us to end up blaming our unhappiness on each other because we didn't resolve our unfinished business before trying to build a relationship. I care about you too much."

Jaxon took her hand in his. The warmth of his skin seeped into hers, turning into an invisible ribbon that traveled upward and wrapped itself so tightly around Ivy's heart her chest ached.

"I don't want to let you go, but I want you to be happy." His chest rose and fell with a deep, heavy sigh. He looked to the ocean for a long minute and then back at her. His expression held resignation, but it didn't completely mask the even deeper hurt she saw in his eyes. "I know you'll paint beautiful pictures because of who you are." He briefly kissed the back of her hand. "I'm so damn lucky you like tacos, otherwise I might never have met you, Ivy Daniels."

Jaxon was trying to make the moment easier. Another sign of his generosity, his strength and reliability. It had been so easy for her to fall in love with him. Amelia was right. She had been stung, but admitting that to him now would just make it harder to let go.

Ivy rested her head on his shoulder, "I'm glad I met you, too, Jaxon Coffield."

The next afternoon, as Ivy rolled her carry-on across the porch to the front of the house at the bee farm, she felt totally exhausted. Even with dark glasses on, the sun was a little too bright for her eyes. Last night, she'd lain awake, memorizing Jaxon's warmth, his scent, the way it felt to be near him. The way the light shadowed his face when he turned his head on the pillow to look at her and held her to his side a little tighter.

She dozed a little on the plane. It helped her to shut out the clock and the map on the back of the seat in front of her tracking the progress of their flight—counting down how close she and Jaxon were to saying goodbye to each other. They'd decided that it would be easier to walk away when they landed and not look back. He had eight days to go before he left Bolan. They weren't planning to avoid each other, but the chances of her venturing out of the farm over the next week were slim.

As she walked in and shut the door, Brooke called out, "Auntie, you're home."

She and Harper came toward her from the kitchen like they had her first afternoon back at the farm weeks ago. It was a déjà vu moment.

Ivy set her purse on top of her luggage. She needed the hug they sandwiched her in more than they realized. Luckily she still had her glasses on, otherwise they would have seen her eyes well up a little.

"How are you feeling?" she said to Brooke.

"Much better."

"Good, I'm glad to hear it." She looked to Harper. "Everything good with you?"

"No complaints here."

Brooke took hold of Ivy's hand. "You have to come to the kitchen. I've got a surprise for you."

"A surprise? Oh really?" Sadness blossomed in Ivy's chest. She wouldn't be able to hear the word surprise without thinking of Jaxon. Somehow, she managed to conjure up a smile. "Just give me a minute to run upstairs. It was a long trip. I'll be right back."

Excitement danced in Brooke's eyes as she let Ivy go. "Don't take too long."

"I won't." Ivy went up the stairs. By the time she was halfway up, it felt as if she was dragging herself to the top.

In the bathroom connected to her bedroom, she took off her glasses and stared at her reflection in the mirror over the sink. Her eyes were red and puffy from fatigue and suppressed tears. She splashed cold water on her face then rummaged through a drawer for eyedrops. *Dang it.* They were in her purse downstairs.

Just as she walked out of the bathroom, Harper came in with her purse and luggage. As she looked at Ivy's face, she immediately grew concerned. "Are you all right?"

"I'm fine." Ivy waved the concern away. "I've been dealing with some weird allergy for the past few days. I just need to put in some eyedrops. They're in my purse. Thanks for bringing my things up."

"You're welcome. Is your allergy because of Jaxon?"

Ivy ducked her gaze and hunted through her purse. "Jaxon? Why would he have anything to do with it?"

"Because he's the one you spent the weekend with."

The certainty in Harper's gaze held back Ivy's denial. Her shoulders slumped in defeat. "What gave it away?"

"Your phone. It rang a few minutes ago with back-to-back calls from the same number. I thought it might be important so I answered it. It was Jaxon. He asked if you were here. I told him yes. I asked if he wanted to speak to you, but he said no."

Ivy sat on the edge of the bed. "He probably just wanted to make sure I'd made it home from the airport."

Harper sat beside her. "What happened? Did you have a bad weekend?"

"No, not at all." A sad chuckle slipped out of Ivy. "It was the best long weekend ever, but Jaxon and I broke up. It was for the best."

"I'm sorry it didn't work out. Every time you came back from one of your long afternoons with him, you looked so happy."

She'd figured that out, too? Ivy had to smile a little. Funny, she'd always imagined Brooke's intuition sussing out the truth about her and Jaxon.

Harper stood. "I better go back downstairs before Brooke comes looking for us. I'll run interference until you get downstairs. The friend you spent the weekend with is supposed to be Amelia, right? You should know, Brooke's hoping it was Von."

No more secrets. It was time to tell the truth. "No, you don't have to cover for me. I'm telling Brooke the truth about me and Jaxon."

"Okay." Harper raised her brow. "But you'll probably want to wait until after your surprise."

Moments later, Ivy breezed into the kitchen. "Okay, I'm here." She released a squeal of delight as Brooke's fiancé rose from a chair at the table.

She'd only talked to Gable through video calls with Brooke. He was even more handsome in person. Did Michael B. Jordan know he had a twin?

Ivy opened her arms wide. "Finally, I get my long overdue hug."

Smiling, he embraced her. "Hello, Aunt Ivy."

As he moved away, Brooke came to his side. The love in the smiles the couple exchanged was even more potent than on screen.

Through the swell of joy numbing some of her emotional pain, she saw her truths clearly. She loved being home. She loved her family. She loved Jaxon. The joy and the pain of love would give her the courage to find her way.

Chapter Twenty-Two

Ivy settled into the Western-style saddle on top of the horse she was riding down the tree-lined trail. Determined not to wallow in the knowledge that Jaxon had left town for good yesterday, she'd decided to tackle something else on her do-again list: horseback riding.

Zurie had lent her Belle, a gentle but regal chestnut horse, for a ride around the property of Tillbridge Stables. Before Ivy had headed out, the stable owner had taken her and the horse through a few paces in the small outdoor arena near the stable.

Brooke rode ahead of her on Gable's horse, Pepper. She managed the large dapple-gray with the same confidence her mother had when she'd ridden horses.

Had she stopped riding horses years ago because she'd been worried of falling off and possibly ending up hurt? Or had she stopped because it was something she and Lexy had done together? Ivy pondered the reason but couldn't reach a conclusion. Either way, this was something she needed to do again. If only she could do the same with painting. She'd tried but she couldn't quite talk herself into moving from a sketch pad and pencil to a brush and a canvas on an easel.

Brooke glanced over her shoulder and grinned at Ivy, a few of her dark curls that had escaped from her hair tie blowing across her cheek. "You okay back there?"

"We're doing just fine." As Belle started to slightly veer to the right, Ivy adjusted her hold on the reins.

Remembering how to ride a horse wasn't quite like getting back on a bike, but she hadn't fallen yet. Honestly, she felt surprisingly at peace. The horse's slow rhythmic gait rocking her slightly in the saddle, the chirping of the birds, the gentle warmth of the morning sun along a light morning breeze all had a soothing quality.

They slowed down as the trail made a few dips and curves.

Brooke pointed up ahead. "Just up that small incline is a place where we can take a break."

"Sounds good."

Apparently, Belle knew the way. She made the climb with very little prompting from Ivy. They halted at the top, and she and Brooke dismounted. Lead ropes in hand, they guided the horses forward.

The grassy area nestled in the trees had a spectacular view of a wide green pasture.

Brooke sighed contentedly as she looked out. "It really is beautiful up here."

"It is." Ivy's palm tingled where the handle of her paintbrush had often rested as she'd worked on a painting. She rubbed her hand over the thigh of her jeans.

That sensation was happening more and more lately, every time she came across a sight or object that was paint worthy. But she hadn't sketched anything since that day on the beach. Her breakup with Jaxon had left her a little hollow inside. Whatever she tried to sketch would probably turn out to be a disaster.

Brooke gave her a questioning look. "So what prompted you to want to do this—go horseback riding?"

"It's something I hadn't done in a while." Belle's soft whinny prompted Ivy to stroke the horse's neck. "It's also something that was on my do-again list—things I once enjoyed but stopped doing. It was something Jaxon encouraged me to start." As she said his name, the pang of loss she'd been fighting hit her in the chest. It was a struggle to breathe against it. Eventually, saying his name would get easier, and her memories of him would fade into the background of her mind. She just had to give it time. Right?

"I'm sorry the two of you split up." Brooke's pained expression looked as if she felt the full force of Ivy's loss. When Ivy had told her about Jaxon, she'd accepted it surprisingly well.

"It's okay." Ivy propped up a reassuring smile. "Jaxon and I had fun. I don't regret it."

"But I do." Brooke shook her head. "Not that you and Jaxon were together but that I said you shouldn't be."

"You were just concerned."

"No, I was selfish." Brooke looked down. As she relaxed her hold on the lead rope attached to Pepper's halter, he started grazing on the grass and Belle followed his lead. "I wanted to feel less guilty about being with Gable."

"What? Why in the world would you feel guilty about that?"

Brooke's eyes were bright as she looked up. "Because the only reason I have a chance at happiness with Gable is because you gave up your chance with Von all those years ago. You would have been married to him, maybe had a few kids. You would have had a happy life with him, but you sacrificed all of that for me and Harper." A tear slipped from one of her eyes. "When you mentioned you saw Von again... I just wanted you back together with him, but it was for the wrong reason."

"Oh, sweetie." Surprised by the confession and touched by Brooke's concern, Ivy reached out and cupped her hand against the wetness on Brooke's cheek. "It wasn't a sacrifice. It was what I wanted to do. Not just because it was what your mom and dad asked of me but because I love you and Harper with all of my heart. I don't feel as if I missed out on anything. I gained so much in my life raising you two."

Brooke gave a tremulous smile. "Really?"

"Yes, really." Ivy gave Brooke a fierce hug. "You being with Gable is like a cherry on top of the icing of the most fantastic cake ever made. You chose a wonderful guy, and you two have an incredible future ahead of you. Your happiness makes me ecstatic. And as far as me and Von, we aren't meant for each other. We wanted different things. We've moved on."

Brooke leaned away to look at Ivy. "And what about you and Jaxon?"

"It was time for us to go our separate ways. We've both moved on, too." As truthful as the words were, they still stung a little. It definitely wasn't the same heady feeling of being stung by love she'd experienced when she was with Jaxon.

The horses starting to fidget created the perfect reason to look away from Brooke's doubtful gaze. "I think they're giving us a hint." Ivy laughed, trying to lighten the heaviness inside of her.

Brooke reached and squeezed her hand. "Are you sure there isn't anything I can do or say to help?"

Ivy shook her head. "I'm fine." Or at least she would be in time. As she climbed back on Belle, something did come to her. "Actually, there is one thing you can do with me."

Eagerness filled Brooke's face. "I'm in. What is it?"

"How do you feel about goat yoga?"

A week later, Ivy sat in a meadow, cuddling a baby goat after the yoga class. Having him standing on her back as she'd executed a table pose earlier had been an interesting experience. The trust in that moment had gone both ways.

"Thank you." As she patted the goat's head, it let out a loud bleat and gently butted her hand. She'd completed another item that was on her list, and she was grateful for the experience, but she couldn't help but wish Jaxon had been there, too. Still, she hadn't been alone.

Nearby, Brooke and Harper chatted with other participants. Harper agreeing to set work aside on a Friday morning had been a nice surprise, and she and Brooke were continuing to get along just fine. Ivy smiled to herself. She'd accomplished what she'd set out to do when she'd left them on their own a few months ago. They had grown closer and their family farm had a future.

As Ivy observed them, her mind wandered, imagining them as moms, raising their children. Teaching the next generation about the importance of the farm. Had they lived, Lexy would have laughed in delight, cradling and doting on her grandbabies as she patiently told them all about the bees, and Dion would have been right there beside her.

Bittersweet emotions filled Ivy's chest as she looked up at the sky. *Lexy, Dion, look at your beautiful girls. They're yours, too. You did good.* The words echoed inside of her as a gentle breeze ruffled her hair.

Yeah, she had done good, but as much as she loved Brooke and Harper, she still wasn't ready to live in a cottage between the bee farm and Gable's house. They'd actually started drawing up secret house plans. She'd discovered them in a file tucked away in a cabinet in the home office.

Ivy spoke to the goat. "I need a little more independence than that. It's time for me to buy a house."

"Was I right?" The real estate agent, Peggy, an older woman dressed in an impeccable pink suit gave her a knowing look. "You said you didn't want a newly built home, but I wanted you to see this place next, just in case you might have an interest. It has so much to offer. Isn't it phenomenal? A spacious great room, eat-in kitchen with a center island, and a walk-in pantry. And wait until you see the bedrooms on the second level. The primary has a powder room and a spa bath perfect for relaxing after a long day."

Ivy glanced around the house. It was the second one Peggy had insisted they check out in the recently developed subdivision outside of town.

They were modern and impressive, but the houses also lacked something. Her gaze landed on the morning room with a screened-in porch and outdoor fireplace. A vision of her and Jaxon relaxing there emerged along with memories of how happy they'd been at his beach house. Then it slowly dissipated. She couldn't live here. If she did, every moment, every room would remind her of being with Jaxon in California. She missed him so much—not just the physical intimacy but also talking with him. Being listened to by him. Hearing him express his unwavering belief in her and feeling it as tangibly as his embrace.

"It's nice," Ivy said to Peggy. "But this isn't what I'm looking for. I'd really like to see an older home."

"Well, okay, if that's what you really want, I have a place. It just came on the market last week. Let's go."

Rather than driving in two separate cars, Ivy had ridden with Peggy.

As Peggy was about to pull out of the driveway, her phone rang. "It's the office. I need to take this. Hello… really?" The real estate agent frowned. "I see. Well, that doesn't sound good. Yes, I'll head over their right now." She ended the call.

"Is everything all right?"

"It will be when I get there." Peggy pulled out of the driveway and sped down the street. "The person who handles our property management clients is out of town, and I've been covering for them. Apparently, a contractor making repairs on the back porch of one of the houses we're managing got his information wrong. You probably know the place. It's the artist's house."

"I do know it." The conversation she'd had with Jaxon about the artist's house surfaced in Ivy's thoughts.

Unlike Peggy, Jaxon had understood her, and he hadn't tried to change her mind about what she wanted for herself. He'd only encouraged her to enhance her vision…to paint. In an odd way, she felt like she'd let him down by not continuing to fill the sketchbook he'd bought her, but it was as if she'd lost whatever inspiration she'd had when they broke up.

Moments later, they arrived at an unassuming white house with blue trim. The grass in the yard was slightly overgrown and so were the surrounding bushes, but the area was obviously looked after.

Peggy pulled in behind a contractor's van in the driveway. "The outside shouldn't look like this. I need to find out why the landscapers haven't been here. We can go through the front door to reach the back instead of walking through the grass."

Ivy wasn't sure she'd heard the woman right. "You want me to go inside with you?"

"Yes. This might take a minute, and my car is low on gas. It's too hot for you to sit out here without air conditioning. And it's not like there's anything to steal in there. It's empty. There are just pictures painted all over the walls. It feels more like a museum than a house to me." Peggy shook her head. "They'll never be able to sell it the way it is."

"It's for sale?"

"Oh no." Peggy shook her head harder. "We've tried to talk them into it. They could get a lot of money. It's a quaint old house, but they don't want to part with it. They'd rather spend a ton of money on upkeep and high-priced security. That doesn't make a lick of sense to me. Come on. You can see it for yourself."

Moments later, as Peggy opened the front door, Ivy's heart started to beat triple time in her chest. She was about to walk in the artist's house and see the murals that she'd only heard about.

They walked inside, and Ivy's breath caught. Vibrant beauty was spread on almost every wall, starting from the entryway into the living room ahead.

She barely glanced at Peggy, who was talking to her as she walked away. "I'll be out back with the contractor. I know you're anxious to see the next house. I'll do my best to move this conversation along."

"Take your time." Ivy walked into the living room, mesmerized by the walls. She recognized most of the images. The artist had painted views ranging from vineyards in Italy to Paris and the Eiffel Tower. She'd woven in jungles in Africa and forests in South America. Image after image, layered like a tapestry spread over the walls.

She could feel the care in them through the tiny details on the grapes, and the bold colors used to magnify the sun. It was in the soft strokes the artist had used to capture the mane of a lion and the fullness of the grass.

Ivy could see the joy and love the artist had wanted to convey...no, *had* conveyed through their art. The murals made her heart swell.

You're the painter you need to be today. Someone who has ideas and memories and dreams that need to be shared... I can't even imagine what your art could do. What you could do.

Jaxon's words hovered inside of her. *You inspire me, Ivy.*

Maybe she could inspire the world, but could she inspire herself to try?

Chapter Twenty-Three

Jaxon loosened his bow tie as he entered the second-floor hotel lounge. He needed a drink. He'd done his duty for the night. He'd come to New York, put on a tux, and attended the award banquet that had been held in the grand ballroom downstairs.

Nicki had been right. The room had been filled with people either sucking up to his father or patting him on the back with tight smiles. At any moment, the latter seemed poised to collectively throw his father to the wolves.

His sister was also right about their father having seemingly changed. Instead of smiling and playing the game, he'd been much more reserved than usual, which had also been reflected in his acceptance speech. It hadn't been filled with the expected self-congratulatory jokes or quips and jabs at his fellow colleagues. Instead, he'd thanked his staff, the colleagues who'd made speeches about him before he'd gone up to accept the award, and his family. That was it, and then he'd sat back down at the family table.

Jaxon ordered a whiskey, straight up, at the bar and took a seat at the counter. The night had ended quicker than he'd expected, and he was glad it was over. He was leaving first thing in the morning for Laguna Beach. He'd turned down the job in Tennessee. He just couldn't see himself there without Ivy. He missed her, and a part of him hadn't ruled out going back to Maryland so he could try to convince Ivy to come to California with him. They'd been good at the beach. He would do anything to get Ivy and their relationship back.

He took a sip of the drink, savoring the bite of the alcohol.

A woman walked up next to him. He could feel her eyes on him, but he didn't bother looking her way. Whatever she had to say, he wasn't interested.

He glanced at her and did a double take. It was one of his ex-partners.

"Hello, Jaxon." She gave him a smile shaded with uncertainty.

"Hello, Lena." He hadn't seen or spoken to the dark-haired woman in three years.

He'd heard she'd married a high-priced defense attorney. Her navy evening dress and jewelry seemed to confirm she'd moved up in the world. Had she been at his father's ceremony?

As if she'd read his mind, she said, "I saw you when you walked into the ballroom. My husband and I were at a table in the back. Do you mind if I sit?"

"Be my guest." He glanced around the lounge. "You have lots of chairs to choose from."

She sat next to him and ordered a glass of wine from the bartender.

Dormant irritation, left over from years ago when

Lena and his other business partner betrayed him, rippled through Jaxon. It was time for him to go. He knocked back the rest of his drink.

"I know this is three years too late, but I'm sorry for what Matt and I did to you." To her credit, despite her nervousness, Lena looked him in the eye. "It was cowardly and unfair." The bartender delivered her wine and she paid for it. Instead of lifting the glass to take a drink, she fiddled with the napkin underneath it. "I know now that the money we got wasn't worth destroying our dream and our friendship. I regret it almost every day. If there was a way I could make it up to you, I would."

He was tempted to just walk away, but the chance to get an answer to the question he'd never gotten to ask tempted him even more. "What did my father say to you? How did he convince you that the right thing to do was to help him betray me and destroy our friendship?"

A stunned and confused look came over her face. She opened her mouth to speak then paused. "You still don't know?"

"Know what?"

She got up and shook her head. "No, I'll get torn apart if I violate the nondisclosure. Ask your father. I have to go." Lena hurried out of the lounge as if wolves were chasing her.

What had Ivy said? Something about regret nipping at your heels eventually catching up and trapping you in place? Lena seemed to be experiencing that fate. It should have felt like sweet revenge, but it didn't. He actually kind of felt sorry for her.

Jaxon glanced at her untouched wine. What had made her leave in such a hurry? And what could his father tell him about his betrayal that he didn't already know?

In the early morning hours, just after dawn, Jaxon quietly carried his bag down one side of a curved dual staircase at his father's house in upstate New York. A skylight above filtered a weak stream of orange and yellow sunlight over the tiled foyer below.

This house felt like an unknown place to him. He'd lived there for a minute when his father first bought it seven years ago, but it had only ever felt like a place to make a short visit to—it had never been his home.

At the bottom of the stairs, the sounds of clattering dishes came from farther down a hall on the right. It could have been the private chef, but the Nina Simone song echoing in the foyer pointed to someone else.

Jaxon found his father in the kitchen. He hadn't seen him since leaving the hotel last night. After having a drink at the lounge, he'd been too keyed up over his conversation with Lena and he wasn't in the mood to see his dad. He'd phoned a friend and they'd met up at another bar downtown. By the time he'd arrived at the house, his father, as well as Nicki and Isaiah, who had spent the night there, were already asleep.

This morning, his dad's short wavy dark hair was combed and his goatee was perfectly trimmed. Dressed in casual slacks and a long-sleeved pullover with the sleeves pushed up his arms, his dad was buttering slices of toast and putting them on a small plate.

He glanced up and saw Jaxon. "You're just in time. Honey is in the cabinet over there, and there should be some kind of preserves in the fridge. And coffee's already done."

"I don't have time to eat. I've got a flight to catch." But he could use some coffee and maybe some aspirin. He had a slight hangover. Jaxon poured a mug of coffee from the full glass carafe sitting in the maker on the counter.

"You used to like toast in the morning for breakfast. Have a seat." His dad tipped his head toward the kitchen table at the far end.

"As soon as I finish this coffee. I have to leave."

"I know you're used to running off, but if you have time for coffee, you can sit down and have a piece of toast with your family."

Running? He was tired of people pinning that word on him. Nicki had accused him of that, and in a subtle way Ivy had, too. Jaxon's temples pounded a little harder. And what was up with his father, acting like they were all one big, happy family? "The only place I'm running to is the airport to catch a flight. And exactly when did we become a family again?" As intended, his comment hit its mark.

His father stopped buttering toast. He dusted crumbs from his hands. "We've always been a family."

"Wow, okay." Jaxon put down his mug. "Since we're all family now, can you tell me why Lena suggested I should ask you about the details of when you and my business partners screwed me over? She couldn't tell me herself since she was too worried about violating your NDA."

His father shook his head and chuckled wryly. "Lena. I always knew she would be the one to break. She can't pick a side and stick to it."

"No." Jaxon shook his head. "You don't get to deflect my question. This isn't about her. This is about you. If anyone can't pick a side and stick to it, it's you. Today you want us to be family, but three years ago, you decided to live by that ethos you told me about in college. What was it?" Jaxon pointed at his dad then snapped his fingers. "I remember. 'Sometimes you have to eat your own young.'"

"It was necessary."

"Which one? Teaching me that philosophy or letting me feel it up close and personal as you took what was important away from me?" Seeing his father wince spurred Jaxon on. He let loose the years of frustration he'd buried inside of him. "The company I worked hard to build. The trust I had with my partners. Did you enjoy ripping chunks out of me piece by piece?"

"No, of course I didn't," his father roared. "You had no idea what was going on."

Jaxon shouted back. "Then enlighten me."

"It doesn't matter now. It's done."

"No, you don't get to do that." Jaxon advanced on him. "You held something back from me about what happened, and either you tell me now or I'm walking out of this house and you will never see me again."

"Please, Dad. He can't leave." Nicki stood in the entryway. "I need Jaxon. We *both* need Jaxon in our lives.

Whatever it is, just tell him." Her baby bump barely showed underneath her oversize sweatshirt she had on with a pair of yoga pants. She looked like a teen. Young and slightly vulnerable.

His father looked to Nicki as if he was in a daze. He went over to her. "How's your morning sickness today? Is it bad?"

"I had crackers in bed before I got up. I'm fine." She threw her arms around him and whispered, "Dad, please."

The bleakness in her eyes as she looked over their father's shoulder at him raised Jaxon's protective instincts. He considered dropping the matter, but he couldn't.

Years ago, a part of him had sensed his father hadn't been entirely straight with him, but he hadn't dug any deeper for answers. Maybe he'd been too angry at the time or just didn't want to hear what his father was capable of. He'd felt as if he had to get away from it all, or one day he would look in the mirror and see less of himself and more of his father in him.

But now he was back, and he needed to hear his father's confession. He needed to hear the horrible parts to know that he never could possibly be like him.

As his father moved out of Nicki's embrace, he gave her a peck on the cheek. "Being upset is not good for the baby or your morning sickness. I made you some extra dry toast and weak tea like I did yesterday. You felt better after having that, right? Like I said, I used to make that for your mom when she was pregnant. It worked every time."

"I'll take the toast now and have the tea when I get back. I'm going for a walk so you and Jaxon can talk."

Nicki accepted the plate of toast he offered her and left the kitchen.

Silence sat between Jaxon and his father.

His dad's expression was unreadable as they stared at each other. He shook his head. "Fine, you want to know everything? I'll tell you." His father made himself a cup of tea.

When he was done, Jaxon picked up his coffee mug and joined him at the table.

Long seconds passed as his father took a drink from his cup. Clearing his throat, he set it down. "The second quarter of the final year of your company, the ideas were flowing and you and your partners were running on all cylinders."

And they were making money for the third quarter in a row. Jaxon recalled how they'd toasted with champagne in his office.

"I caught wind that a larger company wanted to buy you out. I hadn't heard of that possibility from you. Even though you made a point not to discuss business with me, I doubted you wouldn't tell me something like that so I did some digging. I found out Lena and Matt were already in the midst of negotiations without you."

"What?" Jaxon sat back in the chair. "No, they never mentioned anything about wanting to sell. They were as eager as I was to expand."

"Maybe they were, but someone played into their weaknesses—greed and jealousy. Lena liked money, and her family had problems a big paycheck could solve, and Matt, he wasn't happy about what was going on with you and Lena."

"Nothing was going on."

"But the potential was there, and I'm sure the closer on the deal played into Matt's paranoia, telling him that if you and Lena did become a couple, he'd get iced out. He decided to stick it to you before he got stuck. But they were both getting played. The negotiator was lowballing them."

What ultimately happened grew a little clearer for Jaxon. "So instead of telling me about it, you got involved with the negotiations?"

"Damn right I did. You would have walked away not only having your company stolen from you but with nothing to show for it. Whether you knew their intentions or not, your partners were going to screw you. I made sure you walked away whole, financially.

"It was my fault you went into business with your partners in the first place. If I would have just let you develop the philanthropic arm of my company, like you wanted, you would have had your dream and you would have never had to partner up with people willing to stab you in the back for a couple of bucks. You would have stayed protected at the company."

"Protected? Dad, when I worked for you, I was suffocating. I couldn't move right or left without you over my shoulder analyzing and reanalyzing every step I made. I had to leave to find myself and I did. I started a successful company. You should have told me what you found out or let the situation run its course. Either way, you should have trusted me to figure out my situation."

As Jaxon said that last sentence, it hit him as hard as it hit his father—because he knew now that he couldn't go back to Maryland to try to convince Ivy to go with him to California. As hard as it was, as much as he missed her, he had to step back, trust she knew herself and what she needed to do. She needed to take a chance and find herself as an artist, and he had no right to try to take that decision away from her.

His father responded, "Maybe. But you still shouldn't have given away the money I made for you, negotiating the sale."

His father might have changed in some ways, but admitting when he was wrong wasn't one of them. Jaxon wasn't like that. Maybe he wasn't just like his dad after all.

"I wasn't the only one who needed to be made whole." He'd divided the money between the small businesses and artisans his company had partnered with who'd lost their contracts because of the sale, as well as his own employees who'd unexpectedly lost their jobs.

He followed his father's gaze to the kitchen window overlooking the expansive back lawn.

"Nicki is on her way back," his father said. "You know, I've only wanted the best for you two. Your mom was the one who always tried to encourage me to consider the more humane side of things, like feelings." His dad's voice grew a little gruff. "After she died, I didn't know how to do it. Honestly, trying to think in those terms on my own only made me miss her more. The talks we used to have. Our debates." He looked back to Jaxon. "A lot of the conversations I used to have with you before you left reminded me of those debates. I missed doing that with you."

His dad was extending an olive branch to him. Jaxon wouldn't reject it. But it would take time for him to digest and accept what his father had just told him. Having answers about what happened three years ago had lifted an invisible weight from his shoulders. He could now see a way to moving past it.

He couldn't promise Nicki the happy family she'd hoped to have for her child, but he would assure Nicki he'd be around more for her. For everyone.

Jaxon met his father's gaze, finally ready to admit something he'd held back. "Yeah, Dad, I missed you, too."

Chapter Twenty-Four

Ivy awoke before dawn in her bedroom at the bee farm, but she was far from rested. Last night she'd dreamed of the murals at the artist's house. She'd also dreamed of herself sitting in the middle of the flower field at the farm under a deep blue sky, exuberantly painting the view. In the dream she'd been enveloped in a sense of well-being. She'd felt…love.

She'd heard many times about how the unconscious mind was powerful, storing memories and beliefs. Was her mind telling her to go to the flower field and embrace being a painter again? It couldn't be that simple, could it? A tiny seed of hope struggled to appear in the midst of doubt. Ivy threw back the covers and got up.

After a quick visit to the bathroom, she dressed in a pair of navy leggings and an oversize faded blue T-shirt then went downstairs to the workroom. Rolling with the spirit of momentum spurring her on, she packed an easel, painting supplies, and a medium-size canvas in the art portfolio backpack Harper and Brooke had recently given her.

A surge of adrenaline more powerful than a morning cup of coffee hit Ivy as she stuffed her bare feet into a pair of boots at the front door. *I'll find it when*

I get there. What *it* actually was, she had no idea, but she'd figure it out.

In the garage, with her things stowed in the back of the truck along with a spare patio chair, she drove off.

Moments later, she sat alone in the flower field, just her and the rising sun. As she stared at the canvas, trepidation began to overwhelm eagerness. This was silly. What was she doing?

She'd asked herself a similar question on the day she'd gone skydiving with Jaxon. The recollection of him giving her a reassuring grin as he squeezed her hand just before the jump flitted through her mind. Bittersweet happiness came with the memory. Jumping out of the plane. Falling for Jaxon. Months ago, she couldn't have imagined doing either of those things, but she had.

More memories of the past few weeks with Jaxon flowed into her mind. Their first afternoon together. Dancing with him at the Wavefront Bistro. The roadside carnival. Hiking. Skydiving. Their weekend together at the beach house. And then a final vision settled in her mind. The photo of Jaxon as a boy with his mom.

She touched the paintbrush to the canvas. Her first strokes were hesitant, tentative, making her worry for a minute that she should have sketched it out first. Still, she kept going, holding on to the vision of the photo. With each successive stroke, it was as if the brush became energized with the memory. Time hovered, no longer dictated by seconds or minutes, but the drive of her inner creative voice.

Curved and straight lines became the abstract shapes of Jaxon's face and his boyish smile. Swirls of the brush became his mother's wind-tousled hair and her face lit up with laughter. Dips and playful swishes formed the waves in the ocean in the background, the clouds, and gulls floating in the air. She couldn't stop, didn't stop, and when it finally all poured out of her, she breathed long inhales and exhales that caused her chest to rise and fall. She'd done it. She'd captured what was in her mind. In her heart. She'd captured love.

Feeling light and free, she laughed. Managing the farm. Learning to tend the bees. Raising the girls. She'd taken those risks because of love. And when it came to painting, she loved the passion, the emotional connection, the mystery of the muse that still resided inside of her after all this time…and she also loved Jaxon.

As the realization hit, not even the deepest breaths could dull the ache that was burrowed in her heart. She recalled his face as they held hands, as they laughed, as he made love to her. He'd allowed her to discover this piece of herself again, her art, but she'd only been able to get here by pulling away from him.

Ivy added one final brushstroke to the canvas. And just like Jaxon, this painting wasn't hers to keep. She couldn't be with him because even though she loved him, she wasn't ready to say it and he wasn't in a place to hear it.

Back at the house in her workroom, she pulled up Jaxon's number on her phone and tapped out a simple message.

I have something for you. Can I send it to the beach house?

She already knew the address, and it was the most logical place to send it. With Jaxon moving from place to place, he wouldn't be able to carry the painting around. The caretaker could accept or retrieve the painting when it was delivered. What Jaxon did with it after that would be up to him, if he even decided to keep it.

Text bubbles appeared then disappeared on the screen.

How should she respond if he asked what it was? She could say it was a gift, but under the circumstances, wouldn't it seem weird that she was sending him one?

More seconds ticked by without a response. She was about to absently chew on her thumbnail until splotches of paint on her hands stopped her. It was a bad habit anyway, and one she hadn't wanted to do in years before now.

His text finally appeared.

No, dropping it off at the wine bar would be better. It'll get to me from there. Thanks.

It was a perfectly good response. Jaxon wasn't concerned over what she wanted to send him, and he didn't owe her any explanations about anything else. He would probably have Nate send it to him. If he wanted her to leave the painting at the bar, that was what she'd do. His short reply could be his way of setting a boundary, a clear indication stating he wasn't interested in interacting with her any further. She couldn't blame him if that was the case. Sadness made the thumps of her heart even heavier. This painting would be her last communication with him.

Two weeks later, she walked into Charmed Vines, carrying the painting wrapped in plastic, the edges protected in foam.

It was early afternoon and the place was almost empty of customers. Only one staff member was there. A woman she didn't recognize was pouring glasses of wine for customers sitting at the rear counter.

As Ivy approached, the woman smiled at her. "I'll be right with you."

"Actually, is Nate around?"

"Nate? He isn't…" The woman's expression grew inquisitive. "Are you Ivy?"

"Yes."

Her face lit up with a wide smile. "The boss mentioned you might be stopping by. Go ahead and take a seat. He had to step out for a minute, but he'll be right back."

"Okay, thanks." Ivy went to one of the tables off to the side. Since she wasn't having wine, she moved the table tent off to the side, laid the painting on the table, and sat down.

The door opened and two people walked in. Neither of them was Nate.

She set her keys and phone next to the table tent. Minutes ticked by.

Needing something to do with her hands, Ivy pressed down a piece of the plastic wrap that had lifted from the side of her gift for Jaxon. The paint had cured before she put foam protectors on the corners and wrapped the canvas. All Nate needed to do was put it in a sturdy box to send it to wherever Jaxon was located. She should also tell him the painting shouldn't be stored in a humid place if he didn't plan to send it right away.

The door opened.

She did a double take as Jaxon strolled in.

His gaze met hers, and Ivy's mouth dried out.

As he walked to her table, Ivy stood.

They faced each other. On a reflex, she almost reached out to hug him, but the way he held back dissuaded her. He looked good, maybe a little thinner.

Neither of them spoke.

The loss of them not being together anymore squeezed so tightly around Ivy's heart, her chest ached.

Turning away from him, she pointed. "I painted something for you. I hope you like it. I don't know where you'll hang it. You're traveling. It's not like you can keep it in a suitcase, right?" Her attempt at a joke fell flat to her own ears, especially since he didn't laugh. She could only imagine the look on his face. "Okay, I should go." Ivy reached for her things.

Jaxon touched her arm. "Can we talk?"

He was so close she could smell the richness of his cologne. The warmth of his hand soaked into her skin. It was too much. What did they have to talk about? She moved a fraction away from him. "I just came to drop off the painting."

"I only need a minute. Please." The hand he'd touched Ivy with was still in the air as if he wanted to reach out for her. Instead, he let it fall. "We can go to the office. You can tell me about the painting."

She actually did want to know what he thought about it. Would he like it? Ivy nodded.

Jaxon picked up the painting, and she followed down the side hallway into Nate's office.

He put the wrapped painting on a dark wood desk. "Is it okay if I use a cutter to open it?"

"Sure, as long as you don't cut too deep. With the foam corners holding the plastic, you have about an inch to work with. I'm glad you're here. I was worried about it being in a place that was too humid before it could be shipped to you." She sunk her teeth into her lower lip to stop herself from babbling. But why was he there? Just to visit Nate?

Jaxon found a cutter in the top drawer. Standing behind the desk, he carefully sliced the plastic from foam corner to foam corner at the top, then the bottom, and on the right side. He set down the cutter.

As he peeled away the plastic wrapping, Ivy's heart was practically beating in her throat.

He stared down at the painting, unmoving and quiet for a moment. Finally, he spoke. "It's beautiful."

He looked at her.

All of the times Jaxon had looked at her like this, with caring in his eyes, flashed through her mind. Her heart wanted to leap right into his hands, but reality put a leash on it. No matter how much they cared about each other, they were on separate paths.

Swallowing hard, she looked away from him. "Maybe you can find a place for it at the beach house or maybe it's too redundant since you already have the photo."

"I would hang it at the beach house if I could, but I sold it."

Her gaze flew back to his face. "Why? That place was your refuge."

"It was in the past." He walked to her on the other side of the desk and stood in front of her. "Buying this wine bar was more important."

She wasn't sure she'd heard him right. "You own this place?"

"Nate decided that running a business in a small town wasn't right for him." Jaxon took her hand. "But this is perfect for me."

"It is?" She let him tug her closer.

"Yes, because you're here. I want to be with you."

Hope started to spring up but reality reined it in. She closed her eyes, blocking out his face. "You can't move here for me. Someday you might regret it."

"I won't." He cupped her face, and she opened her eyes. The conviction in his held her gaze. "We are *not* your parents. We're not each other's infatuation. We are not opposites. We both enjoy being on adventures. We like tacos, sunsets, and lying under the stars. We're friends as well as lovers. We belong together. Where you are is home for me, and it always will be."

"Oh…" The emotions unleashing inside of her made it hard to speak.

Jaxon stole the rest of the words as his firm lips brushed gently over hers. "I love you, Ivy. We can have forever if you just let yourself see it."

He captured her mouth softly, lovingly. By the time he deepened the kiss she was lost. As she wound her arms around him, her mind replayed images of what they'd shared—from their first night together in South Carolina, to fulfilling her list of wishes together, to the nights of passion they shared. As she became lost in the wonderfulness of those memories, they drowned out doubt.

All she felt was certainty.

Certainty that she had the courage to move ahead into this next phase of her life. Certainty that she could reembrace her creativity. That it was okay to not only want happiness for those she cared about but that she could embrace happiness for herself. She'd found joy in his love and in loving him. What they shared was real. It was hers. He was hers and she was his.

Ivy brought her mouth a fraction from his and whispered, "Yes."

Jaxon leaned away a bit more to look into her eyes. "Yes?" She could hear the need for confirmation in his tone and spot it in his gaze.

"Yes, I see it." She smiled, meaning it with her whole heart. "We belong together. I love you. A part of me will always be afraid of not being able to control the future, but I know we can have a beautiful future together."

"You and me. No turning back. Not giving up on each other." Jaxon's smile reached into his eyes, reflecting his love. "That's what I see for us. Forever."

Chapter Twenty-Five

Six months later

Standing behind the counter at Charmed Vines, Jaxon popped the cork on a bottle of red wine, a premium blend from Sommersby Winery and Vineyard.

A relaxing end to the daily rush… That was the feeling Jaxon was striving for, and from the mood of the early evening crowd at the reopening of the wine bar, he had achieved it. At long last, the renovations were done.

The previously stark black and gray decor had been softened with blues and creams. A mix of retro, jazz, and modern country music, that of course included the latest single from Gable "Dell" Kincaid, played through hidden speakers. Select paintings and photos from local artists added another layer of vibrancy and interest to the space. He had Ivy to thank for the latter. Her insight and eye for details had played a big part in the changes as well as the selection of artwork.

They had also invested in Sommersby. Land adjacent to the winery had come up for sale. Real estate developers and investors ready to build more subdivisions, outlet malls, and other retail spaces had been ready to swoop in for the purchase. Instead, the winery had acquired the land with his and Ivy's assistance and his father's backing. James had gotten in on the deal, not as an investor only seeking a profit, but as a father trusting his son's gut and helping him give the underdogs a leg up. Family-owned businesses like Sommersby Winery and Vineyard and Bishop Honey Bee Farm mattered.

The door to Charmed Vines opened and two couples walked in. A smile tipped up his mouth as his wife of only a few weeks followed them. Not wanting to wait or take away from Brooke and Gable's upcoming nuptials, he and Ivy had exchanged their vows in the courtyard in the back of town hall and celebrated their reception at Pasture Lane Restaurant at Tillbridge surrounded by friends and family. Standing in the wine bar now dressed in a white button-down shirt, a pair of jeans, and bold, gold earrings and wrist bangles, she looked just as beautiful as she had on their special day in her long, fitted satin dress, carrying a simple bouquet of all-white blooms.

Their honeymoon had been just as magical as their new home—the artist's house. He'd tracked down the grandchildren of the couple that used to live there. They'd held on to the house all this time because they'd been hoping to sell it to someone who would continue to preserve and value the art on the walls while living there. After telling them about Ivy, it was clear to the family they'd found the right fit.

It had been a struggle to pull together all of the contractors to do a few gentle renovations before the wedding, but the expression on Ivy's face as he'd carried her over the threshold had been the best present he'd ever received.

Jaxon set the bottle down on top of the order ticket, eager to join her across the room. Wait…was that *his* shirt she was wearing? The fact that it was his made him grin. During their weeklong honeymoon, he'd awakened to find her sitting at an easel painting on the porch connected to their bedroom, wearing only his shirt. Her inner radiance and how sexy she looked had been his inspiration for them christening every room in the house.

The memory, along with Ivy meeting his gaze and smiling back at him, made his heart kick in so many extra beats it felt like it was about to jump straight out of his navy shirt. All of the things he'd felt the first time she'd ever smiled at him were still there—happiness, anticipation, attraction—plus so many other emotions. How had he gotten so lucky?

Just as he started to round the bar, Piper stopped him. "The man standing over there wants to know the price of a painting."

Piper had needed a change from South Carolina and had moved to Bolan. She was also assistant manager of the wine bar.

Jaxon looked to where she pointed. "Thanks. I'll take care of it."

All of the prices for the paintings and photos were clearly marked except for the one hanging in the middle of the side wall.

People often made inquiries about Ivy's abstract painting of him and his mom at the beach. The beauty and artistry of the piece made it naturally stand out.

Jaxon approached the middle-aged man staring at the

painting. "Hello. One of my staff said you had a question. How can I help?"

"Yes." The man pointed. "How much?"

The man's directness reminded Jaxon of his father— or, more accurately, how his father used to be.

Nicki and Ivy had been right about James masking his grief and loneliness behind a callous facade. He and his father were mending their relationship, and James was slowly turning over a new leaf, helping more companies get back on their feet versus dismantling them. It wasn't always perfect but it was a start.

Jaxon replied, "That one isn't for sale, but if you're interested in abstracts, there's a stunning piece in the corner."

"I really like this one. The colors. The mood. Whoever did this painting is a talented artist. I tell you what, name your price, and I'll match it."

Jaxon smiled. "She is talented. The painting is part of my private collection. I'm not interested in selling it."

"Well, if you ever change your mind." He handed Jaxon a business card and walked over to the painting Jaxon had pointed out in the corner.

As Jaxon tucked the card in the pocket of his dark jeans, Ivy looped her arm through his. The man and his offer evaporated from his mind as he became lost in her warmth, the scent of her perfume, and all that he felt for her swelling in his chest.

He raised her hand to his lips and kissed the back of it. "Hey, there, Mrs. Coffield. Can I interest you in a glass of wine?"

"You can." Ivy leaned more against him and whispered, "But first, tell me why you didn't sell my painting. Name your price? You could have charged him double, maybe even triple the cost of the most expensive piece in here and he would have paid it."

Jaxon stood behind Ivy and wrapped his arms around her. "It's not about the money."

In the past, the memory of that day with his mom had always brought sadness. Now, because of Ivy, he could remember the sun, the breeze on his face, and the warmth of his mom's embrace. He could also remember his father's huge smile as he snapped that photo, and later, how he'd splashed in the ocean with them.

Jaxon held Ivy closer. He *could* tell her all of that or he could simply express the most important thing that mattered to him. "When I see your painting of that day with my parents, I'm reminded how lucky I am to have the most valuable thing in the world."

Ivy looked up at him. "What?"

"Your love."

Ivy turned in his arms to face him. Soft emotions reflected in her eyes as she pressed her lips to his. For an all too brief moment, he lost himself in sweetness and passion simmering just below the surface.

"I love you." He'd never grow tired of saying it.

Ivy wrapped her arms around his waist. "I love you, too."

As she leaned more into him, she rested her cheek on his chest, right over the place that swelled with more happiness than he'd ever imagined it could hold. His heart.

* * * * *

Get up to 4 Free Books!

We'll send you 2 free books from each series you try PLUS a free Mystery Gift.

FREE Value Over **$25**

Both the **Harlequin® Special Edition** and **Harlequin® Heartwarming™** series feature compelling novels filled with stories of love and strength where the bonds of friendship, family and community unite.

YES! Please send me 2 FREE novels from the Harlequin Special Edition or Harlequin Heartwarming series and my FREE Gift (gift is worth about $10 retail). After receiving them, if I don't wish to receive any more books, I can return the shipping statement marked "cancel." If I don't cancel, I will receive 6 brand-new Harlequin Special Edition books every month and be billed just $6.39 each in the U.S. or $7.19 each in Canada, or 4 brand-new Harlequin Heartwarming Larger-Print books every month and be billed just $7.19 each in the U.S. or $7.99 each in Canada, a savings of 20% off the cover price. It's quite a bargain! Shipping and handling is just 50¢ per book in the U.S. and $1.25 per book in Canada.* I understand that accepting the 2 free books and gift places me under no obligation to buy anything. I can always return a shipment and cancel at any time by calling the number below. The free books and gift are mine to keep no matter what I decide.

Choose one: ☐ **Harlequin Special Edition** (235/335 BPA G36Y)   ☐ **Harlequin Heartwarming Larger-Print** (161/361 BPA G36Y)   ☐ **Or Try Both!** (235/335 & 161/361 BPA G36Z)

Name (please print)

Address   Apt. #

City   State/Province   Zip/Postal Code

Email: Please check this box ☐ if you would like to receive newsletters and promotional emails from Harlequin Enterprises ULC and its affiliates. You can unsubscribe anytime.

> Mail to the **Harlequin Reader Service:**
> **IN U.S.A.:** P.O. Box 1341, Buffalo, NY 14240-8531
> **IN CANADA:** P.O. Box 603, Fort Erie, Ontario L2A 5X3

Want to explore our other series or interested in ebooks? Visit www.ReaderService.com or call 1-800-873-8635.

---

*Terms and prices subject to change without notice. Prices do not include sales taxes, which will be charged (if applicable) based on your state or country of residence. Canadian residents will be charged applicable taxes. Offer not valid in Quebec. This offer is limited to one order per household. Books received may not be as shown. Not valid for current subscribers to the Harlequin Special Edition or Harlequin Heartwarming series. All orders subject to approval. Credit or debit balances in a customer's account(s) may be offset by any other outstanding balance owed by or to the customer. Please allow 4 to 6 weeks for delivery. Offer available while quantities last.

Your Privacy—Your information is being collected by Harlequin Enterprises ULC, operating as Harlequin Reader Service. For a complete summary of the information we collect, how we use this information and to whom it is disclosed, please visit our privacy notice located at https://corporate.harlequin.com/privacy-notice. Notice to California Residents – Under California law, you have specific rights to control and access your data. For more information on these rights and how to exercise them, visit https://corporate.harlequin.com/california-privacy. For additional information for residents of other U.S. states that provide their residents with certain rights with respect to personal data, visit https://corporate.harlequin.com/other-state-residents-privacy-rights/.

HSEHW25